IMPERFECT HUNT PAPERBACK

A DARKLY FUNNY SUPERNATURAL SUSPENSE MYSTERY - BOOK 5 OF THE IMPERFECT CATHAR SERIES

C.N. ROWAN

CONTENTS

Also By C.N. Rowan

DEDICATION

To Eleanor, Ian and John.
I hope this slightly makes up for the terrible burden of having me as a
younger sibling.
Sorry and all that.

FOREWORD

Welcome to this, the fifth adventure in the imPerfect Cathar series. If you're new to these supernatural jaunts across southern France, I'd advise you to go back to the first book, imPerfect Magic. Not only are you going to miss out on all sorts of bits of the plot, meaning a fair bit of head scratching, but you'll also be throwing yourself enormous spoilers regarding all the mysteries contained in those earlier tomes.

Of course, you're welcome to do as you please. There's no judgement here. Apart from Aicha of Paul's every action of course, but that's well deserved.

If spoilers ARE your literary kink – and again, no judgement – then you should be aware that you're stepping into two particular and potentially terrifying territories. One in Bad Language Land, where swear-words fly thick and fast so girdle your loins for such expletives. The other is British Spellingsia, where U's abound and Z's are shot on sight. So if you see colour instead of color or murderise instead of murderize, you can rest easy, knowing you are simply sailing through strange and foreign climes.

Of course, if you do come across a word you think has been spelt wrong, or any other typos or mishaps, I do want to know. Although this book has been rigorously edited and gone through multiple proofreads, one or two of those sneaky blighters always seem to slip through. If you should trap one, please drop me an email at chris@cnrowan.com and I shall fix it forthwith.

Now, to head to more glamorous foreign lands. Let's board an aircraft and head for the sunny shores of Leicester, England...

CHAPTER ONE
TOULOUSE, 7 JUNE, PRESENT DAY

There's cold as ice. Then there's cold as Aicha...normally. Today? Not so much.

F lying with a control freak is a vision of Hell even Dante couldn't imagine.

I actually enjoy flying on the rare occasions I do it. As long as I go on my own. The whole experience – from the moment you arrive at the airport and huge metal signs guide you towards which grade of car park you're allowed access to up until the moment you get free from the maws of the glass-and-steel giant at the other end – involves following. It's a herding process. That's why I find it relaxing. I don't have to think for a while. Just arrive with time to spare and then go with the flow. Arrow here; queue there. Flash a piece of psychic passport at a perennially bored border guard and then wait in a pen with all the other human sheep till the ground staff shepherd you onboard in groups.

Aicha does not enjoy this. Aicha takes the whole "owner of her own destiny" thing very seriously at all times. People telling Aicha what to do and where to go is like someone following her around, constantly tapping her on the back of the head. With a cattle prod.

So I use my *talent* for the first couple of encounters with airport staff, smoothing away the suspicious glances and ridiculous questions. Problem is, I'm fae now. This is not an environment made for fairy creatures. Except perhaps in the sense of "made to torture them and slowly drive them mad".

You see, they build airports on a gigantic scale to have tens or hundreds of thousands of people tromping through, gawking and chittering and hopefully consuming on a massive scale. That concrete needs reinforcing. Which means rebar concrete – steel bars driven through every column. And I can feel each and every one of them, making my teeth itch, sapping away my fae strength.

So by the time we get to the border guards, I have enough *talent* left to persuade them that the pieces of paper we wave are valid passports even under the intense scrutiny they subject them to, but I've not enough left to stop them from deciding to bombard Aicha with a thousand and one questions.

"Where are you travelling?"

"Why?"

"Where have you travelled recently?"

"Are you carrying anything sharp, anything that can be used as a weapon?"

That she isn't carrying any might well be one reason she's so pissed off. I think it makes her feel the same way most people would strutting through the airport in the nude. She tried to argue for carrying all of her various knives, swords, and other assorted implements of the exceptionally pointy, death-dealing variety onboard with her, using a *don't look here* spell to keep eyes off them. I pointed out that metal detectors go *brrrrrr* even if the security staff don't clock them. Images get flagged automatically by the machines. The poor sucker she convinces magically to look the other way would probably end up answering some very hard questions. They'd lose their job over it. That's not on. In the end, she begrudgingly allowed me to stash them in my etheric storage, where I can have them back in her hands at a moment's notice. She also informed me if I did my usual trick of getting myself killed in some idiotic manner, stranding her without access to them, she'd take great pleasure in demonstrating the usage of each and every one of them on me once she got them back.

By the time we get onboard, Aicha looks like she's been chugging some chemical soup caffeine energy drink for hours while mainlining gorilla testosterone through an IV drip. The cabin crew, masters of human psychology that the job requires them to be, take one look at my companion and offer us two empty rows towards the rear of the aircraft. I think they want the crew at the back to be able to keep a careful eye on us. Keeping us as far as possible from the other passengers doesn't hurt either. I don't care. We've space to relax. That's a win.

The airline's colour scheme, a florid orange against crisp white, carries on throughout the cabin, offset by the muted grey of the seats and the crew uniform. I settle into my row of seats, my bum in one seat and my legs sprawled out over the others, my back half pressed against the window. Then I close my eyes. It'll probably be an hour before we get high enough up that they'll pass round to sell me some much deserved booze. Chaperoning Aicha through the airport is enough to drive anyone to drink.

I'm feeling considerably better being on the aeroplane. The amount of iron composites is pleasingly little. Weight is ever a consideration in aviation, and there are lighter materials to build with. I'm just about dozing off when Aicha drops herself into the seat at the aisle end of my row, booting my feet out of the way in the process.

I sigh. Apparently, now she wants to talk. 'Yes, *laguna?*'

Aicha's scowl could strip the paint off the plane. Seeing as how I'm pretty sure it plays an integral part in the aerodynamics, I prefer she keeps it concentrated on me instead. 'Why can't we just drive?'

Oh, good. We're having this conversation. Again. 'Time, essence, et cetera. C'mon. You know all this.'

'We could do Paris en route then.' My goodness me. There's a truculent tone approaching a whine to Aicha's voice. She really isn't happy.

I shuffle myself further up the window, pulling into a sitting position so as I can look at her properly. 'Aich, we've talked about this. We've got two leads. One is much more clearly linked to De Montfort than the other.'

'But we know there's that rib cage in the capital!'

'Yep. Safely in the care of Leandre – the Lutin Prince and one of the major Powers of France, hell, of the whole of Europe.'

'You think De Montfort cares about that, dickhead?'

I pause for a moment. She has a point. De Montfort isn't going to let anyone or anything get in his way. He wasn't even fazed when he tackled a tower-block-sized snail-dragon. But he'd made sure he knew exactly how to deal with him first. 'I don't think he cares. I *do think* he plans. He's not going to go off half-cocked against Leandre. He'll be plotting and planning, especially now he thinks I'm out of the way.'

'He doesn't care about that. He'll come back if he's killed.'

I frown. That's the sort of ill-thought-out conclusion that Aicha would normally have delighted in tearing strips off me for having. She's taking this whole "trapped in a tiny metal tube and hurtling through the sky at impossible speeds and height with zero control" thing even harder than I expected. 'Aich. Think it through. Quite the opposite. He's spent endless lives plotting how to get this current body so he can have access to *talent*. His reincarnation isn't as simple as mine. It's direct bloodline only. This is the first time in centuries that he's ever had *power*. He'll be protecting that body like a nerdy collector would an ultra-rare Pokemon card. I'm honestly surprised he even leaves the house.' I think this through. 'In fact, I bet he only does when he's supremely confident he's stacked all the odds in his favour that he'll make it home again safely.'

I want to lean over and pat her knee to reassure her. Problem is, I'm attached to my hands. Literally. Something Aicha will modify with extreme prejudice if I patronise her in such a manner.

'I still think we should do Paris first.' Good God, she's sulking. She has her arms crossed, her lower lip jutted out, and she's actually sulking. I've never seen the like.

'We discussed this!' A passing crew member turns a querulous frown in my direction, and I lower my voice, suitably chastened. 'Paris and the surrounding banlieues are packed full of magic creatures and major Talented, several of them fae of origin, Leandre included. All sorts of powerhouses likely to pick up if a potential threat moves into the area. Too risky for a main base of operations. Demon Fart has to have a stronghold somewhere, a safe house or bolt-hole, and family connections are important. Literal lifesavers for him. It's got to be Paris or Leicester, and combined with the discovered bones, Leicester makes much more sense.'

Isaac made that connection because research, obviously. If anyone was going to track down De Montfort, aka Demon Fart, as we've childishly rechristened him, through tenuous scraps of information and obscure knowledge, arcane or otherwise, it was always going to be Isaac. Especially now that he's intellectually supercharged by having his brother Jakob along for the ride with him in his head, as well as two brain-meltingly powerful angels.

About a decade ago, archaeologists made one of the strangest and most exciting discoveries in a long time in the UK. Beneath a school car park, they discovered the body of Richard III, the supposedly hunchbacked king of England, eternally reviled as a villain thanks to a certain Billy Shakespeare. That was interesting enough, but what caught Isaac's attention were the other bones discovered on the same site, including a female skeleton bizarrely entombed in a prestigious sarcophagus. Pretty odd for a woman back in those days. Even stranger was that one archaeologist reported seeing the bones glowing before his chief sent him to have a refreshing cup of tea and a nice lie down, the British equivalent of strong anti-psychotic meds. The funding of the archaeological dig remains shrouded in mystery as well, and somehow, the skeleton didn't end up winging its way for further study at one of the universities or laboratories set up for just such a purpose. It got strangely re-routed and ended up at Kenilworth Castle. Guess which family used to own that?

So Leicester it is. Kenilworth looks like the obvious target, but it isn't the only one. There's an area called Montfort-L'Aumery just outside of Paris. It was a De Montfort residence for a long time. But the odds are still on Leicester and Kenilworth as the most likely location. And I want to go straight to the place where I stand the best chance of getting my hands on the bastard.

Thing is, De Montfort has proven to be endlessly resourceful and an intricate planner. We need to find his hideout without alerting him about our investigation. I don't want him to do a runner. What I want is to make sure he does no running ever again by sawing off his kneecaps with a rusty hacksaw. Tetanus and immobilisation for the win.

'I still think we should have driven.'

Oh good. It looks like we've circled right back round to the start of this conversation. Which I suspect is how the rest of the flight is going to go. I check my watch. About twenty minutes till they start the service, by my reckoning. I can survive the hour or so of flight afterwards if I buy –I perform the requisite mental calculations for the ratio of booze to Aicha's whining– the entire bar.

Probably.

CHAPTER TWO
BRISTOL, 7 JUNE, PRESENT DAY

Shipshape and Bristol fashion. Strange saying. Seems to imply having a large barnacle-covered bottom.

By the time we exit through the swooshing doors of the airport, Aicha is back to normal. She makes this clear when she threatens me with evisceration by nail clipper if I ever mention the flight again. She wraps a *don't look here* around us and thrusts a demanding hand in my face a second after the doors close behind us. A huge part of the stress lining her face evaporates as I pass them all across. Guess they're her emotional support bladed weapons of death. I decide to skip pointing that out to her now that she's armed again.

The weather obviously didn't get the memo about summer having started. We left a heat just the right side of baking back in Toulouse, the sweet spot of the year where you can enjoy being outside from morning until night, without being a walking buffet for the bastard mosquitoes. Here? We've arrived just after nine in the morning, and the chill to the air is being carried deeper into my bones by the wind, which blows hard enough to apparently bypass my flesh altogether. There are warmer mornings than this in February in the south of France.

I decide not to mention it to Aicha. I don't really need to get her riled up about something else already. She's back in hyper-vigilant mode, her eyes scanning from near to far, clocking every movement from here to the horizon. At least we don't really stand out. There are people of every nationality and ethnic background milling around outside, and Aicha isn't the only one with a facial tattoo by a long stretch. It's astounding how purposeless the general movements are. People seem lost, disoriented. After anywhere from hours to days of the airports and airlines directing their thoughts and actions, the people seem bewildered to be in control of their own destiny once again.

I scoop up the car keys with a minimum of fuss from the car hire desk. I considered just stealing something from the car park but decided against it. Getting back off holiday is hard enough. I don't want to add to some poor fucker's post-holiday blues, finding themselves stuck without transport at some ungodly hour of the morning. It isn't like we can't afford the hire prices.

The Kia Sportage I've rented is just what we need. Comfortable but concealing. We aren't about to turn heads as we drive down the street, which is good news. The Koreans make sturdy, cheap cars. Functional and discreet is the aim of the game, however much it makes Aicha's lips pucker in distaste.

'We're trying not to draw attention to ourselves,' I remind Aicha as we pull off.

She looks at me similarly to how she looked at the car. 'Have you seen us? Or *seen* us? Subtle isn't really an option. We both radiate *talent*. Plus, between me being me and you cosplaying as Princess Zelda, people look.'

She has a point. Since we got to the airport, we've spent most of the time being hit on. I tried to make myself look as drab as possible with the glamour I wove, but cities and airports wear me down in this body. The unnatural, otherworldly aura and beauty of it pokes through. It used to belong to Maeve, the Queen of the Winter Court, after all. You don't get much more beautiful. Or deadly. Until Aicha just made her dead -- beautifully.

Aicha herself is stunning too. It's weird thinking about it as I don't see her like that at all, thankfully for both our sanity and my life expectancy. She's like a sister to me. Still, objectively, I can see how beautiful she is. Her dark, almost-black eyes set back into the shadows of her aquiline nose burn with passion and personality. A certain subset of men have a tendency to think that makes her "fiery" and in need of taming, like Shakespeare's Katherina. Said men quickly find themselves choking for air, mainly because of Aicha having kicked their bollocks up into the back of their throat.

Two drop-dead, otherworldly women like us are going to draw attention whether we drive a Prius or a Porsche. I still haven't got used to the las-civious gazes we get from men, often while their wives deal with grizzling infants. The looks we get from their wives are similar, which surprises me. Unless they clock their husbands looking. Then darker, more jealous storm clouds gather in their expressions.

We have to try to be discreet though. I don't want to alert Demon Fart we're coming for him.

I heave a sigh of relief as the satnav directs us away from the airport. Within five minutes, it leads us onto winding back roads that climb and fall away through rolling greenery. The presence of nature recharges me; though the fields lie tended, neat, and precise in their division, the land remains ancient. It reaches out to me through overhanging branches, through the granite, sand, and limestone that form its bones, through restless dreams of days before some jumped-up monkeys smothered it in concrete and tarmac.

By the time we reach Bristol itself, the rush hour has eased, and we skirt the city easily enough. The huge suspension bridge by Clifton provides a magnificent view over the docks and the estuary and the cheerily painted houses on the opposite side set back in rows into the hillside. This is a city built on gradients. You end up with some serious calf muscles living here, I suspect. I wonder what it is about this place down in the south-west, in touching distance of Wales, that makes it such a hotspot of creativity. It birthed trip-hop and drum'n'bass and always seems to be at the centre of cultural originality for the UK. I promise myself a proper visit if time allows. Right now though, we need to get to Leicester.

It's a short enough drive from Bristol that after a fuel up and a coffee grab at a motorway service station, we drive the rest of the way without stopping.

By the time we pull into Leicester, the sun is approaching its zenith, which means it's finally stopped being a lazy git and started providing some actual warmth. The city itself has seen investment in recent times. Modern bulging glass fronts act like makeup that's been slapped onto the long-dead industrial architecture prevalent where money can't reach. I nearly snap a tooth clenching my jaw when we come down the Narborough Road. A bustling melange of bars and fast food, students and immigrants blur by, but it's all the signs labelled De Montfort that throw me. I quickly clock it's the name of a university. Apparently, being a murderous anti-Semite doesn't matter after a few hundred years. Though I suspect it was named for De Montfort's son, the man who was almost king. As it was the same shithead bastard just wearing his offspring's body like a zip-up onesie, I don't really care. They both would've been absolute arseholes even if they hadn't been the same person. Their memory shouldn't be honoured for posterity. Naming a lavatory after them would be more appropriate. I'm aiming to name a shallow grave in their honour...with them inside it.

We park up in a multi-storey car park near the centre of town, then walk down the high street. There was some debate about where to head first. We know the excavated skeleton got sent to Kenilworth Castle, which is outside the city centre, so Aicha was all for heading there and storming it like raiding Visigoths. I felt reconnoitring the dig site and the city itself first to be more sensible — get a lay of the land, see if there are any obvious traces of Demon Fart's involvement. Isaac sided with me before we set off, so here we are.

The city is intriguing. You can see where the money got invested. Swathes of renovated buildings stand proud, if entirely unoriginal – fronts cut out to allow glass panelling; cleaned brick and pedestrianised alleys, all replete with the same mixture of chain restaurants; and quirky pop-ups that masquerade as character but remain money-grabbers. Behind it, though, you can see the real city. Rundown old pubs run down side streets and spill a strange mixture of individuals out onto the pavement. Punks and drunkards, steamed-glass academics and tattooed suits. The mingling is real, and attempts to gentrify the city can't cut the rough diamond weirdness out of its occupants.

The dig site is just a couple of streets over from the high street. They've transformed it into an interactive museum. Our hope is we'll find some official to pump for information. Otherwise, we'll perform a bit of break-ing and entering, see what we can find behind the public façade. Either way, we aren't going to linger right now. I can feel my stomach rumbling, and Aicha's eyes assess every eatery we pass. Hangry Aicha is a horror too hideous to contemplate.

We cut through by the cathedral, the new final resting place of Richard III, unless someone digs him up again in the name of historical science. His statue stands at the end of the open square in front of the church doors, his hand stretched aloft. In it is his crown being waved at the sun. I think it's supposed to be dramatic. It just makes him look like he's auditioning to play tambourine for the Happy Mondays.

I suspect the money spent on the area is directly proportional to the amount of interest generated by the discovery of Richard III's body. Pedestrianised again, the area is all neat green rectangles and pennants on lampposts stamped with the Richard III logo. Prior to this, Leicester was best known for Daniel Lambert, the fattest man in English history. Oh, and Engelbert Humperdinck. Neither brought in the big tourist moolah though. The strangest archaeological story of modern times and a missing king found? That's a draw. Clearly the local council knows it and is ready to do what they need to in order to maximise it.

Various wooden and stone benches squat, artfully scattered among flowerbeds and street lawns. It's surprisingly quiet. I'd have imagined this to be the sort of place people might decamp to from their offices to scoff down their sandwiches during their truncated breaks. But only one bench is occupied. A guy slumps in one corner, dead to the world. He doesn't look homeless, or if he is, it must have happened recently. His clothes aren't super new, but they don't look slept in, however prominently his trainers display their long usage. Outside of that, the only other occupants are a trio of goth kids, black liner face-paint over the kind of white primer that a Parisian mime would be proud of. There are a few ancient gravestones still clustered in the south-eastern corner of the square.

I'm ready to just cut through, to get on our way, but Aicha's hand shoots out, checking me. Were I a normal human, she probably would have caved my chest in. As is, she nearly winds me.

'Something's not right here, *saabi*.' Her eyes rove around, seeking what has set her Spidey sense tingling.

I wave a hand at the group of new New Romantics. 'Was it that the eighties called and wanted their tragic subculture back?'

Aicha's gaze tracks over to the group and stops, fixed on them. Her posture changes to a new state of readiness. In the same moment, their heads snap up, and as one, all their attention turns in our direction. They open their mouths and hiss, and I catch a gleam of fang in each open orifice. Sadly, I don't think they're wearing ornamental teeth caps.

'Vampires,' Aicha hisses.

The three of them glide towards us, taking up position in the most un-hip, undead pincer manoeuvre of all time.

Vampires. At midday. In Leicester. That makes perfect sense.

CHAPTER THREE
LEICESTER, 7 JUNE, PRESENT DAY

If these guys start sparkling, I'm going to set them on fire. Turn them into proper sparklers. Guy Fawkes, eat your heart out. Or drive a stake through them.

I get a better look at them now they've closed the distance. The one on the right is squat, with arms that speak of manual labour and a gut that speaks of daytime drinking. He's wearing a black pork-pie hat, and lightning bolts are painted out of his eyeliner across his cheeks. His T-shirt is some sort of shimmery grey wife-beater, perfect for when you want to look like you live in a trailer park and have a fetish for mithril silver. The guy on the left is tall and broad. His hair is pulled back so tight into a ponytail, I'm surprised he hasn't torn the skin off his face. I wonder if he can still do anything as advanced as smiling. Or talking. It seems impossible without him doing himself an injury. He clearly spends a lot of time in the gym, a fact he takes great pleasure in displaying by walking around topless. He shaved his chest, if I'm not mistaken, and oiled it too. Although he obviously mixed some of that same white makeup primer into the oil, so at least his chest matches his face colour-wise. His eyes have round black circles with splodges coming off like lava-lamp fluid. It's supposed to make him look mysterious, magical perhaps. Instead, he looks like a panda someone just splashed with hydrochloric acid.

The fellow in the middle is obviously the leader. His hair hangs down around his face. It's supposed to be jet-black, but obviously no one bothered to tell him his roots are showing, meaning his natural ginger is poking through. I guess it becomes more difficult to spot these things when you can't see yourself in a mirror. He's tall and thin, which is only accentuated by the floor-length leather trench coat he wears. It must be the equivalent of taking the guts of the Tauntaun that Luke Skywalker cut open on Hoth and wearing them constantly. Only in the middle of summer. Admittedly, an English summer, which means I only need a jumper and a coat instead of a full set of thermals, but summer nonetheless. He's gone for swirling curves off his eyes that are admittedly pretty, though I doubt that's the effect he really wants to go for. The smear lines where sweat has picked up the eyeliner and carried it in smudges down his cheeks aren't deliberate additions, I suspect. The price we pay for style. Even shit style, apparently.

The overall impact is less than menacing. They somehow aren't aware of that fact. They leer at us like we'll somehow be terrified of them, as if they look like deadly creatures of the night instead of monochrome geishas whose makeup artist got pissed on sake beforehand.

'Jesus Christ, this is beyond painful. Actual vampires dressed up as goth wannabe vampires. Is this like cosplay or something? Please tell me this is some sort of surrealist theatre that English undead are into. Is this the "creatures of the night" equivalent of Morris Dancing? Preserving ancient, forgotten traditions or something?' If ever there is a time in my life when I am delighted to be fluent in English, it's this one. It allows me to categorically rip the piss out of these three and for them to understand every word.

Aicha isn't going to be outdone. 'It's like the Insane Clown Posse. Only without the posse. Or being insane. The Lame Clown Trio?'

'Sounds like an experimental jazz outfit.'

'I think it's great they're so open about being into glam rock. What's your favourite Slade song? "Merry Christmas Everybody"?'

The three of them have gone from looking baffled to faintly insulted to deeply mortified. I suspect at least one of them is blushing, but under the layers of eyeliner, it's impossible to spot. They keep trying to speak, but we're not letting them get a word in edgeways.

I point at the leader. 'Hey, I think that one's got some kind of hair and mouth disease.' His lips clamp shut, and wild panic settles in his eyes. 'Yeah – he's got ginger-vitis.'

Aicha groans. 'That's dreadful.' She turns her full-watt attention on him. 'How does that work, by the way? Ginger vampire? Like, does that mean you've lost your soul twice? Are you negative one for souls?'

The outrage in his expression is comedic. Every time he moves, it sends more black streaks running down his face. It makes him look like he's crying ink. Which would, were it to actually happen, be very fucking metal. As it is, he looks like he just got dumped by his partner and sobbed his little heart out in the grimy toilets of the local goth dive. It makes his attempts to snarl at us just look like desperate pleas for attention. I actually find myself feeling sorry for him, wanting to tell him that whoever it was isn't worth it, that there are plenty more fish in the sea.

We leave enough gap in the conversation for him to put his oar in finally. Unfortunately for him, we've knocked him so far off balance, all he can do initially is splutter and spit, apparently incapable of forming syllables.

'Deep breaths. Think before you speak. Let it all out,' I advise in my most soothing voice. He looks like he's having a rough day. Because of us, admittedly, but a rough day still.

He gets hold of his use of language again. 'Who are you? How dare you come into our territory? Are you the Hob King?'

I think this through. 'I mean, I cook a pretty mean stir fry, if that's what you mean?'

Aicha makes a T symbol with her hands, the universal sign for a time-out. 'A moment to speak to my colleague, please?'

The poor little undead fucker is totally lost by this point. He looks left and right, desperately asking for advice and support. By the time his two goons, who look even more confused than he does, shrug their utter indecision at him, we've already taken several steps backwards, forming a huddle to talk privately.

'What's up?' I keep my voice as low as possible and my eye on the vampires.

'What if they work for De Montfort?'

They are also now huddling, obviously trying to come up with some sort of game plan for dealing with our non sequiturs.

I frown. I did not even think about that. 'They said this is their territory.'

'They'd say that if he gave it to them too. Even if they worked for him. Vampires. Egos the size of small planets. Plus, have you seen how they're dressed?'

She has a point. It takes a level of utter ballsiness and self-confidence to strut around a grim post-industrial city like Leicester dressed like that in the middle of the day.

I shrug. 'What are you saying?'

'There're no wards here. None I've felt, anyhow. You?' I know what she's getting at. De Montfort wears a fae body too. Maybe I might pick up some sneakily woven faerie magic that she's missed. I shake my head. Nothing rings a bell magically around here.

She nods. 'Think about it. He travels a lot. Nefarious plans clock up the air miles. Can't protect the city or keep it warded. Plus, doesn't want to draw attention. What would you do?'

I can see where she is going. 'Strike a deal with another Talented or group thereof. Let them keep an eye on the place...'

'...and report back if anyone comes sniffing around.'

Damn. It's a valid point. 'So we can't let them report back.' I turn to head towards them, but she grabs my arm and pulls me back. Apparently, she isn't finished.

'Have you seen their earrings?'

I have to be honest; I've not been paying attention. Their botched-job face-painting has drawn most of my attention. I sneak a peek while keeping my head close to Aicha's.

In one of each of the vampires' ears, there's a skull and crossbones with tiny green jewels for the eyes. I swear silently. 'They're the same as what De Montfort has on his ring.'

She nods. 'Something else. I was having a *look* at that jewellery while you were busy with the banter. They're powerful. Best guess? They send an alarm in certain circumstances.'

I can well imagine what sort. 'Like someone getting attacked with *talent*?'

She nods grimly. 'My thought exactly.'

So we're going to have to take these fuckers out in a two-on-three physical brawl, where they can use all of their natural abilities. Or, rather, unnatural abilities. And we have to rely on our sword skills. While also making sure I don't get this body killed, or I go back to being a Talentless schmuck, the magical equivalent of a reality TV star. Surely a fate worse than death.

Guess I better make sure I don't die then.

We wander back over to the significantly baffled group of goth vampires. 'Sorry for the delay.' I smile brightly. 'What can we help you fine gentlemen with?'

The leader opens his mouth, but I hold up my hand to cut him off, pointing at the shirtless muscle head. 'Hold on a second. Didn't you play the rock saxophone in Santa Carla? What were the two Coreys like? Who was nicer, Kiefer Sutherland or Alex Winter?' The blank looks that come back underline a certainty. They've never seen *Lost Boys*. They need to die.

I wave graciously at their head honcho. 'Sorry, continue. You were just about to tell us what you were doing here and who you work for.'

He nods. 'Quite, well this is where we live and... Hey, hold on. That's what you were supposed to be telling us!'

I frown and look at Aicha. 'That doesn't sound right. I wasn't ever going to tell these bozos anything, were you?'

'Only to go fuck themselves.'

A sage expression spreads across my face. 'True. Very true. So you were going to tell us everything we wanted to know?'

The one in the middle's panic levels are rising exponentially, in direct correlation to his confusion. This conversation isn't going the way he expected it to. 'No. No, I wasn't?' There's a definite question at the end.

'Sure you were! How many of you are in your nest? Who's your master? Who does he work for? All the basics, you know.'

'First line of your address, mother's maiden name, social security number.'

'Sure, Aich. We'll take those too while you're at it.'

I think the fact that we aren't going to suddenly stop being weird and play ball finally sinks in. The Ginger Prince of Darkness hisses, his fangs on display. 'If you want to play rough, that suits us down to the ground. We will feast on your flesh!'

I chuckle. 'Oh, look. He actually believes they can beat us!'

Aicha sighs, throws up a *don't look here* spell, and pulls out her katana/wakizashi combination. 'Just goes to show there ain't no sucker like a bloodsucker.'

I pull my sword from my etheric storage. 'Too damn true, *laguna*. Too damn true.'

The three of them crouch, their fingers elongating out to form claws, their eyes glowing red, ready to pounce. Looks like the fight is on.

CHAPTER FOUR

LEICESTER, 7 JUNE, PRESENT DAY

The setting makes it all feel so Shakesperean, like an undead version of "Romeo & Juliet". 'Wherefore nosfer-art thou, Romeo?'

I might have been merciless in my mockery of the three of them, but that doesn't mean I underestimate the fight we have on our hands. These aren't werewolves. These are vampires.

As much as this trio is doing zero favours for their species by pandering to stereotypes, vampires are still seriously dangerous. Especially when we can't use magic. Lightning quick. Superhumanly strong. The only advantage on our side —other than Aicha, which is always the biggest advantage to have in any fight— is it being midday. I assume the three of them have some serious sunblock mixed in with their mascara. That's how they can rock around, but it should slow them down, slightly at least. I feel confident about winning the fight, but I need to win the fight without this body getting incapacitated. That is a slightly different kettle of undead fish.

The vampires spread out slightly. Conversation is done. Playtime is over. Now we aren't faced by three slightly goofy kids. We're faced by three apex predators. Three apex predators in shitty face makeup, but three apex predators all the same.

I feel Aicha's shift in position. She slides her right foot forward, raising the katana into a cross guard. Good. She's clocked the situation and is taking point. I take a step backward. I'll play a defensive role, guarding our rear. We both angle our bodies — not yet back-to-back, still facing our opponents but ready to close up when the moment comes.

It comes. Fast.

Even with me being ready for just how rapidly they move, they almost catch me out. Beer Belly blurs, seemingly out of existence. Next moment, he's nearly on top of me. The only thing that saves me from being disembowelled is where I'm standing. The strands of perfectly manicured grass beneath my feet practically scream at his unnatural presence as he steps on them. To my fae senses, at least. But it gives me the early warning I need.

I pivot back and twist my wrist to catch his claws on my blade edge. Sadly, he has two sets of weapons, having two hands. I have only one. The second set of claws slashes across my left arm, and my bicep explodes into fiery pain. By the time I swing my blade around to counterattack, he's gone again. Back where he started, he licks the crimson drops from his fingertips like a kid cleaning the sugar off after gulping down some sticky sweets. Damn. That was way too close. And only the first foray.

Things are going better for Aicha. Obviously. The leader and Sax Man have quite correctly identified her as the bigger threat and are harrying her as a pack. Have you ever seen one of those sixties martial arts films, where everything's been slightly sped up to make the fights seem even quicker and more impressive? It's like watching one of those. On fast forward. There's a jerky unreality to it. The brain insists humanoid bodies can't move at that speed even as the eyes insist that yes, they actually can because there it is, happening right in front of them. Both Beer Belly and I pause to admire the action, though I keep a close eye on him in case he tries to sneak attack.

King Ginger is pressing her from the front, bobbing and weaving like Jackie Chan as Drunken Master, attacking from different angles and heights, searching for an opening. Sax Man is hounding her left flank. He's trying to play the strategic game, seeking a gap in the action, a momentary lapse in concentration where he can strike. He makes chivvying forays in, slamming forward like greased lightning, his claws outstretched, then blurring back to the edges to seek a new opening.

Aicha doesn't have to be as cautious as I do. She blocks most of the attacks, of course. She keeps her katana concentrated on the leader, her eyes tracking his disjointed movements. Her wakizashi parries the incoming "bulldozer strapped to a jet engine" assaults from the muscle-bound Sax Man, catching his razor-sharp, elongated nails on the small blade to turn him aside. That doesn't mean she isn't cut though. Thing is, she doesn't care. She's happy to take a cut here, have a chunk of flesh torn away there. Well, happy might be the wrong word. She isn't a masochist. She's just tough as nails and able to regenerate instantly. Compared to what the Nazis did to her, these sorts of injuries are nothing. She protects her blade arms, of course, to keep her weapons. Every time she takes a hit, she makes sure she pays one back to whoever dealt it out. The result is that while she might be slick with her own blood, she heals straight back up. The vampires might not bleed in the same way, but they heal slower too. They both have multiple wounds that would incapacitate any lesser species. Sadly, they've obviously fed recently. The black sludge oozing from their cuts knits their flesh back together, albeit slower than Aicha recovers.

The result is the battle is fever-pitched but evenly matched. The two of them are enough to keep her too occupied to concentrate on making a clinical strike either straight through the heart or by cleaving their heads from their necks, and they can't do her any permanent damage. I've just decided to re-engage my vampire, risk be damned, so I can get in and help her when the battle changes. For the worse.

The vampire leader falls a step back. I watch as he coils spring-like, then he leaps at her, his claws spread wide, hammering down from above like a tiger finishing the hunt. Aicha can't move away fast enough. She bends back and has no choice but to bring up both blades, using them to catch the extended nails and transfer the vampire's momentum into a spin, sending him crashing off to the side.

It is, however, exactly the opening Sax Man has been waiting for. He dashes in low and hard like an American football player going in for the tackle. Lunging forward, he tears through her right hamstring. Aicha cries out and sinks to one knee, her leg giving out under her.

I cry out in sympathy and start forward, only for Beer Belly to dive at me low, going for a shootfighter move to pull me down and grapple. I strike wildly at him, desperate to get to Aicha, severing two of his outstretched fingers, then crying out again as he rips through the flesh on my shin. Only the hardness of the bone and the slight deflection I caused when I detached his digits stop him from tearing my entire left leg off. I roll to the left, kneeling myself, my sword raised in a hanging stance above my head.

Luckily, losing his fingers has discouraged Beer Belly from immediately trying to finish me off. I sink my left hand into the grass, seeking the essence of its seeds. Funnelling my magic, I touch the potential of the seeds' myriad states – the change from dormancy to shooting growth – and channel it into my left shin. I feel the flesh regrow, reform as my body's cells respond in sympathy to that latent possibility in the lawn, stimulated by my *talent*. I just have to hope using magic on myself won't trigger the vampires' earrings. But it's that or being out of the fight. Three versus one won't help the injured Aicha even if they leave me alone rather than finishing me off. I need to get healed and quickly.

In the momentary pause, while Beer Belly concentrates on regrowing his severed fingers and I on my shredded shin, I fix my eyes on Aicha. Sax Man hasn't pressed the advantage thankfully, but he has backed up, obviously happy to continue to snipe from the sidelines. The leader, though, is unrelenting, striking at the kneeling Aicha with vicious swings, a constant spitting blur of claws, raking at her as she blocks as many as she can, blood streaming from the many places she can't.

I see him go in for the killing blow. His hand angle changes, his palm cupping to bring the razor-sharp edges into the perfect alignment. It comes down, aiming for her neck, shaped just so, meaning that even as Aicha instinctively pulls backwards, the index finger blade still connects to her carotid artery, slicing straight through.

It's a death blow to anyone. Anyone except Aicha. I saw what he didn't. She also clocked his movements. Not only that, but she angled her head to present her neck very precisely, just so. As his nail cut through her neck, she dropped her wakizashi and now claps her left hand to the back of his head.

She's too slicked-up to get enough grip to do much damage even with her incredible strength. What she *can* do, though, is force his face into a certain position. I realise what she's going to do about a moment before she does it, and it's magnificent. Genius. She pulls him into the jet gushing from her neck, drenching his face in her lifeblood and spraying it into his eyes. He staggers back, blinded, clawing at his face as she raises her katana, her neck already healing, to parry an incoming attack from Sax Man, snatching her wakizashi back up off the floor in the same fluid movement.

It's brilliant. She's basically copied the defence mechanism of the short-horned lizard and used her own blood to repel the assailant. The vampire leader lurches away and instinctively paws at his face, trying to clear his eyes. He might be a vampire now, but he was human once, and being blinded in the middle of battle has sent him into a state of complete panic. He's acting on instinct, so as he desperately tries to wipe the blood out of his eyes, he wipes it from his face as well. As the liquid comes away, so does his make-up. He's under the shade of one of the trees at first, so doesn't notice...until a step back brings him out into direct sunlight.

The vampire screams as the rays hit unprotected skin, and we hear the sizzle and pop of it turning into crackling. The accompanying roast pork smell is a paradox, both appetising and stomach-turning at the same time. If he moved quickly before, now he's a distortion on the air itself. One moment there, then gone. With that one move, Aicha has more than evened the fight. The advantage is now ours.

Sax Man charges in, desperate to seize back the initiative. Of course, Aicha is ready for him. Her neck wound has healed and so has her hamstring. She ducks under the flailing claws, places her shoulder into his solar plexus, and drives herself back up to standing, transforming his furious energy into a flip that carries him sailing through the air. With a back-snapping crunch, he impacts on the paving tiles next to the bench like a comet entering its emo phase, right where the scruffy, potentially homeless fellow lies, still fast asleep and oblivious to everything happening around him.

This, though, is too much, even for his state of stupor. He cracks open an eye, yawns, stretches, and swings his legs round to pivot himself into a sitting position. He blearily scrubs at his face, fumbles in his pockets, and produces a lighter and a suspiciously long, half-smoked roll-up. The sweetness to the acrid smoke as it drifts over once he lights it up confirms it isn't tobacco.

I hear him crack his neck, and then he turns his attention to the prone vampire who is still winded from his short-lived introductory lesson to the principles of flight. He bends over, peering down at the prostrate figure.

'Ey up, cocker. What's crackin' here?'

I've always thought my English is impeccable, but the farther you head towards the Scottish border, the thicker and more impenetrable the accents become. I don't think there's another country in the world where intonation and slang change so entirely within a half-hour drive. Hell, half an hour in America is popping to the corner shop for a lot of the population. Here, it means they sound like two different countries entirely.

This chap has an accent from the north, though where exactly I'd struggle to tell you. Quite a bit farther north than Leicester, that much is sure. It has a warm burr to it that matches with his gentle, albeit slightly dazed smile. His scraggly stubble half-hides a face that probably would count as affably good looking when not waking up on a park bench. His clothes are scruffy — jeans that sit in the middle ground between loose-fit and properly baggy, a striped hoodie with frayed cuffs, and a simple silver chain underneath it. This falls out as he bends over, and the vampire hisses in fear, throwing his arms up across his face like the full-on drama queen he is.

'Oh, reet. One of them, are yee?' He leans farther forward, and for a moment, I think he's going to cuff the vampire round the ear. Instead, he grips the earring and tears it out through the bottom of the lobe. Bringing it closer, he examines it while the vampire shrieks, clutching his shredded ear. He shrugs and tosses it into the nearby flowerbed. Then he peers again at Sax Man.

'Flippin 'eck, yee've made a right old mess there, lad. Let's get thee cleaned up, ey?'

His *talent* builds around him, and it both speaks to mine and raises my magical hackles at the same time. I can use nature in any aspect, but this body I'm in is Unseelie, a creature of the Winter Court. I'd swear down that the person in front of me is human, but there's a touch of frost, a breath of Winter intermingled with the smell of fresh-cut morning grass. It's as if he's human and fae, both Seelie and Unseelie.

Waves of *talent* break over the creature at his feet like the dawn's first tide drenching a rocky inlet and then it's gone. The vampire squeals and starts writhing in agony, his makeup having vanished. All of it. Including his sunblock mascara. Leaving him lying prone, topless, smack bang in the midday sun. That roast-pork smell quickly changes to the charring odour you get when you forgot to take your dinner out of the oven. For several hours. Sax Man's complexion is altering just as rapidly, turning charcoal black and flaking off. The vampire has time to form another O of agony with his mouth, issue a last high pitched keen. Then he explodes into a pile of dust and ash.

Beer Belly has been as agog throughout all of this as we have, but seeing his mate transform into cinders and not the fun kind from the pantomime with ugly stepsisters is enough to give his brain a right royal kick up the arse. He turns to flee at full speed, incomprehensibly fast.

For me, anyhow. Apparently not for Aicha. A throwing knife lances its way from her hand and intercepts his turn radius, cleaving his left ear from his head to pin it to the nearby tree, magic earring and all.

Perfect. That's my cue. I summon my *talent* and push up through the tree's roots, into its branches, to the very tips. Then I persuade the tree that the seasons have sped up, that they're whipping past at a lightning pace, the years skipping along in seconds. The branches shoot out along the trajectory I've calculated, growing at a spectacular rate. Right through the chest of Beer Belly.

He has enough time to look down, realise what has happened, and then say, 'Oh...' before he, too, explodes into dust. It forms a wonderfully neat pile just at the foot of the tree that so effectively skewered him. I thank it, giving the trunk an appreciative pat as I pass. Then I turn my attention to the stranger who so effectively dispatched Sax Man.

He swings himself up off the bench and absent-mindedly dusts at his rumpled clothes, mashing ash from his joint into the fabric as he does so. Looking back up, he gives us a lopsided grin. 'Good work there, our kid, but might have been a grand idea to ask him a few questions afore yee shut his cakehole permanent, like.'

I look at Aicha. She glances back. Then we both stare at this strange Talented who is halfway between a hobo and a high fae apparently. There are so many questions, so many answers we need to get. One is more pressing than all the others though.

'Cakehole?' Aicha voices.

The man or fairy or whatever he is scrunches up his forehead. 'Cakehole, aye. Gob. Yee *meawth*, yee wierdos.'

I run the *meawth* through the part of my brain that handles translating strange and obscure languages, from Aztec to Atlantean, and finally I penetrate the dialect.

'Are you saying "mouth"?' Good God, it's harder than translating what Lou Carcoilh, rest his soul, or Franc, piss on his, said.

'Aye, bingo. Top marks an' all.' His grin hasn't faded in the slightest. It doesn't seem to bother him that we're struggling so hard to understand him. Perhaps making sure people don't quite get him —and thus underestimate him because of it— is a part of his natural defence mechanism. I make a mental note not to commit the same error.

A sudden, terrible thought strikes me - this must have been how the vampires felt when talking to us. I decide to pull the conversation back to the matter at hand. 'Look, don't worry about the vampires. There's still a way to grab some information. First things first... Hold on, sorry. Is that bothering you?'

While his smile remains fixed in place and fixed on me, his eyes keep darting every half a second down to the two piles of ash. The longer it goes on, the more the smile seems strained and the more his gaze keeps flicking like a strobe-light between the piles and us.

He sighs and nods. 'Sorry, mon. Not your fault, right fucking bothers me that it bothers me, it does. Racial stereotyping, that's what it is. Still, no good getting a cob on over it.' He stops, pats himself down, obviously looking for something. After checking all of his pockets and scanning about anxiously on the floor, he goes to rub his chin, obviously bewildered. Doing so knocks the joint from his mouth. He half-catches it, fumbles again, and just snatches it from the air before it falls to the floor.

'Fucking A,' he mutters and takes a hard drag on it. The disappointment that writes itself on his face when he realises it isn't lit anymore would've been heart-breaking if it had been over anything actually serious. He pats himself down again. Aicha leans forward and picks up his lighter from where he left it on the bench before he can start the whole rigmarole again. He nods his thanks, lights up, and inhales deeply. Then he looks at us, that same slightly baffled look back on his face.

'Right, what was it we were talking 'bout again?'

I don't know how I'm going to keep Aicha from killing him. I'm not sure I'll be able to keep myself from doing it. Only centuries of dealing with irritating Powers keeps me from screaming in frustration at the stoner magician. Instead, I take a deep breath and point at the two piles of dehydrated vampires.

'You were telling us why these bothered you so much?'

The guy winces. 'Oh, fucking 'ell. I'd forgotten about them. Still, I'd forget me own head if it weren't screwed on. Ah, bollocks to it.' He waves his hands, and I feel his strange fae magic rise again. The next moment, the two piles of dust vanish. It's bizarre. There's no mysterious gust of wind that comes and carries them off. The earth doesn't split open and swallow the vampire ash whole. Just one moment they're there; the next they aren't.

The not-fae-but-not-human-apparently guy brushes down his jumper again, and I can't help but notice that the traces of ash he dragged down it earlier have also gone. In fact, despite him having literally been asleep on a park bench, with the accompanying image of being homeless that conjures up, he's spotless. His general crumpled style and half-baked demeanour means you think his clothes are dirty. It's only when you look properly, you realise they aren't.

'Fuck a duck, I 'ate that.' His smile finally wavers, and he looks distinctly glum now. 'Pandering to fucking stereotypes. Bastard genetics. Still, no use getting het up about it.' He perks up and turns his smile back towards us. 'What was it we were discussing again?'

This guy is a complete paradox. Clearly massively Talented but also obviously stoned out of his gourd. He should be annoying –and, honestly, with us being on a tight schedule and his all-round weirdness making my brain feel like it's been dumped into a bath filled with the itching powder of curiosity, he is a bit– but somehow he isn't as bad as he should be. Underneath the wreaths of weed smoke and the five-second memory, he has a guileless charm about him. He seems genuinely friendly. Plus, he isn't trying to kill us, which makes for a pleasant change.

I give him the benefit of the doubt and make another effort. 'You were about to tell us who you are.'

He flashes another thousand-watt smile that transforms his face, lighting it up from the inside. 'Oh right. Fuckin 'ell, right rude of me. Beg pardon and that. Craig.'

He sticks his hand out. It's weird, this English obsession with a firm handshake instead of kissing people on the cheeks like normal people do. Still, when in Rome, as they say.

'Paul', I say and, 'Aicha,' as we shake. He looks me up and down as we do so, and I can see the approval on his face. He does it subtly, isn't obvious or rude about it. Still, it's weird.

Oh. So this is what objectification feels like. Got it.

I can see Aicha studying him like when a kid catches a massive spider under a glass and they can't quite decide if they're going to keep looking at it, let it out in the garden, or set it on fire with a magnifying glass. I understand. He is fascinating...in a car-crash-in-slow-motion sort of way.

'So, Paula,' he starts.

'Paul.'

'Paul, right,' he corrects easily. 'Would I be correct in saying that yee might have a little touch of the Fair Folk about yee?'

'This body, yes.'

'Explains why you're such a stunner, doesn't it?' He gives me a bawdy wink. I should probably feel insulted, but there's such a harmless naivety to him, instead I find myself gabbling out an explanation.

'Look, I should probably tell you, I'm not really a woman.' I try to ignore Aicha's snort of laughter behind me. This is going brilliantly.

His eyes pop a touch, but his grin never wavers. 'Bloody 'ell, yee can't half pass! They'd love yee in the clubs up north, I tell yee!' He drops his voice a touch and leans forward. I try to concentrate on what he's saying and ignore what sounds like childish sniggers from over my shoulder. 'I'll be honest with yee. I couldn't care less what's between yer legs or what used to be, lass. Long as you're happy, I'm happy. Proper modern man, me.'

Okay. This has just taken a very unexpected turn, fast.

CHAPTER FIVE
SALZBURG, AUSTRIA, 10 FEBRUARY 1939

I t will do me good to get in out of the cold in more ways than one. Winter in Bavaria has never been a joke. The mountains stretch long fingers down to poke the people with their cold reach well into the months of spring in many places, but the outdoors carries a whole distinct, different chill to the air at the moment. One not related to the weather. A people divided, distrusting, suspicious of lifelong neighbours, let alone scruffy-looking, dark-skinned foreigners. It has replaced the once welcoming, wide-thrown arms I associated with the locals last time I passed through. An impoverishment of spirit seems to have spread more viciously than any malady might have through the Germanic people for all the talk of reclaimed national pride. The rest of the world might only now be stirring awake as to what goes on behind increasingly closed borders, but it's no surprise for those of us in Talented circles. We can see what everyone else has been closing their eyes to.

As such, there're not many places I have less desire to travel to at the current time than Germany and Austria, and yet here I find myself, stomping snow from boot treads like I can shake the niggling disquiet and distaste that lingers from my journey. The roads to arrive at this roaring hearth have not been warm or welcoming by any stretch of the imagination.

Here, at least, I'm guaranteed an open-armed reception. Through frosted glass, electric lights –still, such a marvel to me so many years on– spring to life and then Johannes throws the door wide open and seizes me in an exuberant embrace, practically jumping up and down with me in his arms. It's been many years, but he's still a boundless ball of energy, no doubt having discovered some clandestine occult secret recently, yet still finished in time to go out and drink the whole neighbourhood under the table until the early hours. And considering this is Bavaria, that's no simple task.

Though I do wonder, seeing what lies outside the front door, whether Johannes has been quite so ready to go out and mingle as he did historically.

For now, though, I'm just glad to see my old mentor. He stands taller than I and twice as broad, dressed in a simple white shirt and brown waistcoat. His face is that of a handsome man in his mid-thirties, with a bristling red beard. He's a brilliant bear of a man, as rugged and as raucous as he is intelligent and educated. Which makes me think of Isaac and how very different they are for two people who are so alike in certain ways. Both scholars, both certified geniuses in their occult fields. And both capable of breaching dimensions in a way never since replicated. Magicians of legend and with good reason.

He hurries me inside, slamming fast the door against the wind's bitter, jealous swirl, and hurries me towards the reception room, where the fire crackles merrily, inviting in its offer to thaw out weary fingers. Books cover the walls, much as in Isaac's sitting room, but there's none of the careful haphazardness that defines my friend back home. Everything is neatly put away, stored in its meticulously organised place. Rare grimoires worth small kingdoms are stored alphabetically or chronologically rather than being used as a support for a pile of equally valuable tomes. I've often encouraged Johannes to come and visit us, but it's probably better for the condition of his heart that he never sees Isaac's workshop.

A wooden table, its curved carved legs splayed to support the mighty oak surface as though bowed by the weight, occupies the left side of the room. Sturdy but simple wooden chairs line it, and the top comes replete with a small keg of what I suspect will be remarkably tasty dark Bavarian beer, unless Johannes's tastes have changed dramatically since last I passed by. It looks like it would have taken several men to carry the table in here. Mind you, Johannes always did like the strong, rugged type almost as much as they like him. I'm sure he would've had no problem getting someone to lend a hand, although I also don't doubt he could've moved it himself with ease if he so desired.

Two turquoise-shaded wingback chairs pulled up and angled towards the fire bring back happy thoughts of drunken debates in similar setups with my old friend. Between them, a huge male hound lounges in the radiant heat, the sheen of his sable black fur glinting in the firelight. He pops his head up at my entrance, his tongue lolling out before he springs to his feet and lollops over.

'Paul!' The affectionate growl never changes the strangeness of hearing a dog speak. Even if this dog isn't really a dog. Not anymore, anyway. The creature looks up at Johannes. 'Faust, you never told me Paul was coming!'

Johannes ruffles the creature's head, causing an instinctive preen and doggy grin. 'I wasn't sure when he was, if he was, Mephy. I sent the letter, but I had no reply.'

I sigh. 'The post across Germanic borders is no longer reliable, and I was afraid to draw attention to you from the wrong sorts. We Talented are in high demand with a certain part of these damned so-called National Socialists.'

It's a strange thing to see grimness in place of the usual gregarious expression my friend wears. 'Indeed. I suspect we'll be on the move ourselves

soon, though they'll not find capturing us any easy task what with Mephy...
Mephy!'

The Doberman-shaped being has jumped up and is setting about
humping my leg. 'Mephistopheles! Not cool!' I push at his head, trying to
separate my thigh from a very specific part of his anatomy that's pressed
against it.

Mephistopheles looks up at me, his tongue still hanging out the side of
his mouth. 'Hey, it's not my fault your leg's so bloomin' sexy. I'm just doing
what comes naturally.'

And therein lies the truth of Mephistopheles — the one and only known
and provable case of a demon coming to and staying in the human realm.

First, let's clear up a few misconceptions about demons. In the same way
that angels aren't heavenly stooges who've drawn the short straw in the
whole "free will" stakes and have to do whatever some overbearing creator
demands, neither are demons some pointy-horned sadists getting their
kicks from prodding the damned with their pitchforks. Those are human
simplifications applied through lenses of misinformation and prejudices.

The Bene Elohim, aka: angels, occupy the higher dimensions, where beings have transcended from the physical, the limitations of flesh. Demons
exist in the lower planes. That doesn't mean they're evil or cruel, though
they can be. It means they revel in the corporeal, delight in the base urges
of the body. The way Mephistopheles describes it, the lower dimensions
are one long continuous Roman orgy all day and all night, stopping only
to gorge on the most extravagant and taste-buds-overloading dishes their
peculiar Talent can produce. Things like work or duty or commitment are
incongruous to them. They do whatever they like the moment the thought
occurs to them. They can't imagine living any other way.

Which is why despite demonology gripping the seedy mind of many
a socially inept and embittered young Talented, we aren't knee-deep in

denizens of the lower planes. It's very simple really. They think our reality is boring. Totally lacking in decent entertainment. Basically, we're a bunch of puritan prudes, and they don't want anything to do with us. The very few times anyone has successfully managed to summon one, demons have done everything they could to fuck back off to their own dimension as quickly as inhumanly possible. Usually by turning the summoner inside out and stringing their internal organs like bunting from the chandeliers.

Except, for some reason, Mephistopheles. I'm not sure how or even why Faust summoned him. I know it wiped out the Hotel zum Löwen and several neighbouring buildings in the ensuing spreading blaze in Staufen im Breisgau. Luckily, he faked his own death at the same time as it made him persona non grata in the Prussian states.

Whether it was something about the particular working Faust did or about him personally that bound Mephistopheles here, I have no idea. Faust won't ever discuss the details, not even with me. And Mephy gives him a strange look whenever I raise it, that sort of half-resentful, half-exasperated but entirely affectionate glance an old married couple will share. I can't help but think their relationship must be something along the same sort of lines as with Isaac and Nithael, that somehow, in the course of whatever working he used to open the pathway through, their essences became intertwined. So for as long as Johannes is here, so is Mephistopheles.

Thing is, demons never learn much at home about impulse control. And Mephy doesn't see much point in changing that just because he's in a different dimension. So when he sees a leg he wants to fuck, he doesn't bother with flowers and diamonds. Doesn't matter whose leg it is. He just ups and ruts.

I wisely don't bring up his visit to the Bavarian Court in the sixteenth century. It still makes Johannes wince and turn redder than the particular member Mephistopheles rubbed up against — Albert V. Repeatedly. He earned his title of Albert The Magnanimous that day by not executing them both on the spot.

After using a conveniently placed poker as a lever to separate Mephy away from canoodling with my lower extremities and by distracting him with a sizeable chunk of deer leg, we settle down into the fireside chairs, tankards in hand. An amicable clink and appreciative first swig, then we settle down to business.

'So what's the matter, Johannes?' I don't want to beat around the bush. We've been friends for near on four hundred years, and never once in that time has he asked me for help. 'What can I do to aid you, man?'

He sighs, wiping the froth from his thick red beard absently with his sleeve. ''Tis not for me, my friend. A problem has arisen for another, a colleague of sorts. A brilliant if occasionally foolish man with a fabulous mind and an obsession with your past that has caused him all sorts of problems.'

My ears prick up at this. 'My past? What do you mean? He's followed my studies?' I can do without that; I'm quite happy to stay anonymous. I've no need for fans or stalkers, thank you very much.

Faust shakes his head. 'Not your individual past. The collective one of your people. The Cathars.'

Oh. One of those. 'Is he another of these blasted Polaires? Waltzing around claiming to be Esclarmonde's reincarnation?' I ran into the Countess of Caithness once to see how she was, this woman claiming to be that most practical and Perfect of women. Let's just say she didn't manage to fill the rather large shoes she asserted were hers.

'No, though I believe he knows them. He passed quite some time over in the Pyrenees, around Montsegur, I think.'

'I've not heard of any Talented setting up round there?' Not that it's surprising. I avoid that part of the Pyrenees like the plague. Not exactly packed full of happy memories.

'He's not Talented. Well, not as I can *see*, anyhow.'

Now I'm really intrigued. I can't imagine why Faust has called me here to get involved if the fellow's some unTalented scholar. 'So who is this chap? And where do I come in with all of this?'

Johannes is about to answer when there comes a light, hesitant knock at the door, the sort of noise made by someone who's not sure what they're more afraid of — that there's no one inside or that someone is. He flaps his hand at me to stay seated as I half rise, then hurries down the hall to the front door. Even craning myself around into an eminently uncomfortable angle, I can't see who the guest is.

Faust comes back into the room, leading a man who's taken the first step into middle age. His strong nose and dark eyes aren't features particularly in vogue in Germany at this precise moment. A prominent forehead suggests his hairline is moving rearwards, though what he has is still thick, slicked back, and black, fixed in place with gel no doubt. He's no warrior; he doesn't have the physique of a pugilist, but there's something to him that suggests he possesses a will and a drive that might lead him to walk across hot coals or razor blades to get to what he wants to know. The sardonic quirk of his eyebrows can't hide that desire for knowledge burning underneath. It's a gaze I've seen before in men who've uncovered great secrets. And often paid great prices for them.

I couldn't give a damn about that though. A second later, I leap to my feet, cross the room in a blink, and have the man pinned against the wall in a heartbeat, already reaching for a knife. Faust blocks my arm, holding my wrist gently but firmly.

'What, now, Paul? Such poor faith in me. This is my guest I spoke of!'
His tone is mild, but there's reproach in there. I'm in his house. We're safe.
It's not my job to be assaulting his invitees.

I look askance at my host. The first reason why I have this man hoisted
up by his throat is his long trench coat, replete with the epaulettes marking
him out as a high-ranking member of the SS, the German secret service,
a murderous bunch if ever there was one. Apparently, though, this isn't
enough, so I pop his lapel, revealing the badge under it. A rope-tied sword
in a rune-inscribed oval.

'He's with the fucking Ahnenerbe, Johannes!' I can't keep the hiss from
my voice. Good God, I want to kill this bastard stone-dead.

The Ahnenerbe — the Nazi natural philosophers and archaeologists
digging for objects of *power*.

Hunting the Talented wherever they can find them.

CHAPTER SIX

LEICESTER, 7 JUNE, PRESENT DAY

Getting propositioned by strange English fae magicians wasn't quite how I expected the day to turn out.

I'm still somewhat knocked off balance by getting hit on. Aicha, bless her, rides to my rescue before Craig can try any harder to get me out on a date. 'So we got names. I don't mean to be rude, but I don't actually care if I am, so there's that. What are you?'

This pulls Craig's attention away from me and back to the situation at hand. He gives a sweeping bow, elegant as a Victorian courtier. 'No offence taken, lass. I'm the Magus of Blackburnshire, King of the Hobs.'

Bloody hell. Those are two big titles to be bandying about. I open my *talent* up and *look* at him. He keeps his own power tightly reined in, but I can tell there's a metric shit tonne of it. Meaning there is a lot more to Craig than first meets the eye. The thought strikes me again that this is almost certainly deliberate.

I replay some details of our chat with the vampires in my head. 'Hold on, so it's you the Kiss rejects were looking for?' They'd asked me if I was the King of the Hobs.

'Well, more they were aware I was looking for them, like. Been a fair load of 'em coming up my ends, moithering me and tryin' to take me territory. Seemed to be coming up from down 'ere, so thought I'd come 'ave a poke about, like.'

I furrow my brow. 'So why were you asleep on the park bench then?'

Craig chuckles, looking a touch embarrassed. 'Oh, that. Smoked far too much of this far too fucking early for me own good, like, didn't I? Daft bastard that I am.' He takes another toke to emphasise exactly what it was he'd been doing too much of.

Colour me shocked. I would never have imagined it. Still, I wonder if he has any other useful information for us. 'Any idea who the vampires are working for?'

'Well, they're vampires, lass, so for their own damn selves would be my guess. I get what you're getting at though, like. I 'eard rumours they are all buddied up with someone. That's why they're getting all hoity-toity, thinking they'll come and have a reccie up in my end of the woods. Cheeky sods. Finding out who and having a small word in their shell like is the main reason I'm 'ere.'

Interesting. Looks like our aims align, assuming he's telling the truth. Funnily enough, though, I find myself trusting him. And not just because he wants to take me out on a date.

'Okay.' I walk over towards the car park on the other side of the black-painted railings, to the west of the cathedral. I'm not sure what the building on the other side of it is. A mixture of old industrial factory and modern glasswork, it looks like a school, but the lack of pupils suggests otherwise. I'm not really too interested in what it is though. I'm more interested in the large black SUV parked just on the other side of the fence. Or rather, by what's underneath it.

I stop by the passenger side door. 'Are you okay under there?'

There is a long pause filled with silence. I clarify. 'I know you're under there. Your soles are poking out,' I say as kindly as possible.

'Oh, so he does have two soles!' Aicha adds brightly.

I groan. 'Ouch, *laguna*. Right, I'll ask you again. Are you okay under there?'

Further silence. Then –

'...Yeeees?'

The word is drawn out, thick with uncertainty. Still, we've broken the ice. I plough on.

'Are you the last vampire? Leader of the ones who attacked us?'

Another pause.

'...Noooo?'

I mean, top marks for audacity. It's never going to work, but the Good God loves a tryer. I play along.

'So what are you doing under that car?'

More silence.

'...Having a nap?'

Ouch. I can hear him wincing as he says it. He knows it's stupid the moment it comes out of his mouth. He was doing so well.

'Comfortable place to have a nap, is it?'

'...Yessss?'

Okay, he's really struggling now. I walk around the car to where his head is and lean down. 'Okay, good effort. Nice try. Thing is, there's far more comfortable places to grab fifty winks. Like the park bench. Over there. In the sun. That was comfy, wasn't it, Craig?'

'Bloody right! I only meant to snooze for five minutes. That was at nine o'clock this morning, like!'

'So you've got two choices. First, I can drag you out of there and accompany you over for a nice long, probably eternal lie down on that lovely, comfy bench. Or you can tell us all about who you're working for and your connection with De Montfort.'

The vampire hisses, which might have been scarier if he wasn't currently cowering under what's effectively a shuttle bus for a large family, hiding from the daylight. 'I can't tell you anything!'

'Then it's time for your daily dose of Vitamin D,' I say cheerily and reach down to drag him out by his earlobe.

The vampire hisses and spits like a cornered cat, scratching at my wrist. Normally said action would have resulted in half the blood in this body pissing out under the car with him, but he pulled the hand back before he could cut too deep as the sunlight hit his black nail varnish. Guess it isn't very sun resistant. Neither is his ear. As he pulls himself back under the safety of the car's chassis, it comes off in my hand.

'Oh, dear.' Between him pulling back in horror and agony and my firm grip, his crispy fried earlobe snapped off. 'Is it supposed to do that?' I look over at Aicha and shake my head sadly as I toss Demon Fart's earring away. 'They just don't make Nosferatu like they nosferatused to.'

'Hashtag sad.' She cleans globules of the black tar blood off her weapon. They splatter next to the tyre of the SUV. Close enough that the vampire underneath can see exactly what they are.

'Stop! Please, stop!' The Ginger Lord of Darkness whimpers. I don't feel too sorry for him. His ear will regrow quicker than his roots do. If we leave him alive.

'So tell us all about De Montfort and his connection with your nest.' The good humour drains from my voice. He knows just how serious I am.

This vampire isn't done trying though. 'We don't have any connection to the University. Our master forbade us to hunt there.' The hopeful tone to his voice that we'll buy into his innocent misunderstanding would be cute if we weren't in such a hurry.

'Hey, look!' I crumble the disintegrating ear into ash between my fingers. Bending down, I use the black residue on my fingers to write 'twat' in English on the pavement next to the car, then draw an arrow pointing underneath. I hum pensively. 'Aich, if we cut off all the parts of his face, do you think we'd have enough to make a sidewalk painting? We could title it "Stalling Knobhead And The Price He Paid For Wasting Our Time". What do you reckon?'

'Down to try.' A sudden grin, brighter than her gleaming blade, spreads over Aicha's face. 'Hey, would that make him a NoseForArtU?'

Oh, damn. Damn, damn, damn. How did I miss that one? Cursing internally, I turn my attention back to the terrified vampire. 'Would you like to try again? Remember, you've still got "phone a friend", although if I see you reach for your mobile, I'll redo your makeup with the charcoal I make out of your hands. Capiche?'

He caves. Course he does. It's the only sensible course of action. We killed his backup, and if he comes out from under the car, he's a dead man or deader man considering he's already undead. 'I don't know much.' I think even he can hear how weak a starting line that is.

'Well.' Now that he has crumbled, literally in the case of his ear, my tone brightens once more. 'Let's start with what you do know, and we'll decide how valuable it is and how many limbs the information you hold back is going to cost you. Sound fair?'

'What happens if I answer no to that?'

'I snap appendages off until you say yes.'

'Yes. That sounds totally fair.' The vampire's voice conveys how utterly miserable he is. I might feel sorry for him if he didn't try to kill me. And if he wasn't an undead bloodsucking fiend. With terrible makeup skills just to add insult to injury.

'Good! Spit it out then.'

I can almost hear him gnawing his lip. I wonder if vampires accidentally cut themselves when they do that. Maybe that's why they're so arrogant. Bashfulness leads to lip laceration. 'I really don't know much.'

Hearing the hesitation, I consider applying more threats, but we've already terrified the guy. He'd be close to a heart attack if his heart were still beating. 'I've never heard of De Montfort. Wait!' He feels my hand close around his leg. Apparently, that's excellent motivation. 'I haven't, but I know who you mean. The fae who gave us our earrings, right?'

'Right.' I let go of my grip. Looks like he gets to keep his limbs. For now.

'Okay, so yeah. I know him. He had to put the earrings in. Something about a spell on them. Him and the master have been working closely. It was him who helped us set up here. Told us we could use this as a base of operations to expand our reach northwards.'

'So your dick'ead of a master is 'ere in Leicester?' Craig leans in, and I feel the *talent* building. There's definitely more to him than meets the eye.

There's silence from under the car. The power in the air builds further. Then soft choking noises emanate from underneath.

'Stop!' I say sharply, both to the vampire and to the Magus. 'Stop trying to answer that question. You can't, can you?'

'No.' The choking noises stop, at least. I was worried he would kill himself trying to respond.

I turn to Craig. 'He's under some form of geas. Probably part of the bond with his Master. Giving us that information could directly lead to killing him or harming his nest-lord. He's physically incapable of telling us.'

It's a sensible move by his liege. Vampires are vermin and treated as such by the rest of the Talented world. They're pests, spreading out from a spot, consolidating their power base until they can take over. No respect for the unTalented, no care taken. All they want is to feed, and they'll happily murder their way to a full belly. They'll also show no respect for the boundaries of other Talented. Means that even those who don't really care about the non-magical folk don't like vampires. Those like me who do? Really despise them. They're all superhumanly quick and strong, and the older ones can develop a form of *talent*. Strange and dark and twisted but *powerful*. Like cockroaches, they get stamped out, their nests destroyed as soon as any neighbouring Talented find out about them. Like cockroaches, they always survive though. Seems like that's what has brought this Magus of Blackburnshire down to the Midlands of England. They've encroached on his territory. He's come to return the favour. With extreme prejudice if he's any sense.

None of that matters too much to me though. I've bigger fish to fry than territory squabbles in another country even if it involves vampires. I pull the conversation back to what matters to me. 'What about De Montfort? What did he get out of you being here?'

'Guards.' I can hear the miserable tone of the vampire's voice. He isn't directly betraying his Master, so he can give the information. He knows he's revealing information that can hurt his nest though. Luckily, he's more worried about the immediate hurt we can lay on him. 'We keep an eye out for any Talented coming into town and deal with them if they do. Plus, there are certain areas he has us keep watch on at all times. Like here.'

'The cathedral?'

'And the visitor centre over the way.'

Of course he does. Cunning bastard. It's a smart move. De Montfort doesn't care about territory like most of us do. His driving force is his nefarious plan with the bones, whatever that involves. Getting a load of super-tough cannon fodder and setting them up as sentries around any potential loose ends protects him and acts as an early warning system. Especially with the natty skull-and-crossbones earrings.

'Where else is guarded?' An excellent question from Aicha. Brilliant thinking. By telling us where he wants protecting, it might reveal potential weak spots.

'Umm, the university. De Montfort, that is. Those are the main two at the moment.'

Hmm. Not entirely helpful but not totally useless either. If I were De Montfort, I'd be tempted to have the vampires stake out the university just because of the shared name. Anyone coming here to investigate him might well follow that connection. Of course, he might also have it guarded because of a more direct connection. Either way, it's worth investigating if the visitor centre is a dud.

I raise an eyebrow at the other two, an invitation to ask any further questions. Both give slight headshakes to say they're done. I have one more to ask. 'When were you expected to check in again?'

'Tomorrow morning. Just before dawn, we have a shift change. Time to head off and feed quickly, then get some sleep. It's a long shift.'

Twenty-four hours is a serious amount of time to be on duty. Sounds to me like the vampires need to unionise. Though I'm not sure that works when you have an all-powerful dictatorial father figure in charge. When said "father" also likes to be referred to as your Master, you're into a whole world of weird trauma to boot.

One last question pops into my head. 'How many of you are there in your nest?'

Silence. That slightly choked silence that tells me we've hit up against the limits of what he can tell us. I try a slightly different tactic. 'More than twenty?'

A slight grunt comes from under the car. 'More than fifty?' The same noise again. 'More than a hundred?' There's a half-whine, half-expulsion of air that I take to mean we're in the right ballpark numbers wise. Fucking hell. A hundred vampires. That's a mess we could do with avoiding.

I judge that we've got as much information out of this schmuck as we're going to. I push my *talent* into the earth, searching. Deep down, I find what I'm looking for buried under the concrete. A dormant thistle seed carried by insects or the tiny natural movements of the earth always happening under our feet. It takes only some gentle coaxing and some investment of *talent* for it to grow.

It smashes out through the tarmac, cracking the even surface like Jack's beanstalk breaking out of the barren earth. The sharp-spiked stalk comes up straight under the top left of his back. Thanks to my power, it cuts through his body as easily as it did the car park. I feel it come out the other side, its head blossoming into a flower as it bursts from his chest cavity, annihilating his heart in the process. He explodes into ash instantly. Looks like he used all the blood he drank previously, trying to heal from the sun damage. What's left of him will help nourish the little weed that killed him.

At least now there's no way he'll be going back to report on us. I turn to the other two. 'Right, that gives us till tomorrow morning before they realise something's amiss, all being well. Seems to me we need to have a sit down and chat. Discuss what's going on, share a bit of knowledge. Find out any shared goals...'

'Eat some food before I tear your tongue out and strangle you with it. Less talking. More eating.'

'And apparently, stop Aicha from getting too hangry as well. Pub?'

Craig grins that half-baked, half-charming grin. 'Scran wi' a couple of crackers such as yourselves? Why, I'd be mad to say no. It's a date.'

It isn't a date. Despite what he thinks, it definitely isn't.

CHAPTER SEVEN
LEICESTER, 7 JUNE, PRESENT DAY

Off on our definitely-not-a-date. Also to feed Aicha before she kills someone in cold low blood sugar. Probably me.

We head back up to the high street. I spotted a decent-looking pub as we made our way to the cathedral called The Tree. A sign noting vegan-friendly food caught my eye. Of course, we aren't in France anymore. There isn't the same deeply ingrained cultural suspicion of anyone who volunteers to forego the delights of consuming dead flesh. I seem to remember reading somewhere that veganism is the fastest expanding culinary market over here. We French still get baffled by flexitarianism.

The menu highlights this effectively. There's an entire separate vegan/vegetarian/gluten-free section. The options are mind-blowing. There is a serious possibility I'll never leave England. It's equally possible I might just camp out in this pub for the rest of eternity.

We wend our way through the bar area, which looks like a hipster's dream of a Victorian snug. Bakersfield-style armchairs covered in distressed green leather sit between stools and high-backed wooden seats. The pile of board games are a nice touch. Still, we've no time to enjoy ourselves. Outside of indulging in the culinary delights, of course.

We take a seat outside. There's a rear terrace with a mixture of wooden benches and tables and functional plastic seating. Although it's compact, the high walls give a sense of privacy, and I find the trees and creeping vines soothing. My fae nature gets antsy in built-up areas. The amount of iron composites around us might not be enough to slow me down, but it's like dunking an allergy sufferer's head inside the filled bag of a vacuum cleaner. My eyes itch, I've got a bunged-up nose, and I feel like I'm running a heavy cold. At least the bar isn't decked out in the a-la-mode industrial fashion. Otherwise, I'd probably break out in hives.

Both the bar and the outside are packed, but we grab a small round table we can perch around. A simple spell keeps our conversation indiscernible to anyone nearby. Once we place our orders, no one else needs to hear what we have to say.

We fill in Craig on most of what's happened. I'm not sure how much he takes on board, to be honest. He's added a spell to the cone of silence we've established that deodorises his smoke when it hits the barrier. As a result, he spends the entire meal puffing away on a joint I can only presume has been rolled in the American way – without tobacco. The fact it looks more like a cigar than a cigarette means he didn't skimp on the amount of weed he packed it with. I use a teeny amount of my own *talent* to keep the smoke away from my mouth. I don't want to catch a contact high. It's hard enough to avoid ordering one of everything off the menu as is; I don't need to end up getting the munchies as well.

The northern wizard looks intrigued when we talk about De Montfort, even if it takes us about ten goes to explain the whole reincarnation thing we both have going on.

'So he comes back in the bodies of your kids?' He scratches at the growth on his cheeks. I'm not surprised. It makes me itch just looking at it.

'No.' I try again. 'It wasn't ever my kid. It was his.'

'And you pick and choose the body you want?'

'Not normally, no. That only worked in Lyon because Isaac is such a genius.'

'And this Jack of Plate was really De Montfort?'

I avoid banging my head on the table. Just. 'No.'

In between all this, we get Craig's story from him. He lives up north, near Blackpool, which is, according to him, the English version of Las Vegas, though something about the quirk of his mouth as he says that makes me suspect he isn't being entirely truthful. The gist of it is that vampires went up north, trying to muscle in on his territory and take him out in the process. He skirts around what happened, but I pick up they're getting too close to his home. He has a teenage daughter called Emme. I get the impression he has a pretty laissez-faire attitude to life. Seems like the threat to her well-being, though, is enough to stir him to action. So he's headed south to find out where the vampires are coming from and how they became so audacious as to assault the Magus of Blackburnshire directly.

Talking about his title brings me to one of the most intriguing questions I have about him. 'Look, both you and that vampire called you the King of the Hobs.'

'Aye, that's right.' He's taking a break from his spliff for a moment, during which, he's attempting to shovel the entirety of his plate –some sort of chicken curry that, to be fair, smells absolutely amazing– into his mouth.

'I mean, how does that work? Aren't you...' I'm not sure how to put it delicately.

'Human? Aye, funny story, that.' I can see a three-way battle of desires going on in his head, between wanting to tell the story, finish his food, and inhale his weed. Although, considering how he's eating, maybe it's more inhaling his food and finishing his weed. Like most of us, though, the opportunity to tell an origin story, particularly a peculiar one like the one I've asked about, wins out.

'So, basically, right, my great-great-great-great-great-I-don't-fuck-ing-know-how-many-greats-grandaddy were a hob, reet? And he weren't just any hob, but were King of the Hobs over in Faerie. Anyhow, he did someat or other that upset the big chief bitch Maeve over there. Got her proper riled up 'n all. Asked me pops once what he'd done was so bad. Apparently, he got absolutely smashed at a do she were throwing, where he was in charge of clean up. 'Cept he got rat-arsed on the elderflower wine, dint he? So next day, when Maeve comes down expecting her ballroom to be proper shiny-like, instead it's still completely trashed with the Hob King passed out in a pile of his own puke on her throne. She didn't see the funny side. Lacking much of a sense of humour, by all accounts. Right hard-ass.' He frowns, visibly straining to think back through his hazy recollection of our conversation. 'Did you meet her at all?'

We got as far in our own story as telling him we'd planned to go to Faerie but not that we'd managed it. I wave a regal hand downwards at the body I'm wearing. 'Meet her? You're looking at her right now.'

He spurts his mouthful of food out, although, to give him his due, he turns his head sufficiently that it sprays into a nearby plant pot rather than on me — or even worse for his life expectancy, on Aicha herself.

'You're fuckin' Maeve? Christ on a bike. Beggin' your pardon, yee mag-isterial self. I thought yee were Paul.'

Apparently, the shock has made him forget my whole "reincarnating in dead bodies thing". That or the copious amounts of cannabis. One or the other.

I make a calming gesture with both hands. 'I am Paul. This was her body. She's not using it anymore.'

Craig's eyes pop wide open. It highlights the pinky-red colour they've turned. The shade deepened during our conversation. He looks really, really high. 'You killed Maeve? Fucking 'ell, fair play, like. Talk about ding, dong, the witch is dead. Crackin' work, lass. How did it happen?'

I shrug. 'It was her own fault. She committed Aichacide.'

'But how do you kill the fuckin' Queen of the Winter Court? That's mad as fuck.'

Aicha cradles her pineapple juice. 'I found sticking the pointy end of a sword into her repeatedly was a good start.'

We've drifted off the point. I get the feeling this is a regular occurrence with Craig. 'You were telling us about Maeve and your ancestor.'

He tips his pint in acknowledgement to me. 'Right! So, anyhow, yeah, Maeve's vexed big time, proper raging over the mess he made, especially over her throne, right? He's still snoozing, so fucking gone he ain't even realised the boss lady's rocked up. Anyhow, she wants to bring maximum misery on him — not just him, either, but his offspring and every descendent forever and ever, amen; you with me? So first thought's probably some spectacularly bloody execution, but that's letting him off the hook too damn easy, that's what old Maevey is thinking. Can't have that. So she stands and thinks about what's the worst thing she can do to him. What's the shittiest, lowliest, crappiest creature in all the known bleedin' universes? Easy answer that. Humans, innit? So she makes a spell, changes him into a piddling human, and banishes him off to Earth, good riddance to bad and messy rubbish, right?'

He stops. There's a momentary conflict over what's his priority — taking a breath or taking a drink. His unwise decision is to try to do both simultaneously, leading to him spluttering into his beer.

'Sorry, wrong pipe,' he says once he regains the ability to speak. 'Right, where was I?' I have to wonder for a moment if he means regarding the story or his current position in space and time. I wouldn't be surprised if he's forgotten both. 'Oh, yeah. Okay, so great-great-shit-tonnes-of-greats-grandpappy goes over to the Dark Side, becomes human over in our world and all that. Thing is, he's still the King of the Hobs. Maeve ain't thought that through, mainly 'cos for her, no one else's royal status is worth a bean. 'Cept that's right important still for the hobs. Hobs is all about cleanliness and order and structure. And eating the gizzards of anyone who fucks with them too. 'S why they were over in Winter, after all.

'So the old fella gets banished 'ere, but the hobs still need him as His Nibs, get me? And thing about hob royalty, by their rules, only way the title can pass on is by death, willingly going to the offspring, or by abdication. Not big on the usual "stab you in the back and nick the crown off your head, son" way of most royal successions, bless 'em. Well, the old boy's not daft, is he? He realised, thanks to holding on to the crown, he's got access to his magic still. Makes life a damned sight more comfy, like, over 'ere. So when the hobs came popping across for a cuppa and asked him to resign, he politely refused. Then spanked the shit out of the nearest one to make his point, like.'

He takes another drink of his beer — without nearly choking to death this time. A successful improvement. 'Anyhow, long story short, it's mainly a ceremonial title these days, what with Maeve being a reet vindictive bitch, fucking champion at holding a grudge 'n all. Still, does mean I get to have access to some nifty fae magic despite being a puny human, int it? So, yeah, cheers!' He salutes us with his glass, then downs the rest in one smooth movement.

It's an amazing story, even if translating both Craig's northern dialect and broken pattern of speech takes some doing. I've never heard of a full human having access to fairy magic the way he does. Sure, there's Gwendolyne, but she's a fae-in-waiting. Generally, half-fairies and their gradually watered down offspring have touches, flares of the *talent* their original ancestor had. Nothing like what Craig wields though. No wonder he holds the title of Magus despite being apparently permanently stoned out of his gourd.

That's a question in and of itself. I feel like we've got to where I can ask him that without fear of insulting him. 'I hope you don't mind me asking, but what is with the whole...' I wave my hand at the chunky, clearly incredibly potent spliff he's lit up again. I can't think of a polite way to put it. 'The whole Cheech Marin impression?'

Craig looks at the spliff, confusion creasing his brow, like he can't re-member what it is or where it's come from. He takes another drag just to remind himself. It seems to work. 'Oh, this? Well, I'm fae, ain't I? Sorta.' He says it like it answers everything.

I've just got back from Faerie. I don't remember seeing them all passing the bong around while we battled it out with their nobility. 'I'm not following.' Honesty seems the best policy.

He takes the hint to elaborate. 'Well, I'm all about nature, ain't I? Con-nected with Mother Earth and all that woo-woo stuff, right? So way I see it, I can either go dancing 'round a maypole with me knackers hanging out or else get connected with 'er another way. Getting me smoke on helps me link into my power. Since I like having access to my power, right, I smoke. All the time. Plus —' He gestures wildly. I'm not entirely sure at what. Then I realise it's just a general gesture at everything outside of us. 'Have you seen reality, like? It's all a lot more bearable when you're baked, honestly. Does my nut in, otherwise.'

Funnily enough, I can understand that. There's a certain undeniable logic there. I look over at Aicha and see the same understanding mirrored in her expression. It doesn't matter who you are in life. How much money or power or *talent* you have. The world can be a dark and unwelcoming place. Once you become part of the magical world, it only adds another layer of danger and double-crossing to life. It's hard for those who want no part in the politics and power plays. Sure, Isaac has withdrawn from it all to a degree, but he has Nith as protection, a mind-bogglingly powerful angel from a higher dimension. And even then, he gets dragged into my bullshit plenty of times. I can appreciate the attraction of the old "turn on, tune in, drop out" mantra. If getting high makes life easier for Craig and keeps him in tip-top form *talent*-wise for when the challenges he can't avoid come, all power to him.

We've caught up on each others' backstories, as much as is necessary, at least. It underlines my gut feeling that we can trust this Craig. Our major concern is he'll fall asleep in the middle of a battle or forget he's supposed to even turn up to it. I'd take flaky over snaky, though, any day.

'What's your next plan of action then?' I get straight to the point. Probably a good plan, considering the magician's ability to get distracted by the bubbles popping in his beer.

'Eh?' He pulls his attention back to me with some effort. 'Oh, yeah, right. Further investigation and all that, hey. See if I can dig up the location of the main nest. That'd be right good, get this all done and dusted. With the emphasis on dusted, if you see what I mean. Like, if you kill a vampire, they turn into dust, poof.' He makes an explosion gesture, followed by slow raining movements of his fingers to symbolise the falling ash.

'Yeah, we got it.' It wouldn't have been a bad joke if he didn't spell it out. 'So looks like the vamps and De Montfort are working together. Seems our interests are aligned. Fancy carrying on the team-up for the time being?'

He grins a cheeky, shit-eating grin that should put my back up but somehow doesn't. For an incomprehensibly powerful fae-magic-wielding Talented, there remains something charmingly innocent about him. 'I'd love to team up with you, lass. Any time.'

Looks like he isn't done hitting on me though. Oh, good.

CHAPTER EIGHT
LEICESTER, 7 JUNE, PRESENT DAY

I heard Richard III despised tall Talented. Apparently, he hated Lank Casters.

Suitably refreshed, with the tanks refilled thanks to a hearty meal, we head back over to the Richard III centre. It's a fascinating place, all semi-holographic projections and interactive displays. The dig sites themselves are on display. Unsurprisingly, there are no lingering magical traces. It's been over a decade since the exhumation of the skeletons. They have bones behind glass, but they're copies, plastic versions of the originals. We riddle the clearly knowledgeable and passionate staff with as many questions as we can think of short of, 'Where can we find these specific bones so we can steal them?' which might upset their professional demeanour. They enthuse about the story of the dig, but all they can tell us afterwards is that they've gone to various archaeological departments for further study and preservation. Excluding King Richard himself, who's re-buried in the cathedral facing the site.

Eventually, we speak to a wiry grey-haired chap. Approaching the later end of middle age, his vim knocks twenty years off him when he speaks. He works in direct partnership with the University of Leicester, which was the driving force and chief authority behind the dig itself. They took charge of dating and identifying the remains found. We turn the conversation around to the skeleton in the sarcophagus, to his intense delight. His passion for the find runs towards obsession, and it clearly delights him that we're interested in details outside of King Richard III himself. Sadly, he doesn't know anything about the information we have, that it's gone to Kenilworth. I see him hesitate though.

'Was there something else about those remains?' I don't want to dig too hard and raise suspicion about our motives. I can see something has clicked in his memory though. Luckily, this is a man who loves to share, indeed who gets paid to share his enthusiasm about this particular subject on a daily basis.

'Now that you mention it, yes. One funny thing. I was here on-site as they all got parcelled up, packaged, and sent off. I seem to remember one got sent to De Montfort University, which didn't...' He hesitates. 'Well, it didn't make much sense.'

'Why not?' I continue to press delicately. We need this information. I don't want him to clam up.

'Well, no offence to De Montfort University, but it's not their area of expertise. They're a great university,' he adds hurriedly. You can tell he's desperate not to speak ill of anything to do with his city to visitors. 'They just don't have the equipment to deal with that level of archaeological find. Not like Leicester University. Plus, Leicester Uni were involved in the project from start to finish.' He polishes his glasses on his museum-branded polo-neck T-shirt. 'I think it was a council decision. Something to do with being fair, making sure everyone got to share in this tremendous success story for the city. De Montfort opened up their own Heritage Centre, you know? Built it round the ruins of the Church of Annunciation, where part of their own campus is. I think that was the reason they gave us for that course of action.' I can hear the doubt in his voice. It was obviously strange enough to stick in his mind. That makes it worth investigating in my book.

We thank him and head back outside, regrouping in the afternoon's warmth outside the cathedral where we dealt with the Goth Squad.

'What do you think?' I ask Aicha.

'Nothing there, *saabi.*' Her eyes rove over the visitor centre as if she can see through it, searching out some hidden clue we've missed so far. 'Only other thing is the computer system.'

It's a valid point. We could try to break in, hack their computers. Problem with that is technical know-how. I look over at Craig. 'Are you any good with computers?'

He smiles back. 'Oh, aye! Proper good. Love computers, me. They're not so much fans of me though. Fuckers are always breaking down or the hard drives seizing up or whatever. Costs me an arm and a leg every time.'

Okay. 'So if we need to completely melt down their servers and lose all the information stored in them, you're our man?'

'Absolutely. No worries, like.'

Not exactly what I wanted to hear. I sigh. 'I really hoped we'd have something more to show for the visit. We're on a time limit now. We've only got till tomorrow dawn before the vamps and by extension, presumably, De Montfort know something's amiss. Considering the layers of scheming he's demonstrated so far, I don't doubt he'll end up in the wind. So what do we do next? Follow up on the De Montfort University lead we just got? Or head straight for Kenilworth Castle?'

Aicha gets straight to the point. 'The skeleton might have stopped at the university, but it ended up at the castle. Can always come back and break into the campus later if the castle's a bust. Follow the bones.'

Craig shrugs. 'There's been nowt so far pointing me towards the nest or any other vampires, like. My next plan is to come back here in the wee hours, catch whoever comes to take over from them other daft buggers we killed. I ain't got any plans, like, till then.'

I feel torn, but I know why. It was my idea to come to Leicester first rather than going straight to the castle. I want that to have been the right decision, but honestly? Meeting up with Craig has been cool, and he's useful to have as an ally, albeit temporarily, and finding out about the vampire connection is no small titbit of information. I've shown our hand though. The last thing I wanted to do. The whole idea was to scout out cautiously, without alerting Demon Fart to our presence. Particularly not to my continued existence or unexpected freedom. Now we only have the rest of the day and the night before he knows that something is wrong.

I wanted the university lead to be solid, to be the trail of breadcrumbs that leads us straight to his door, but I have to be honest. It doesn't fit. Arrogance is a definite character trait of Demon Fart's but so is sly cunning and caution. I don't think he'll be camped out in an institution that bears his name, however much that might tickle his pride.

I sigh. 'Let's head back to the car.' Looks like we're driving over to Kenilworth after all.

It isn't a long drive. The castle is just on the other side of Coventry. The M69 (a name that causes Craig to wiggle his eyebrows lasciviously at me, to Aicha's delighted amusement in the back) leads us most of the way. Driving the last small stretch brings us through one of the charming rustic villages of the English countryside. They're genteel in the extreme, practically begging you to stop and take afternoon cream tea. Thatched roofs and exposed timber beams come as standard. So does comfortable wealth, if I'm any judge.

During the drive, I give Isaac a ring and update him on our various malarkeys since arriving in England. He's just as concerned as I am by the alliance between De Montfort and the vampires. We just have to hope it's a marriage of convenience and won't stand up to any serious test.

Isaac's been investigating Kenilworth in the meantime and has some ideas about where will be best to look. 'There's no blasted archaeological centre there, my lad.' I can hear the frustration even over the phone line's distorting crackle. 'It makes zero sense for them to have sent the skeleton there, especially from such a prestigious dig.'

'Magic?' I ask.

'The magic of money, more like.' Aicha's cynicism is, as usual, well founded.

'There's a definite money trail, aye. Probably a combination of the two.'

No surprises there. The ultra-rich are the most capable of sorcerers, simply waving their bank balance until everything they want to go away just disappears. Isaac has traced shell account transfers and some sudden lavish spending by certain councillors and figures of authority involved in the excavation. He couldn't follow it back to De Montfort –he isn't Jonny Lee Miller in *Hackers* or anything– but there's enough proof of curated and covered-up corruption to identify definite meddling by someone outside of the project.

We pull up in the castle's car park, which is little more than a strip of scrubland on the opposite side of a bridged ditch. It's like a model of the site itself; exiting, we cross over the ancient moat, along an earthen walkway where the sides fall rapidly away, the grass-covered artificial slopes re-joining the natural roll of the undulating verdant landscape. Our elevated position gives us a breathtaking view in all directions. The clear summer air only adds to the impression of being able to see half the way back home.

We pass the ticket booth-cum-gift shop and get into the castle proper. It isn't difficult to guess where we need to target our investigation. Most of the structures have long crumbled, only certain walls still standing proud, stone-solid where frivolities like roofs and flooring have fallen by the wayside.

There are two exceptions. At the bottom of the internal slope sits a cheery Tudor building. Once a stable, it now serves as a teahouse. We're all glad to grab some caffeination and have a quick poke around. The right-hand side is a museum about the history of the castle, including De Montfort's role. I have a shufty about while Aicha and Craig order the drinks. It quickly becomes clear that unless Demon Fart is hiding out in a space the size of a broom cupboard, he isn't in this building. It's a huge open space, architecturally not much changed since the days it held horses. If anything, even more open with the separations for the individual animals removed.

That only leaves us our most likely target for investigation. Leicester's Gatehouse. The one building still standing to a degree where it can be considered liveable, functional. Isaac said if Simon's on the site itself, he'd be there, but it was worth crossing the teahouse off the list. Not least because it got me coffee. I've killed enough people today to merit a caffeine hit.

As we tromp our way across the grass towards the gatehouse, Craig suddenly grabs our arms. 'Hold yer horses, like.'

If there's one thing I've learned over the centuries, it's that if you don't want to end up wearing your toenails as eyebrow piercings, it's probably a good idea to stop *immediately* when a super powerful magician tells you to. I freeze in place. My foot hovers centimetres above the ground. There are worse things than IEDs hidden in the magical landscape.

'What is it?' I hiss anxiously. I appreciate the save if I'm about to blow myself to smithereens unintentionally, but I'm also aware I currently look like a constipated chicken mid-wing flap. If I'm going to look a damn sight more glamorous than usual, what with the heart-stopping, gorgeous body I'm wearing, I don't want to break the illusion. Call me vain. Then run for the hills, you suicidal maniac.

'There. *Look.*'

I do as he suggests, opening myself up more fully to my *talent*. We all pulled in our abilities as much as possible. We've not seen anyone wearing a whole shit tonne of greasepaint since arriving, but Simon might well have other agents in play than the vampires.

Just in front of us is a ward line. Luckily, not immediately – a good metre or so away, so I put my foot down with a sigh of relief. I didn't spot it. Even though I'm wearing a fae form, I'm still not really used to the way fae *talent* works. The grass itself forms the warding. Blades twist themselves together, intertwining into shapes reminiscent of Celtic knots. The energy created is of nature itself, so it doesn't blaze brightly even with my *sight* fully open. We're damn lucky we've someone with us more used to fae magic. I'd have blundered straight through that without even noticing. Best case after would have been we lost the element of surprise. Worst case? We became the elements of surprise. Being broken down into your component atoms and molecules is always a surprising thing to experience.

I look over at Aicha, who's crouched down. Luckily, she had the good sense to throw up a low grade *don't look here*. It isn't enough to make us light up on any nearby Talented's magical radar, but it'll stop the group of bored schoolkids whose attention is anywhere other than on their teacher's droning lecture from deciding to come and check out whatever interesting shit we're up to.

'Can you undo them, *laguna*?' Ironically, this is both my normal job and is better suited to my magical skill set. This is fae magic, and I normally do the magical lock-picking. Aicha does the magical lock-smashing-it-to-smithereens. Problem is, this is a subtle working. It'll involve me using my fae magic with a level of finesse I've not mastered yet. Like picking grains of rice out of a bowl with chopsticks. Except in an earthquake. And with my hands wrapped in parcel tape. And possibly concrete.

Aicha rocks back on her heels. 'Undo them? Yes. Without whoever set them knowing it?' She looks up, making direct eye contact. 'Doubt it.'

The look tells me everything. We'll be tipping De Montfort off. Any hopes of a stealthy approach will be dead in the water. Doesn't matter how quickly we close the remaining distance. By the time we reach him, he'll be ready for us.

CHAPTER NINE
SALZBOURG, AUSTRIA, 10 FEBRUARY 1939

J ohannes pulls me back again, still gentle but insistent. 'That's why I called you, Paul. To help Otto here.'

'Oh, I can help him, all right.' My lip curls, as if the savage distaste for the fucker in front of me is bringing out my inner animal. 'I'll help separate his head from his fucking shoulders.'

'Paul! Enough!' Suddenly, I find myself on the other side of the room. I've no recollection of getting here. My hands are clamped to my sides with a red glow, tied by the rope of *talent* Johannes has thrown around me. Apparently, Faust has had enough of me ignoring his request to calm down. I don't bother struggling. We're in Faust's home, with Mephistopheles watching me, those weird, intelligent eyes in that pointed-snout face. I don't have even close to the magical muscle needed to overcome the two of them in this environment. Looks like I'm going to have to listen after all.

Johannes tuts and wanders over to me with my tankard. He lowers his voice. 'If I let you have your hand back for your drink, will you promise not to *push* the mug through his head and just enjoy your beer? At least until I've finished talking?'

Damn, he knows me too well...although I'm loath to waste good beer on a fucking National Socialist; I'd have gone for the old "quaff and kill" manoeuvre. But Faust knows a promise will hold me. I nod begrudgingly, and he hands me my drink. At least I can brood beerily now. Until I get enough of this incredibly strong booze down my neck. Then I'll brood blearily.

Johannes pours another drink for the visibly shaken Nazi. Boohoo. I'll shake him till his eyes fall out if I can get my hands on him again.

Johannes leads him to his previous chair by the fire, then pulls a new one over for himself to sit in. My own chair lies politely empty. I get the impression it's a bit of a message. I can rejoin the conversation when I can behave like a grown-up. Boo – being an adult sucks. Doesn't bother me to stand over here against the wall, being childish. I stick a middle finger up at Johannes. As it's on the hand still clamped to my side, he doesn't see it. The snigger from the floor by the fire tells me Mephy does though.

I still want answers. 'Faust, what the fuck is going on? I thought you said you were ready to get the hell out of Austria due to these scumbag fuckers taking over, not inviting them over for a piss up?'

Johannes pours himself another drink along with a large bowl that he puts down for a very appreciative Mephistopheles, then slumps into his chair. 'Paul, Otto didn't get a choice regarding joining the SS. He certainly didn't when it came to becoming a member of the blasted Ahnenerbe. Himmler himself ordered him to. I'm not saying he's a saint, but since he opened his eyes to the price to be paid for the Ahnenerbe's dream, he's been the source of all the information I've got and promulgated out among the Talented. The man's saved a lot of lives in recent times. We need to repay the favour. Tell him what you did.'

He addresses the last part to the man, who is nursing his beer close to his mouth and chest, as though afraid it'll disappear. Otto's head pops up, and I'm struck again by the feverish intelligence behind his eyes. The man's that sort of dangerous dreamer whose reveries could change the world. Not always for the better. I suspect a certain Austrian now running this country might have a similar regard.

But there's a defiance there as well, and I like it despite myself. I'm a sucker for a rebel. It's a strange expression for someone wearing such a conformist outfit.

Otto glances at Johannes then, encouraged by what he sees, he looks back at me, lifting his chin. 'I resigned.'

I blink, shocked. 'You quit the SS?' I can't imagine that went down well if Himmler had hand-picked him.

He gives a bitter bark that's almost a laugh and almost a lament. 'Oh, that wasn't the problem. After they caught me for the second time with Pieter, my options were narrowing. Death or the camps.'

A gay high-ranking SS officer? The hypocrisies of the so-called master race laid bare once more. 'If that isn't the problem, what is?'

There's a bitterness in the man's smile. It comes when we know we've done something both stupid and entirely necessary, when we're faced with a choice having no good outcome, and the one we end up with is even worse than expected. 'I quit the Ahnenerbe.'

Jesus Christ riding solo on an oversized tandem bike, that wouldn't have gone down well, I suspect. 'How did they take it?'

'About as well as you might expect.' The former Nazi, former Ahnener-bian holds up his hand. On the centre of his palm is a swirling mess of what looks like Futhark runes. For a bunch who believe in the superiority of the Germanic people, they sure do wish they were Scandinavian a lot of the time. It's aglow with an old-rust-orange coloured power.

If I'm not mistaken, the Ahnenerbe have marked Otto with the equivalent of *Treasure Island's* Black Spot.

'Any idea what it does?' I ask the man. He's pale but resolute. I don't think he regrets quitting even if it'll cost him his life. The worry is, it might cost him more than that. Magic like this – dark, twisted magic? The price might be his soul.

Otto shakes his head. 'No idea but nothing good.'

I glance over at Johannes. 'You can't undo it?' I find it hard to believe that between him and Mephistopheles, they can't resolve the problem.

Faust sighs, absent-mindedly scratching Mephy between the ears, to the demon's immense satisfaction, judging by the rumble from his belly. 'We can mask him temporarily. But he swore a magically charged blood oath on joining the cult. It's bound up in his soul. If we tear it out...'

He doesn't need to say the rest. If they do, it'll shred the man's essence to smithereens. He'd be dead. Worse than dead. Probably not what he was looking for when he reached out to Johannes.

A thought occurs to me. 'Why did Himmler force you into the SS and the Ahnenerbe?' Gay or not, if it's because he came up with some enterprising way to identify and exterminate non-Aryans, I'll vote for the soul shredding.

The man smiles a small, sad smile. 'He was a fan of my work. Still is, probably, even though I'm sure he'll be glad when I'm dead. My books about the Cathars brought me to his attention.'

Books about Cathars? There's been this sneaking interest, at least among the esoteric societies, both Talented and deluded, in the Crusade of late, not least because of Grail hunters. It's not something I've been terribly worried about, what with having destroyed said Grail myself hundreds of years ago. But I do remember someone mentioning something about a book with some interesting takes on the whole mythos and the Cathar movement. Interesting in that they were totally, utterly, and spectacularly wrong, but it was written with a poetic flare. I can't remember who mentioned the book to me. But I do remember the author's name.

'Otto Rahn. You're Otto Rahn, aren't you?'

He smiles bashfully. 'At your service, sir.'

Otto Rahn. The man Heinrich Himmler believed in so much, he built an entire room in his castle, all ready to display the Holy Grail when Otto recovered it for him, so high was his confidence.

No wonder the Ahnenerbe are ready to hunt him to death. I can't imagine Himmler will be best pleased that he's no longer getting that particular shiny trophy. Especially after all the building costs.

I feel vaguely sorry for the idealistic young academic sat in front of me. His obsessions brought him to the attention of people he didn't want to get noticed by. Although, maybe that's just an assumption on my part. Just because he's homosexual and he's bailed on the Nazi movement doesn't mean he didn't have shared ideals regarding racial purity. Either my thoughts must be clear on my face or else Johannes knows me even better than I think. He waggles his hand back and forth. Okay, so the man's not a full-blown fascist, but he's no saint either. I'll pull more details from one or both of them later.

'So what happens next? Why did you send for me, Johannes?' Fascinated though I am to quiz the scholar on his beliefs regarding my long-lost people and our long-destroyed treasure, I still don't see how I fit into this puzzle. I'm sure Rahn would love to ask me a whole heap of questions if he knew the truth about me, but I doubt Johannes called me here to satisfy his intellectual curiosity in the middle of running for his life.

Faust is about to answer, but Otto interrupts. 'I fear that my time draws short, marked like this. If I am to die, I would make one last pilgrimage to Montsegur, one last search for Lucifer's Crown, for the Grail, before I am taken. When I made my decision to leave, I wrote to Johannes to ask if he knew any who might protect me and guide me across the Alps. I do not seek salvation, sir. Only a last chance to finish my life's work.'

'All very commendable.' My tone may sound harsh after the earnest entreaty, but I still don't see why this is *my* responsibility. I turn to Johannes. 'Why me? Why can't you get your friend across? You said you were readying to leave.'

Faust has the good grace to look sheepish, at least. 'The key point is readying, Paul. I'm unable to do it without Mephy, and if I were to leave now, I wouldn't be able to secure the endless secrets and treasures I guard, not even mentioning all the tomes and grimoires I have concealed here. Everything needs to be tied up tightly and secured before I go so that the Thule Society and the Ahnenerbe don't get their greasy little paws on them. There's too much risk beforehand, and keeping Otto here until I'm ready would be too likely to draw their attention. He's quite the beacon right now.'

Okay, I get it. 'So you want me to keep him safe and act as a decoy at the same time? Keep them looking for us while you lock up the rest of the goodies in Bavaria they haven't found?'

Johannes looks both embarrassed and relieved. 'Quite. I've no idea what they'll throw at Otto, but I'm sure you'll be able to handle it. We owe him a debt, the whole community, for the information he's fed to us. This is how we repay that debt.'

Otto sits up, straight-backed but with an earnest, pleading look on his face. 'Please, sir. If you fail, I die. It is fine; if you did not try, I'd die for sure. All I ask is that you try. It cannot leave me in a worse situation than if you do not.'

I'm not going to lie; I'm pretty pissed off by the whole situation. I've already heard enough rumours and seen enough people disappear off the Talented radar to know that the Ahnenerbe are not to be trifled with. The last thing I want is to draw their attention and their ire. Hunting me down and capturing me will be no straightforward matter, but that doesn't mean

I want a bunch of well-funded, highly trained magical fascists on my tail. I'm not sure this supposedly redeemed high-ranking SS officer is deserving of that sort of risk-taking.

Still, Johannes has always been a good friend, and he welcomed me with open arms when I turned up on his doorstep, no questions asked, fresh from my death at the hands of the Chief Inquisitor in the chambers beneath the Vatican. Now he wants a favour. I'd be a poor sort of friend if I didn't step up to the job.

So against my better judgement (which is suggesting I head for the hills or, rather, the mountains and leave Otto Rahn to sort out his own self-imposed mess), I walk over and sit myself down. Johannes released my bonds as soon as he saw I wasn't going to immediately kill Rahn the moment he did so. I just didn't want to sit until I was sure I wasn't going to bolt for the door. Instead, if I'm going to get involved in this bloody mess, I might as well be comfortable and have another beer while I do so.

'Right,' I say, passing the empty tankard to Faust. I could have topped it up on the way over to sit down, but fuck it. He's asking a lot of me. He can get me a fresh beer. 'So what's the plan?'

Otto Rahn looks across at me blankly. 'I already said. Cross the Alps into France and go to Montsegur.'

Oh, right. *That is* his plan. Not going to be any difficulties with that, what with him being a highly wanted man by the German authorities, secret police, and occult Talented magic-users.

I have the feeling I'm going to need quite a few more tankards of that strong beer to get through the rest of this conversation.

CHAPTER TEN

KENILWORTH, 7 JUNE, PRESENT DAY

Walking through unknown fae wards is a good way to qualify for the Talented equivalent of the Darwin Awards. Posthumously.

A polite cough comes from over my shoulder. Sadly, as the person making said cough has been smoking heavily since we met and presumably every day ever previously too, this is enough to set him off into a wracking set of phlegmy, hacking wheezes. Each one seems to only tickle Craig's throat further. It takes him a couple of minutes to regain control over his respiratory system.

'Fuck a duck, soz about that, like. Chest's proper feeling that kip on the church bench.' I'm not convinced that's the cause of it, not by a long shot. Seems rude to point that out though.

Craig carries on, oblivious to the doubtful expression on my face. I suspect he's entirely too wasted to pick up on such nuances anyway. 'What's the crack then? Worried about the ward, like?'

I'm going to have to spell it out, aren't I? 'Yes, Craig. We can get past the ward, but then he'll know we're coming. Sort of ruins the whole "our chief weapon is fear, fear and surprise" routine, if you know what I mean?'

His face practically splits in two with the width of his grin. 'Ooh. Ooh! Monty Python. Nice one. Knew yee was a cultivated lass...lad...a person of culture, if yee gets me. Loving that. Proper large.'

As much as I appreciate my pop culture references being picked up on, this is hardly the time or the place. 'Thanks. Doesn't alter the problem though, does it?'

Craig's grin doesn't budge an inch. 'Oh, aye. It kinda does, like. Well, in the sense there ain't no problem 'ere, like. I'm the flipping King of the Hobs, me!'

Aicha's gaze is so stone-like, it would draw top marks from a basilisk judging panel in a staring contest. 'And he was Queen of the Fae briefly. And Leo DiCaprio is the king of the world. And Kate Winslet is the queen of selfishly hogging a floating door and letting her boyfriend drown unnecessarily. What's your point?'

'Why d'you think it were so important for ol' good queen Maeve to 'ave me old man gone once she made him human? Proper cruising for a bruising with him still having his magic. He'd a been in her chambers next night, slitting her throat if she hadn't banished him off to the mortal realm quick chop.' He leans towards us, still looking very pleased with himself. 'Hobs are the cleaning crew for the fae realm, right? Well, anywhere we go, basically. Probably deliberate, to be honest, written right in to whatever the magical equivalent of our DNA is basically, like, which is why I kick so bloody hard against it. Contrary bastard, I am.'

Impossibly, his grin seems to get even larger. 'No point having a bunch of eternal cleaners on your staff if they haven't got the flipping keys, now is it, like?' He leans back, pulls out a crumpled joint from somewhere, and lights it up, making rapid little sucks to get the end burning properly. Then he takes a lung-buster of a drag. It seems like a reward for himself for having the answer to our problem. Though the reward it actually gives him is another prolonged coughing fit.

Once he stops hacking away and calms himself down with another hit on his doobie, he turns his attention back to us. 'Maeve couldn't have us lingering about once she'd done us dirty like that, like. Fae wards don't work on hobs. We can just walk right through 'em, and they never even notice we've been there.'

That is...brilliant. I basically gave up hope on us getting the drop on De Montfort. Suddenly, it looks plausible again. Of course, there's a flaw in the plan.

'That's all very good for you,' Aicha says. 'What about us? I've already had dickhead here go off wandering about behind a fae ward on his own, and it ended with him getting his magic eaten. Like the complete and utter dickhead he is. Let's avoid repeating dickheadery, shall we?'

I thought my mastery of English was good. Aicha can make the same compound words up and humiliate me just as thoroughly in English as she can in French. Or Arabic. Or any other language she uses. Basically, she's world-champion level at polyglot insults. At least when it comes to me.

'Oh, aye, don't sweat like it's cracking flags, love.' I have no idea what he means, but he makes it clear with his gestures. He offers us each an arm like Dick Van Dyke accompanying Mary Poppins and her gender-fluid best friend on an afternoon stroll. Then he tips me a wink. 'Shall we, ladies?'

I can't see there's much option. I loop my arm through his. Aicha rests her hand lightly on the crook of his other arm. I hear her mutter, 'If there's any singing, dancing penguins, I'll burn the place to the ground.' Looks like she had the same mental image as I did.

Craig chaperones us forward. I take a deep breath as we step over the boundary line. I can't stop myself from wincing slightly in anticipation of possible atomic disassembly. Nothing. Looking over my shoulder, I see the ward is still there. So are we. There aren't any blaring alarms, no giant white globes rolling down the path to subdue us. So far, so good.

Craig turns his head, his charming smile slightly undone by my need to weave my head backwards to avoid him burning my eye out with the tip of his joint. 'Shall we, milady?'

We shall. We shall indeed.

"Gatehouse" is a pretty underwhelming title for a building that is, in effect, a miniature castle all of its own. Robert Dudley built it to woo (successfully, by all accounts) the so-called Virgin Queen, Queen Elizabeth. Hexagonal towers linked by stone crenelations make up the main part of the building. On the other side are what look like two enormous terraced houses stapled onto it, industrial-style chimneys poking out the tip of the extenuated roof points. The whole place puts to shame the mini-chateaux style of construction that became all the rage among the landed gentry of France a couple of centuries previously.

Much of the building is taken up by displays about the families who have lived here and Dudley's love affair with Elizabeth. Fascinating but not what we're after. A couple of corridors off the main rooms labelled "Staff Only" pique our interest. We hang back, observing the employees circulating, their wary eyes inspecting visitors to ensure their hands stay behind carefully positioned cordons, that fingers keep an acceptable distance from irreplaceable antiquities. The staff often dip off through the one panelled door, seemingly either to take an officially sanctioned break or just to briefly escape the bombardment of inane questions. No one goes through the other. Not one of them even so much as looks at it. In fact, as we observe the faces of other visitors, no one else even seems to see it. We reach silent agreement. If Simon De Montfort is in this building, he's on the other side of that door.

You'll find it hard to believe, considering recent events, but there are periods in my life when I'm not at constant risk of hideous and painful death. Occasionally. It doesn't matter how much of a lust for adventure or a penchant for disaster you have. If you live for centuries, there's going to be some downtime eventually. These days, it's an opportunity to finally make a dent on the glut of high quality, highly addictive TV programs and books liberally bestowed daily to a public entirely acclimatised to such an output rate. I lived through decades where any book of interest being published at all was a rarity and where the material inside was often drier than the paper it was printed on.

Luckily, living with or close by Isaac, I've always had a wealth of texts on hand. Literally. Tomes were worth their actual weight in gold during various epochs. And sure, there were travelling troubadours and occasional theatre troupes, but my limited patience for studying (in the case of Isaac's book collection) and other people (in the case of public entertainment) meant that, much like a needy, attention-fuelled child, I had to learn to entertain myself.

One way I did that was by learning various skills. Skills that, indubitably, I could replicate more easily magically. Did I really need to know how to juggle when I could make the balls swoop like swallows through the air with a thought? No, but it stopped me going on a murderous rampage because of weapon-grade levels of boredom in a particularly bleak week in the winter of 1795, so it was a win all round.

Another skill set I learned and have used more than once since is lock picking. It's a straightforward matter to move tumblers with hardened air, taking the shape necessary to lift each one. Despite what the films show you, it's a whole different matter doing it with hairpins and random jiggling. Luckily, I have a lock pick kit. Unluckily, it's in my etheric storage. And I've no idea what even that small amount of magic usage might do in terms of drawing unwanted attention inside De Montfort's wards.

'What's the warding situation in here?' I ask Craig quietly out of the corner of my mouth. 'Can I use a small amount of *talent* without giving the game away to De Montfort if he's here?'

Craig nods reassuringly. 'Oh aye, nae bother, like. Long as yee don't start doing fucking Gandalf-style firework displays, you'll be reet.'

One other problem occurs to me. 'I'm going to need both my hands to do it. What's going to happen if I let go of your arm?'

The Magus of Blackburnshire, King of the Hobs, sniggers. The kind of laugh only someone permanently high as a kite strapped onto the back of the Space X rocket can manage. 'Oh, yeah. Yee never needed to hold onto me arms, like. I were just being a gentleman. Can yee imagine how dapper I looked, having yee two bobby dazzlers one on each arm though?'

I'm not quite sure if I'm going to kill him or not. What amazes me even more is that Aicha hasn't already. Truly, every day offers opportunities for personal growth.

He reassures us he can mask us, so I pull my lock pick kit from my etheric storage and set to work. When I was in practise, I'd have had this done in a couple of minutes. Rustiness and my desperate attempt to be entirely silent means it takes more like five. For all I know, De Montfort is on the other side of this door. If he hears me scrabbling and scraping away, we'll be walking into the equivalent of Tony Montana wielding his machine gun at the top of the stairs, only without the backup of a small army to take him down. If he hasn't just done a runner instead.

By the time I hear the faint *click* that tells me it's done, I'm sweating in what chauvinists would say is a most unladylike fashion. My rebuttal? They've obviously never got a woman to work up a sweat, which means they're both missing out and failing as lovers. I ease the door open, and we step inside.

The door reveals a corridor. It is dark-wood panelled, matching in style to the Elizabethan elegance of the display rooms we've come through. This is obviously still an original part of the building. The difference is these walls are bare, no ornate gilded paintings or artfully displayed sculptures. The quality of workmanship regarding the panels' finishing elevates them towards a level of art themselves, but otherwise, this corridor could be considered functional compared to what we've seen so far.

There are three doors. One on each side and one at the far end. We creep forward. I have to remind myself to breathe, to keep it constant and quiet. Otherwise, I'll end up half-choking myself in my desperate attempt to be silent and breaking into a coughing fit or something equally stupid, giving the game away.

Chunky keyholes in locks are ideal as peepholes. As long as there's light on the other side; otherwise, you just get to see a load of pitch black. That's what Door One and Door Two show me, the side doors. Door Three? I hit the jackpot.

I can't see too much on the other side of Door Three, but the clean white walls and loaded work surfaces I do see speak of some form of workshop or laboratory, but my eyes don't linger on them. The man directly opposite draws my gaze as much as he draws my ire, anger rising up from the pit of my stomach to flood every nerve extremity till I feel afire with rage just from the sight of him. His back is turned to me. I've only seen him in this body twice, both for brief periods of time. Each a moment of utter misery, of loss and failure that have engraved him on my memory. The body of the child of Susane, a child I believed myself to be the father of. The murderous, rapacious, villainous whoreson bastard himself. Simon De Montfort.

I don't dare speak. I hardly dare breathe. Keeping hold of my fury's demand to rend him limb from limb with my bare hands, to remain in control and not go full-on barbarian berserker takes all my mental energy. I look over at the other two. Raise an eyebrow. My instinct is to blow the bloody doors off. Pull the magical equivalent of a sawn-off shotgun and go full-on Omar from *The Wire*. Thing is, my tendency to rush in guns blazing has cost me dearly recently. Worse, it has cost other people even more. I find myself second-guessing my instincts now. Maybe there's a better way to go than the equivalent of a SWAT team battering ram?

I try to express all that with my eyebrows. Craig has no clue why I'm waggling them up and down like a pair of breakdancing caterpillars. His bemused expression confirms that. But Aicha, ever-reliable, borderline-psychopathic Aicha, understands me perfectly. She's berated me enough times for piss-poor prior planning and rightly so. The smile that lights up her face is radiant. Its warmth speaks of her delight at me finally –finally!– learning. She steps forward. Pats my shoulder (her equivalent of a full-blown hug). Peers through the keyhole. Thinks for a moment.

Then blows the door in. She doesn't even need to huff and puff.

Guess it's time for some action after all.

CHAPTER ELEVEN

KENILWORTH, 7 JUNE, PRESENT DAY

Little prick, little prick, let me in. I'm going to set fire to your chinny chin chin.

Instincts can be buggers sometimes. They've kept me alive a whole host of times. Even more often, they've led me deeper into appalling trouble. The problem with relying on them is you aren't the only one who has them.

It is, as with most of Aicha's plans, a stroke of genius. She hits the hinge points a millisecond before she *pushes* the door with her not-inconsiderable *talent*. So instead of the door swinging back and smashing open against the wall to the side, it sails clean across the room. Directly at De Montfort.

If it'd caught him, it would have knocked him for six, magical fae or not. Sadly, he can also react instinctively. Instead of turning at the noise, which most people would have done, resulting in him taking a flying door to the forehead at speeds only slightly below the sound barrier, he hurls himself sideways. Looks like his instincts serve him well. The bastards. I send a mental note to my own ones that they owe me a save at least as good in the near future.

Still, it's almost worth him not getting crushed by it to see his face as he pokes his head up from behind the desk and sees us. To say we've caught him off guard is an understatement. He goes white as a sheet, his face making that repetitive goldfish 'O' shape I've made myself more than a few times recently. Surprising the complete and utter shithead might only be a minor victory measured against the entire war, but Good God, it's a satisfying one.

In the split second of the door sailing across the room and De Montfort performing his ninja roll, I take in the room itself. It's like a macabre version of a school science lab. The surfaces are all clean and white, with various equipment on the sides. Microscopes, what looks like a spectrum analyser, rows of test tubes and Bunsen burners. I suspect the latter get used for alchemical purposes that would blow the average science teacher's mind though.

Where De Montfort was working, two skeletons are arrayed. For a moment, it makes me think of those plastic ones you'd see in a classroom, used to demonstrate anatomy. Except I don't think these are plastic. And they aren't held together by wires or pins either. They hang in place, pulled together by an almost magnetic force. A magnetic force made of raw power. Which isn't surprising because each one of the bones in the skeletons are awash with incomprehensible amounts of *talent*. There's enough in just a single one to make a power-hungry magician drool at the possibilities of what they might achieve if they possessed it. Strung together like that? It'll draw you like moths to a flame...if you're a megalomaniac. It makes me want to run screaming as fast as possible in the opposite direction. I suspect this is the healthier reaction.

Sadly, De Montfort doesn't stay on the back foot for long. He still carries the sceptre he nicked off us in a back holster like he thinks himself the fucking Crown Prince of Eternia, and he pulls it free before I even clock him moving. I guess centuries of military service and surviving without *talent* have him honed like a well-oiled machine.

What happens next is fast. By the time I clock the sceptre, he has it aimed directly at my chest. I didn't have time to see it move. I certainly don't have time to watch the rest of the *talent*-imbued bones link their power to it. It's instantaneous or as near as damn it as makes no odds. We might have caught De Montfort off balance, but it looks like his answer to that is that attack is the best form of defence. Faster than I can move, faster than I can think, a bolt of *talent*, putrescent off-green that speaks of long-suffered rancid disease and endless rot, comes shooting out of the end of the rod. My reactions are good but nowhere near good enough to avoid it. It's going to hit me, and there's nothing I can do but brace myself for whatever fucked up thing it's going to do to me.

My reactions might not suffice, but I'm not Aicha. De Montfort, having spent hundreds of years fighting wars, might consider himself the embodiment of a military man. Aicha is all that, then some. She's done the same, and she's a *woman*. Not only does that make her tougher by nature (don't start talking to me about denser muscle mass or whatever; women have periods and childbirth. They win every time), it means the odds have been stacked against her for centuries. However badass De Montfort has learned to be, Aicha is that multiplied by oestrogen.

There are limits, of course. She doesn't have time to weave up a shielding spell. She probably could pay him back, hit him just as hard with a magictov cocktail while his attention remains focused on me. Problem is that ball of energy. Best-case scenario, it's going to dissolve my corpse into some gooey, gloopy mess, and I'll be back to square one, in a Talentless body. But there's something about the spell he's thrown at me. Even in this instant, where everything feels slowed down, and I can track its trajectory, the unavoidable path it's arcing along to smash into me, I can feel it. A darkness, a power, that sense of the colour of rot isn't just an image of the magic, it feels like what it might do to my very soul. Honestly, in this split second, I'm not sure I'll be coming back from this one.

So, Aicha – well, Aicha Aichas. I might not have the reaction time to move out of the way, but hers lets her move into it. She launches herself like a pre-coiled spring under tension directly into me, sending me sprawling sideways, my head twisting against the movement of my body, my eyes still tracking that ball of power as it splashes across Aicha's form. My mouth can't even form the first syllable of denial, of pleading with reality for it not to be true, for us to switch back places before the agony carves itself into her normally immoveable expression, and she starts to dissolve.

It isn't like the shit-wizard, where his body liquefied, dribbling down itself into a pool of once-human by-product. This is more like acid. Where it splashes across her, the magic eats her away, leaving nothing behind. And it spreads. Quickly. The green energy rolls across her body, devouring in both directions. Before I can take the first step in her direction, it's spread up to her chin. I watch helpless as her jaw disintegrates, as her nose disappears, as it steals the light from her eyes and takes her eyes with them.

In a matter of seconds, Aicha is gone.

CHAPTER TWELVE
KENILWORTH, 7 JUNE, PRESENT DAY
By the Good God, this isn't how it was supposed to go. Not in the slightest.

I start towards where she was, stop, start again. It's stupid on my part. Wasteful even. She sacrificed herself to keep me alive, and here I am, ignoring the most dangerous enemy I've ever faced, not paying him any attention. I can't help it. All my attention is focused on where she was, waiting for her to reform, willing her to reappear. Aicha regrows almost instantaneously. Agonisingly but instantaneously. It kept the Nazis busy, finding ways to dismember and disintegrate her in original and different methods over the five years they held her captive. They never managed to make it stick.

Apparently, De Montfort has.

She doesn't reform. Doesn't come back. She doesn't rematerialise from a left pinky tip with a quippy cult reference and a sack-full of violence to unleash.

I stare at the space where she was, trying to make sense of it. I can't. It doesn't make any sense. Aicha is a thousand times more capable, a million times more sensible than I am. I've said before that there are no true immortals, but if I had to lay money on one making it till the sun went cold and life itself became extinct, I'd have bet the farm on Aicha.

Except she doesn't come back.

Movement pulls my attention away. Through blurred vision, my stinging eyes see De Montfort opening a portal. It isn't big or flashy, just a small gateway through to a dark wood-panelled room on the other side. He pushes the two skeletons through and is about to step through himself. I raise a hand to stop him. No, not to stop him. To blight him. To hit him with a hundred years of famine, of drought, of the suffering of a nation when Nature herself turns her back on them, all condensed into a single moment. I draw on every dram of my fae essence.

Not quickly enough. He's gone.

The portal snaps shut, leaving nothing but a blank white wall. I consider obliterating that instead, but it'll do nothing to make me feel any better. I feel hollowed out by the emotional equivalent of a melon scooper, an emptied husk. Given time, the emotions will come flooding back — rage, shame, guilt, despair. I'll be a walking flask filled up with the most toxic cocktail of emotions possible, ready to pour it out on anyone or anything. I know that's coming. I've been there before. Not long back. Right now, I'm going through the motions of destructive suffering. Soon I'll be lost to it, drinking it down till it consumes me too.

I turn to Craig, ready to rage at him, to demand why he didn't help, why he didn't stop De Montfort's escape. Except I see why.

He's placed a barrier of his own –no easy working inside someone else's wards– across the splintered doorway. It's holding what looks like a small army at bay. They're either disgruntled National Trust employees come to vent at our destruction of an antique door to make our grand entrance or vampires in De Montfort's service. Going by the elongated teeth, the claw-like hands, and the glowing red eyes, I'd say the latter. Or both. I can well believe the National Trust is an equal opportunities employer.

'Soz, like. Bought you as much time as I could.' Sweat rolls down Craig's forehead. It drips into his eyes. Must sting. I can sympathise. Mine feel red raw already. There'll be time for that later though.

Right now, I want to honour Aicha in a way that seems both befitting and cathartic.

I pull my sword from etheric storage. My fae magic wraps its way up from the pommel, entwining it like the vines around Sleeping Beauty's castle. I intend to put this lot down for longer than a hundred years though.

'Drop the barrier,' I grate out, my sword raised in guard. 'It's clobberin' time.'

That one's for you, Aicha. As are all of the next ones too.

CHAPTER THIRTEEN
KENILWORTH, 7 JUNE, PRESENT DAY

Good God my heart hurts. Just when you think it can't possibly be filled with more pain, Life finds a way to fill it to the brim.

The restraining magic dissipates, and the vampires surge into the room. That's fine. Be the tidal wave. I have no objection to being the breakwater.

I come at them, almost swifter than they can close the gap despite their inhuman speed. The fury arrives now. The first emotion to come and fill me up. I embrace it, ride it, allow it to fill every atom. There's a bargain however. I insist on a partnership. I'm not about to go off into a berserker rage. This one is for Aicha. It has to be surgical.

Literally, in the case of the first vampire I meet. I keep my sword razor-sharp at all times. Despite that, cutting through bone is a good way to chip your blade or end up with it blocked, lodged halfway through. Not if you bring the right weapon, the right movements, the right exact precision strike points like Aich can. Could.

I'm not half the warrior she was, so I do what she'd have wanted me to. I cheat. Powering up the Talent enrobing my blade till it blazes like a lightsaber, I sweep in and down at the first vampire. He stretches his arms out, reaching for me, looking to seize me, probably to tear my throat out. He'll find that hard to do with only stumps left from the elbow onwards. I consider taking his legs off at the knees, pruning him like the Knight from Monty Python's *Holy Grail*. Kandicha would have appreciated that. Still, there are a lot more of the bastards to kill. Letting Craig die just to make the death comical wouldn't have been Aicha's choice. She saved me. I need to do the same. I reverse the flow of my blade, pivoting my wrists in a figure of eight to bring it up to shoulder height, and decapitate the vampire on the backswing. Boom. Dusted. One down, Aich. One down.

I dance. I dance a deadly routine, through lethal opponents, my blade my partner leading my steps, my anger laying down the choreography, my mind directing. Right foot forward, pivot, and turn. Impale, explode, drop, and roll. Kneeling feint, then exploding up to shove the point through a brain. Twist and split, spilled grey turned ash. Step one, two, and drive an elbow plexus deep. Sweep the leg, then back two, three. Mirror the movement through the neck. Letting the blade travel outwards like a rotational lift, the momentum cleaving three more heads from shoulders. A pirouette of death. A whirling dervish of devotion to precise and certain limb separation.

I don't know how long I carry on for. Nor how many I kill. When your enemies explode into ash, you can't really verify afterwards, and I'm too lost to the rhythm of my movements to keep a running tally. All I know is that at some point, there's no one left to kill. No one left at all except a very white-faced hob king. He pulls a joint out with trembling fingers and lights it, though it takes several goes for him to get his fingers to work well enough to get the lighter to ignite. He drags long and hard.

'*Fucking 'ell, like.*' Well, I can understand why he needed so long to put together that particular piece of linguistic poetry. 'That was brutal, lass. Remind me not to fuck with yee ever.'

Looks like he isn't so keen on that date after all. Mind you, I must look a state. The thick tar-like excuse for blood the vampires' arteries contain has mingled with my pouring sweat, so it runs down my face and clothes like oil or the stuff Baron Harkonnen bathed in. I don't know if they managed to cut me. Certainly, I still have all my limbs, but outside of that, I'm still too numb to feel any injuries. The rage is dissipating. I'm not ready to feel any of the emotions yet to come.

I grab a piece of white fabric off a counter, either a hand towel or a lab coat, one of the few things not liberally coated in muck and dust now in the once pristine room. Using it to clear my vision, I look around.

To say we trashed the place is an understatement. The work surfaces are smashed to smithereens, even more than the door is. All the fancy equipment has been converted into fancy scrap, having been sent flying and disassembled with extreme prejudice. If there were any clues here before, I doubt there are any now, at least not any still intact. I don't feel too worried on that account. There's not been any computers or piles of convenient paperwork full of receipts and billing addresses from the get go. I've seen the two major clues. Those De Montfort made sure to take with him.

The room looks like a miniature volcano erupted in the corner or like someone put a bucketful of cinders in front of a high-powered fan. Black powder coats every surface liberally. The demolished furniture, the once-white walls, the floor, the roundish object where Aicha disintegrated...

I blink. Look again. Dash forward. Sweep the ashes aside. Wipe at the thing. Wipe at my eyes. Try to clean them both enough for me to see what I hold in my hands. Hoping I'm right. Terrified I'm wrong.

I'm not. For once, Good God, love me, I'm not. It's a head. Not just any head. Not a shrunken head a la Harry the Hunter from *Beetlejuice*. Not one of the vampire heads I decapitated, implausibly still whole. It's both more and less plausible than that. It's the head of my best friend. Aicha Kandicha.

I say more plausible because when regeneration is one of your signature moves, I guess finding you regrowing should neither shock nor amaze. I say less because it's never taken her so long. Aicha's healing propensity is almost instantaneous. Outside of her encounter with Maeve, I've known nothing to slow her down before. She missed a fight, for fuck's sake. If Aicha is missing a brawl, it doesn't seem a huge assumption that she's completely dead.

I can't tell you how pleased I am to be wrong even though seeing her like this hurts my heart. The pain reforming causes her is categorically immense. It's so bad, she can't hide it, can't stop her newly reformed features from grimacing in extended agony. The lack of lungs and vocal cords means she can't talk yet. Luckily, she can move her features though. When she mouths, 'Dickhead' at me, I maybe shed a tear or two. Luckily, being a sweaty mess, it gets covered up by my already slightly sodden, dishevelled general state. I hate her being in such terrible pain, but if she can insult me, she'll be all right.

I crouch down next to her, waving Craig over to join us. He double-takes when he sees Aicha's cranium, even more so when he sees her blink, sees her neck starting to form underneath her chin.

'Stone the crows, you two are a right fricking freaky-deaky pair, aren't you? You' —he gestures at me— 'some sort of badass sword master ninja warrior woman and you' —he points down at the head by his feet— 'able to come back from being killed even when you do something as totally mad and ill thought out as jumping in front of a super-powered magic bolt! Is this what you two do for kicks all the time?'

I look down at Aicha. Her expression is perfect. She's completely forgotten about whatever inconceivable agonies are wracking her reforming nervous system in this instant. There isn't any place for that. The immeasurable outrage coated across her face rules supreme.

I can't resist. My hand goes in my pocket, then out, snapping a photo on my phone almost without conscious thought. 'That is one for the family photo album.' Truly a moment I'll treasure for eternity or however long a slice of it I manage to exist for.

As her lungs reform, I suspect Craig is about to receive a reaming out, the likes of which he's never encountered before in his life. Before Aicha can lacerate him, subjecting him to the Ego Death of a Thousand Cuts from the Razor Sharp Tongue for his character analysis of a moment ago, he redeems himself. Enough, at least.

He sweeps up the lab coat, for lab coat it is, that I wiped myself down with earlier. Flourishing it out like a matador's cloak, he lets it billow down gently over her reforming chest, covering the exposed muscle tissue before the flesh forms. It covers her modesty. Aicha doesn't care about me seeing her naked. I doubt she would about Craig either. Exceptional long life and regenerative abilities reduce your body modesty to close to zero. It's the thoughtfulness of it, the utter care he applies to make sure it flutters down as softly as possible onto the exposed, re-knitting flesh.

Then he pulls out one of his seemingly unending supplies of pre-rolled joints from wherever it is he keeps them and pops it into her mouth. 'That looks right painful, like. Here, grab a chuff on that if yer lungs are back in action.' He sparks up his lighter and holds it out. By the tiny flicker of the flame dragged in magnetically to the end of the spliff and the accompanying *puff puff* noise like the world's smallest steam engine designed for a mouse-sized amusement park, it looks like her breathing apparatus is reforming. Aicha doesn't enjoy getting drunk or high as a general rule of thumb. When your thumbs haven't even regrown yet and are going to hurt like fuckery when they do, you're allowed to toss said general rules out of the window. Preferably a twentieth story window.

Aicha's expression eases slightly, even if it glazes a similar amount. Damn. I don't know what homeboy is rolling, but it has to be some seriously potent shit to be having that sort of effect on a Talented that quickly. Outside of taking advantage of the luxury of actually being able to get pissed out of my skull after Franc's death —and didn't that end fucking badly? — I have too many very lethal, very motivated enemies to enjoy getting high. If the last few months have shown me anything, it's how justified I am being paranoid when straight, let alone when high, but I make a mental note not to get into a sesh with Craig however tempted I might be.

While she slowly fills out again under the lab coat, I update her on what has happened since she caught Demon Fart's Hadouken straight to the chest. Craig interrupts a couple of times, particularly regarding my dispatching of the vampires. He gets supremely over-excited till he's gabbling, tripping over his own tongue, the main gist of his tale only just distinguishable underneath all the times that 'fucking' and 'like' get liberally sprinkled through his sentences.

By the time we finish the story and she's smoked Craig's spliff down to the roach, it looks like she's mainly regrown underneath the lab coat. I pull out a change of clothes for her and set them next to her head, ready for us to vamoose and leave her some space to recoup and get dressed. She spits the spliff butt out to the side.

'Where's...De Montfort gone?' Her speech remains rough, uneven. Talking still isn't easy for her. Agonising pain always does make forming coherent sentences hard work.

'France. Not sure where.'

Craig's eyebrows shoot up. 'How d'yee ken that, like? Looked like he coulda just popped next door for a cuppa and a bit of scran. All I saw were a hoity-toity room done out wi' the same dark wood panelling as this gaff.'

I laugh. 'You're right. Difference is the wood panels in here don't have Fleur de Lys motifs on them. Either he planned for us seeing him popping through his escape hole and had them added to throw us off his scent, which is implausibly over-prepared and cautious even for that shithead of a prepper, or it was a building from a similar time period but back home.'

'So...what now?' Aicha's voice is still barely above a creak, hardly more than a murmur. Man, my Santa-like list of all the ways De Montfort has been naughty, all the lumps of coal I need to hammer up his rectum with a croquet mallet, just keeps getting longer and longer.

I pat her shoulder. Seeing as how she's regrowing from the head down, I feel confident that'll be fully flesh covered by now. Tapping exposed subcutaneous layers full of newly formed nerves, even gently, would be a dickhead manoeuvre.

'Now you get dressed and rest. Then —' I look her dead in the eye, let her see exactly how serious I am. 'Then we hunt down that fucker and kill him until he's dead. Possibly even longer than that.'

I have bones to pick with Simon De Montfort. Two almost complete skeletons worth to start with.

Chapter Fourteen

KENILWORTH, 7 JUNE, PRESENT DAY

Every day provides an opportunity for new growth. Which is fortunate, considering how often we get bits chopped off us.

I owe Craig an apology. I slaughtered all the vampires in my incandescent rage. I didn't think about the whole "keep one alive to question them about their nest". He's riding shotgun for us, but his mission is to get more information about the vampires attacking his domain. Disrupting their partnership with De Montfort probably helps, but it doesn't solve his issues. He takes it like a trooper though.

'Don't bother yer head about that, like.' He grins that scruffy, charming grin that makes his eyes twinkle even through the perma-glaze the weed coats them in, like the American-style doughnuts that probably haunt his dreams every night. Or morning, passed out on a cathedral bench. 'One of the knobbers dropped his phone, like, in all the' —he mimes some sort of mix of bushido and Shaw Brothers' martial arts films— 'swoosh, clang, *ahhhh*, dead. Found a phone and guessed the unlock pattern. The cockstride used a V. Quick mooch through his GPS location history showed some spots he was hanging round on the regs, over Nottingham way. If yee two are all good, I'll go and have a poke about there, see what I can turn up before I head back up north, innit.'

'We've got it from here, Craig. Listen – I owe you one. If you ever need a hand' –I produce a plain white card– 'give this number a call.' It's the number to a phone we keep permanently at Isaac's, a line people can always get a message to me on. My mobile phones don't last long enough for me to remember numbers as a rule of thumb.

He nods his thanks and turns to go. Then he turns back. 'Hey, if yee come back these ways again, I want that date. Deal?'

I feel mean to disillusion him, but it needs doing. 'Craig, honestly, we're about to go to war with the most devious *talented* individual I've ever come across. I love having fae power at my fingertips, but honestly? The chances this body survives much beyond the next week?'

'Bookies are running even odds.' Aicha looks better. She's dressed, but she can't quite hide the existential weight she's carrying from the pain she's suffering, the worry it's causing her.

I whistle. 'Those are some generous bookies. Point is, next time I come back over here, I almost certainly won't be in this body. I'll be in a new, less glamorous, less *talented* one. And almost certainly male again.'

He pretends to think it over, rubbing his chin, squeezing his brows together. Then the easy-going, half-cut, charming grin comes back. 'I don't give a rat's arse, me. Next time, we're doing it, aren't we?'

Well, blow me down with a feather. Top marks for persistence. My interests don't really lie in that direction, but at the very least I'll have a laugh going out and getting pissed with him. I owe him that much.

'Well then, I guess we are.' I make an attempt at a curtsey.

'Christ, he's having a stroke. Do you know the AVC recommendations?'

Ah, Aicha. Ever there to prick the balloon of my ego.

I flip her off as Craig dissolves into laughter. Then with a proffered fist-bump to each of us, he heads out the door.

'What about us then, *saabi*? What's our next move?' We need to talk more about what happened to her here. I can see she needs something else to focus on for now though. Some other form of distraction.

'Now? We head back to France ASAP. Specifically, Paris. I'll fill you in on the rest as we go.'

Now it's time to get back on the hunt. The game is afoot.

I ring the hire car company and arrange to drop off the car at the London rental office by Saint Pancras. How we arrange it is they scream at me it's impossible, then I tell them I'm doing it anyway, so name a figure to make it happen. When they pluck a figure out of the air, sufficiently extortionate to assuage their outrage and their greed, I authorise the payment, and we jump into the car and head for the M40 motorway to make our way to the capital.

I fill her in as we go. 'Did you notice the two skeletons at all?'

She gives me her blank-faced "are you a complete moron? Of course you are" patented expression. 'The two ones with enough *talent* to make them visible from the moon? They might have caught my attention. Dickhead.'

Fair. 'What did you notice about them?'

She pauses. Thinks. I can see her piecing it together from her memories, perhaps visiting her own equivalent of my mind palace. 'They weren't complete.'

Bingo. 'Not quite. Did you catch what was missing?'

Again, the intense thought face. 'The skull and right hand. Left leg and arm bones on one.' Internal examination again. 'Right leg bones, rib cage, spine. Left collarbone and shoulder blade on the other.'

Good. 'That matches my assessment. So where are those bones?'

She thinks, just normal deductive logical thinking this time. I see it click. 'The hand, leg, arms, and spine – those make up the sceptre.'

'Right! I reckon he's waiting to add those bits last 'cos he'll need to dismantle the very useful dimension hopper to get them. That'll be the last thing he does. So what does that leave?'

Pause. 'The shoulder blade and collarbone.' I have my eyes on the road, but I can almost hear her eyes widening from the other seat. I love catching her by surprise, showing I can actually think things through, that I'm not just a pretty face. Not even a pretty face normally. 'The skull! The rib cage!'

My head bobs back and forth, caught up in her excitement. 'Exactly. We might not know where the shoulder blade or collarbone are, but we know perfectly well where the skull is. And we also know, unless it's the one in the other skeleton and we're too late, where a rib cage packed full of dark magic is now stored.'

'Paris. Leandre.'

'The Lutin Prince himself. Which we know because...'

'We let Al-Ruhban give it to him. Dickhead.'

My eyes widen as I glance at her. 'What?'

She stares at me in silence, "you're a dickhead" repeating clear in her eyes. I look away only because I have to look at the road. Honest.

And then I groan, remembering our flight to England and how she mentioned the rib cage. Repeatedly. 'You already clocked that as our next move.'

A slow clap comes from the seat beside me, and I can feel each clap on the back of my head.

'Well, er, going to Paris then would've been wrong.' I ignore the fact that had we gone to Paris and caught him there, the outcome probably would've been the same as what happened here. 'Ahem. Anyway, my suggested plan is this. Give Isaac a call and put him on high alert. We already know De Montfort gave Torquemada's skull to Ben and kept an eye on him. That doesn't mean he can replicate the Enochian runes and the magic-nulling serum Ben made...'

'But it doesn't mean he can't.'

'Yep. We head to Paris, organise a pow-wow with Leandre, and get him on board with the risk posed by De Montfort. Perhaps persuade him to let us take the rib cage to study. At the very least get access, so Isaac and Jakob...'

'Isakob.'

I pause. Grit my teeth. Then sigh. She deserves the win. 'Fine. So Isakob can get a good look at it and compare the magic it carries against that of Almeric's skull. Either way, alert him to the danger, get him onside while we hunt down De Montfort.'

Aicha weighs my plan, assessing it like a pawn-shop jeweller trying to work out if the "family heirloom" offered by the guy looking like he wants to scratch his way out of his own skin is worth a centime. Eventually, she passes judgement. 'That's not entirely fucking stupid, *saabi*. Congratulations.'

High praise indeed from Aicha. She isn't finished though. 'I still don't get why he gave Ben the skull. Looks like he's been hunting down all the bones. Why gift some away?'

It's a valid question, one I've been mulling over myself in the occasional moments of downtime since our last clash. 'No real idea. I mean, he needed Ben's skull. I guess, with the resident magician/angel combo, perhaps he didn't fancy his chances. Maybe he hoped I'd kill Ben or he'd kill me or we'd both weaken each other sufficiently that he could just sweep in and pick up the reliquary pieces while we lay bleeding out in the dust? Either way, it didn't seem to work out for him. He got the drop on Lou, but we kept the one skull safe, thankfully.'

We lapse into silence, Aicha digesting what I've said, trying to poke at my theory's many flaws like a dancing bear to see if she can make it pirouette without tearing our heads off. Talking of metaphorical wild animals, there's a big-assed elephant in the room we need to discuss. More woolly-mammoth sized, in fact.

'Aicha, what happened with your...' I feel lost for words. I try to mime regrowing a body, which, let me tell you, is not easy while driving at high speed down a motorway. Certainly not without looking like you're having a seizure.

Aicha's tone is bleak. 'I don't know, *saabi*, not really. Something in that magic came very close to cancelling out the Aab-Al-Hayaat's effects. It was touch and go. I felt the dark calling.'

She felt the dark calling. Such a simple phrase, but it still sends shivers down my spine. Maybe it's the thought of losing her. Maybe it's the thought of my own dark place I was called back to again and again, not too long back. I wonder, not for the first time, if there isn't some integral part of me still left behind, under that cave in Faerie even now.

I force myself back to the problem at hand. 'What could cause that? Is De Montfort that powerful? Is it because he's got Melusine's sceptre?'

She's silent for a moment. A moment that stretches almost to where I'm not sure she's going to answer. She does though. 'The sceptre certainly. Well, the bones as a whole. The power that hit me was...incredible. I felt it as it burnt through every fibre of my being. Twisted. Darkened. But familiar.'

'Familiar? Familiar how?'

'I tasted it in my tongue before it dissolved into nothingness. I felt it in my nerves as they disintegrated. It felt like your magic, Paul. Distorted, but it still felt like you.'

I avoid ploughing into the lorry pulling out in front of me but only just. She has completely blindsided me. 'Felt like me, how?'

'Felt like your magic. Not the "you're a wizard, Harry" Hogwarts wannabe magic. The "Bill Murray in *Groundhog Day*" magic. I've been with you as you died far too many times, you careless dickhead. Know what it feels like when you go. What it feels like when the vacated body breaks to pieces. That...' She drums her fingers on the dashboard, an arrhythmic pattern. I wonder if it's to dredge up the memories or to drive them away. 'That was what it felt like when the spell broke mine down.'

I don't know what to say. It seems illogical, unreal. Of course, De Montfort has the same Grail-gained reincarnating abilities or a close cousin variant thereof, and he threw a powerball at her. It wasn't his power though. He drew it from the bones, channelling it through the grave-robbed sceptre. I think of the skulls, of how I felt that similarity between the *talent*, how I just knew the first skull belonged to Arnaud Almeric, who'd been splashed with the same essence out of the broken Grail. How it calls to my power and draws me to reincarnate in bodies nearby it over closer, more convenient corpses to me.

The affinity Aicha felt isn't between my reincarnation *talent* and De Montfort's. It's between it and the bones themselves.

Chapter Fifteen
SÖLL, AUSTRIA, 11 FEBRUARY 1939

It isn't a comfortable journey to the mountains despite the transport Johannes somehow laid his hands on. Motor cars are still scarce and liable to scrutiny. Mind you, anyone moving around in the area now is likely to draw attention. Especially when they're a long way away from the Aryan ideal.

In this regard, at least, Otto's SS uniform helps out. With us facing unknown forces sent by the bastard Ahnenerbe, I'm loath to burn any *talent* I can conserve, even for a low level *don't look here*. So I rely on his credentials to get us past any roadblocks and accompanying hard questions. Part of me panics each time we have to stop in case they ask for paperwork, aware that Rahn's a wanted man. So far, the three silver pips and stripe of his *obersturmführer* epaulettes get us waved through without any further demands.

Considering the man is an invaluable source into the veiled machinations of the SS occult agencies and that I'm the source of the answers to the questions that have plagued him his whole academic life (not that I'm about to reveal that to him anytime soon), conversation is surprisingly stilted.

I try again. 'So how is that? Living with a curse?' *Jesus Christ, smooth Paul.*

The blank fish look I get is entirely merited. The peculiar combination of watery eyes jam-packed with intensity behind it is unnerving though. 'Terrifying.' The monotone delivery sounds like a Brit discussing the weather.

We lapse into silence once more. It's a difficult one. I know I should be shaking him down for intel, but it's easier said than done. He's not so much a closed book as one that's been placed in an iron casket and then welded shut. Then buried. Under the foundations of a ten-storey building.

Still, never let it be said I'm a quitter. 'Have you ever seen anything like it before? Have you any idea what it might mean?'

'That I'm a dead man.' Silence reigns.

I'm just cursing myself for even bothering when he sighs, and a tiny bit of the starch that seems to have leached into his posture from his crisp uniform disperses. 'I apologise. I have spent so long now guarding my tongue, wary of every word I say, that I might anger this one or intrigue this other in the wrong way. I am not used to speaking candidly anymore.'

The man worries at a strand of his hair that has fallen forward, then seems to realise, slicking it back into place. 'I cannot tell you exactly what it does other than it is a contract. There are certain...' He hesitates, clearly searching for the right word. 'Certain forces who have made deals with the Ahnenerbe. They are attracted to the dark energies, delighting in the malice and mischief contained within, and are willing to work side-by-side in exchange for their freedom to operate as they wish against any designated as...undesirable... If a target is assigned, the deal is they will hunt them down. Not that many of the Ahnenerbe object to hunting.'

So basically a supernatural hit contract he carries as a visible mark for the Talented to see. A contract that the darkest, most naturally evil of creatures are waiting to carry out. Brilliant.

The drifting snow isn't a blizzard, but it's persistent. It shades the world, obscuring distance, hiding hairpin turns as the road wends upwards, twisting round the rising foothills that sit like progenies of the towering Alps ahead. It's strange. I'm from the mountains. The Pyrenees are safe territory for all their creatures and crevices. Here, I'm out of my element. These peaks grasp at the sky and tear the clouds downwards to wear them like the death ring the man next to me fiddles with. A part of me thinks the farther we go into the wilderness, the easier I should feel because we're leaving the world of Men behind, where uniforms and rules shape reality. Problem is, there have always been sharper claws hidden out in the wilds, waiting for the unwary.

As the heaviness of the precipitation increases, I'm intensely glad we're in a car, that we don't have to try and hike our way through these untamed highlands. Which is, of course, when the engine seizes up.

We don't have to bother wasting time figuring out the car is dead, and that's the only good thing about this. The sort of screeching and banging that comes from under the bonnet as the car drifts to a halt, only carried by momentum a few extra metres before the gradient and gravity win out, means we're well outside of the realms of my technical know-how to get it going again. I yank on the handbrake before we roll backwards, and we both jump out. Luckily, Johannes supplied us both with well-fitting boots and furred coats, so I won't need to use my limited power just to keep us alive.

Otto swears, his cold composure cracking under the pressure. I guess the bite of the February mountain air swirling around us is cooler than even his temperament. It's good to know he's affected by such mundane things, at least. So far, considering he's on the run from both the German secret services and the *secret* secret services, he's not seemed particularly fazed. I suspect nothing gets him excited...unless we start to discuss the

Albigensian Crusade. No doubt, if we did, he'd delight in telling me all the things wrong with my version of what happened. Having said that, the whole "being threatened with the concentration camps for homosexual clinches" says he must have some human passions somewhere, buried deep underneath all that ice.

For now, though, I have more pressing matters than my imposed companion's lack of social skills. Despite being obsessed with magic, Otto is entirely unTalented. He's gone round to the front of the car to fuss over it, waving his hand through the billowing smoke as if, were he to clear it away with a stiff breeze, the motor will start working again. I, on the other hand, can see the glowing orange swirls through the bonnet. They're eating through the engine, turning the metal the same colour as the magic, ageing it instantly. Rusting, seizing it up.

That's a hex, if ever I saw one. Not good news.

Swinging a rucksack full of emergency provisions onto my back, I push Otto away from the car. 'Leave it. It's dead. So are we if we don't get moving.'

His eyes widen. 'That wasn't natural?' At my headshake, he pales. 'They've found us?'

'Not necessarily.' We need to get off the road. I can see a few houses nestled into a plateau, with woods stretching behind. Easier to elude pursuit.

'What do you mean, not necessarily?' *Ah, he is human.* I can hear the edge of panic forming in his tone. He fiddles with his ring as we hustle down the small dirt road, aiming for the gap in the trees behind a chalet-style log cabin.

I shrug. 'It was a targeted hex, but they may well have been using your curse marker as a homing device, something to cause general damage to any vehicle you're in.' At that, a thought occurs to me, and my eyes narrow.

'Which is a good point; why haven't they just struck you down at a distance with a death curse?'

Rahn holds up his hand, displaying the ring covered in twisted runes and symbology. 'Why do you think I haven't taken this detestable thing off? It keeps me safe from such attacks.'

I take a good *look* at it as we hurry into the shelter of the woods. It's imbued all right. A good deflective warding, enough to keep targeted magics off him, at least at a distance. Clever stuff. No wonder attempts to strike down the German high command have failed. We all assumed the buildings were heavily warded. Apparently, they carry their own personal wards with them instead.

We don't have time to appreciate the intricacy of the magical design work right now though. I've told him half the truth. It's not necessarily the case that the spell-caster is nearby just because the engine exploded. But I'm willing to bet they are. There's a prickling building on my skin, like the early warning of an oncoming storm front. Someone or something *powerful* is coming.

By the pricking of my thumbs...

I've no idea if whoever's chasing us can trace Otto by his mark. If I had to guess, I'd say not with the ring blocking it, but it's weird, dark magic, tied up in death and suffering in ways that make my skin crawl. There've been times over the centuries where my paths have crossed with Talented who specialise in this sort of tainted sorcery, who channel misery and death into magic. I always avoid them like the plague if possible or wipe them off the face of the earth if it isn't. I've certainly not delved into studying their ways and weavings.

Whether they can or not, there are other ways to find Otto even with his defence against magic. Cast out a net; look for the moving blank spot. I'm hoping that's how they're looking for us, from still some distance off. If so, covering ground means that, hopefully, by the time they get here, we're somewhere else entirely.

Of course, that would be too easy.

Whoever, whatever's after us, they aren't trying to hide. They want us to know. I can feel their power now, my hairs bristling as it rubs against me. They're near, not far from where the car died, and they're closing fast. I need to do something to buy us some time. We're almost at the woods, where it'll be easier to lay some false traps, lead them astray, hopefully. Allow us to find a vantage point, somewhere we can have the upper hand. I'm hoping to be the ace in the hole. The Ahnenerbe won't know Rahn's got Talented protection, so they won't come armed for bear. Possibly.

Of course, depending on who's coming after us, armed for bear might be their natural state of being.

We're metres away, and I'm about to break into a run, forcing Otto to do the same, when I see them.

Shit. Kids.

Three children near the last cabin, playing around the trees, a quiet giggling game, muffled by scarves and snow.

Three delectable treats to charge up their Talent, if whatever's after me is as twisted as I think they are.

They've not seen us yet, but they will. I grab Otto's arm, pointing as I do. 'There, those kids.' My gesture's furious, on the edge of panic, willing him to understand. 'Get them away, inside. Make them leave. Do you know which way's west?'

He nods, pulling a pocket compass from his jacket. Good. 'Head due west as far as you can. Here.' I scoop down, handing him a stone, *pushing* a fragment of my essence into it as I do. 'Take this.'

I watch as he drops it in his pocket. Honestly, I've no idea if I'll be able to track it as I normally would with that ring on, but it gives me more of a chance. Whether it works or not, I'll be leading his pursuer on a merry dance. And, more importantly, keeping them away from the children.

'Go.' I push his shoulder roughly, stirring him to action. 'Get them away and then go!'

I fling the rucksack into his arms as they come up instinctively to catch it, then turn my back on him. If he doesn't get those kids away, I'll kill him myself.

I rub my hands together, trying to work some warmth back into the flesh, which has chilled beneath my gloves from the mountain's bite. I don't like being hunted. Let Rahn run like a startled rabbit. Once those kids are safe, he's on his own until I catch up with him. If I catch up with him.

Now, though, it's time to deal with whatever's after us.

If I can.

Chapter Sixteen
Approaching London, 7 June, Present Day
Turn again, Whittington! Go on, give us a twirl. Looking fabulous.

There are things to get done before we get back to France. Not least, organising actually getting there.

Silence lapses inside the vehicle. There's a lot to think about. Not that I think either of us expects to come up with some moment of deductive genius, a spark of inspiration that solves the case, then it's tea and biscuits and pats on the back all round. Nope, if this were a TV detective show, we'd not even be at the point where they really start finding clues yet. We're a long way from the last joke where everyone freezes with a cheesy grin on their face, and it fades out to the credits. Maybe though, just maybe, we might be heading in that direction, finally.

I need to call Isakob –never let it be said I don't do anything for my friends– and update them on the madness we've been through. While we talk, I get Aicha to book us onto the Eurostar, the train between England and France.

On the phone, outside of verbal ticks, it's almost impossible to tell which of the two brothers I'm talking to, so we reach an accord that Isaac holds the reins to save my head melting with trying to figure it out mid-conversation. Melted heads tend to mean you miss important bits of information. Especially when, like me, you are a bear of little brain. Which makes Aicha "Piglet" of course. I'm not feeling suicidal enough to tell her that though. Not today, at least.

There's not much in the way of revelations. The sympathetic magic between the two mostly assembled skeletons and the sceptre fascinates him, of course, and he wants to study them in greater detail. I point out he's welcome to ask De Montfort for a lendsy, but I don't think he's likely to get a favourable response. He also assures me that the wards both around the house and the Toulouse region are at maximum strength. Even with the realm-hopping powers of Melusine's rod, De Montfort will have difficulty bypassing the restrictions put in place by the two Bene Elohim residing inside Isaac. Dimensional travel is something of a forte for them.

I don't dream for a moment that De Montfort isn't working on a plan to extricate Almeric's skull from their hands. I just feel it's a sufficiently new kink in his plan given he hasn't got there yet. Going for the rib cage in Paris or else the shoulder bones if he's located them elsewhere first makes far more sense. He's had plenty of time to plot and prepare. I can say a lot of bad things about Simon De Montfort – and do so regularly. At loud volume. Punctuated with the most obscene and graphic foul language I can muster. But he knows how to both lay and execute a plan meticulously. The cockheaded batwanking cuntlefish.

I mention the possibility of Isaac joining us in Paris if Leandre doesn't want to let us leave with the rib cage but will allow us to study it.

'Aye, lad, perfect. I'll need a little more time, but then we'll join you.' Isaac sounds evasive. It makes me suspicious. He's up to something.

I get straight to the point. 'How much time? What's going on, 'Zac?'

'I'm not sure.' There's a hesitance to his voice. I can tell he wants to say more, that he's desperate to share, but something holds him back. 'Trust me, lad. It's nothing bad. I just don't want to get anyone's hopes up. If it works, it might just help us even the odds.'

Intriguing. I'm not burning with curiosity so much as the steering wheel is getting covered in glowing red question marks, honest. I can wait. He'll tell me when he's good and ready. No problem.

'C'mon, 'Zac! What are you up to?' Five seconds. I lasted five seconds. Not bad, all things considered. Where "all things" are the sum of my inquisitive nature and poor impulse control.

'No.' Damn it. I know that tone. It's a tone I've wheedled and whined against like the truculent eternal adolescent I apparently am many times over the centuries. Despite my best efforts, I never got him to change his mind. I doubt this will be the first time. 'I promise if it works, you'll be the first to know, lad. Leave it at that.'

I know when I'm beat. After I promise to keep him updated – a promise I can understand him extracting from me after the booze-fuelled misery cruise I took around the streets of Toulouse on my return from Narbonne, which feels approximately a zillion years ago, we hang up. Aicha has sorted out our tickets, and we're fast approaching the M25, the ring road leading us to London proper. Well, fast is how we have been approaching. Now the traffic is building up, meaning we've slowed down dramatically. It isn't going to get better from here. Once we get inside London proper, I'll need every single one of my two brain cells to follow the sat nav instructions and navigate the capital's streets. I get Aicha to pay the congestion charge online after a handy reminder flashes up in pixelated orange on an overhead electric signpost. Now there's just one more thing to do before we get on the train and head to Paris.

'Do you still have Al-Ruhban's number?' I should have it myself, but I'm rubbish at staying in touch with people. Aicha might not be gregarious, but she does a much better job at maintaining contact. Her friendship is hard won but harder to lose. See my recent actions if you need a good example of that.

She huffs her annoyance, though whether at my lack of organisation or having to deal with the car's shitty touchscreen, I can't be sure. I'll go with the latter. Sure, why not? A few moments later, Al-Ruhban's rich vocal tones fill the car.

'Hello?' The caution in his voice is entirely natural. Considering how many of us Talented burn through phones like, well, burner phones, caller ID is never going to be our friend. I've no idea if Aicha has some pre-arranged pattern of ringing, then hanging up like we do; I'm distracted trying to get around the family sedan sat in the middle lane doing half the speed limit without getting crushed like Frogger by the other cars doing double it as I pull out into the fast lane. But either way, such patterns can be copied easily enough. Still, something makes me a touch uneasy. Last time we met, Al-Ruhban was all open arms. I guess decades involved in the capital's Talented politics will change a man. Guess they'll change a half-man, half-djinn too.

'Al-Ruhban, it's Aicha. Are you home? Need to visit.' I want to look at Aicha, see if she has the same feeling about his initial greeting. I also don't want to die in flaming wreckage made of twisted metal. Tough choices, but I keep my eyes on the road. My developing allergy towards death makes me feel like a sweet-toothed diabetic. I really don't want to lose this body, but I suspect, eventually the choices will get too damn tempting.

'It's not the best time.' Okay, something is definitely going on. I decide to get involved.

'Al-Ruhban? Paul here. Good to hear from you again, dude. Totally get that whole not-the-best-time thing. Problem is, we've had a similarly utterly shitty-beyond-fucking-belief time on our end. Remember the present you got from us the first time we met? That's turned out to be a lot more important than any of us could have imagined. We need to see it. We need to speak to the Prince.'

The silence hangs over the line like a freshly scrubbed lead balloon. Guess that news hasn't gone down as well as I hoped.

He speaks eventually. 'This really isn't the moment, *saabi*.'

'Why?' My frustration's mounting. His answers are the equivalent of playing a game with a friend who keeps tutting or sucking in a breath or saying things like, 'Oof, really?' every time you're about to make a move. Enough to make you doubt yourself but annoyingly vague. I don't have time for vagaries. I need a damn good reason. That I can then tear into teeny, tiny pieces and jump up and down on. Because whatever he says, we're coming to Paris to talk to Leandre.

His long-suffering sigh carries all the frustrated weariness of a middle manager dealing with ineptitudes and unrealistic expectations aimed at him from both above and below. 'Paris is practically on lockdown. Movement is limited. The Prince isn't seeing anyone.'

Ah. That might throw a small spanner in the works. Where the spanner has an explosive charge strapped to it. And "the works" are the cooling facilities of an ageing nuclear generator.

But we still need to see the Prince. Whether the Prince wants to see us or not.

CHAPTER SEVENTEEN

LONDON, 7 JUNE, PRESENT DAY

Of course Paris is in lockdown. Of course it is. Why would it not be? Anything else might actually be vaguely helpful.

It takes a whole heap of badgering and persuading bordering on a petulant whine, but eventually Al-Ruhban agrees – with a long-suffering sigh – to see what he can do about getting us to his and setting up a sit-down with Leandre. He doesn't know what has caused the restrictions. No one has contacted him specifically, not yet at least. General information gets passed around via a pirate radio station broadcast across Paris and the nearest suburbs. Apparently, someone has enchanted the transmitter so only Talented can hear it. To everyone else, it sounds just like static. The info coming out for the last couple of days has been crystal clear. Stick in your area. Don't move around. Don't call us; we'll call you.

By the time we navigate through the baffling network of backstreets and main roads to drop off the hire car, Aicha not having torn her door off and used it to beat to death the delivery van drivers who seemed to consider blocking every narrow alley their Good God-given duty (Though she might have scorched 'Twat' into one of the vehicles when we discovered our ten-minute wait had been to let the driver grab a sandwich. I can live with that. She didn't engrave it into his forehead. He can count himself lucky.), Al-Ruhban calls us back as we approach Saint Pancras. We give him our ticket numbers and arrival times so he knows that time's limited.

'Okay,' he says, sounding harassed. That might be our fault for harassing him. I have too much stress of my own to feel in any way guilty about that though. 'I can't get in, but I've contacted a friend. Scarbo works as a messenger-slash-delivery-boy for Leandre. He can get around even under lockdown. He'll pick you up, then get you over to me. We'll work out the rest from there. Maybe he can get a message to the Prince for us?'

'You trust this Scarbo? What have you told him?'

'I trust him. He's been a good friend to me since he got the Thirteenth District back in the nineties.'

This is news to me; last I heard, a jiuweihu, the Chinese equivalent of a kitsune, ran the quarter, occupying the top floor of one of the Tang Brothers towers, the businessmen who control vast swathes of the Paris equivalent of Chinatown. Granted, my lack of knowledge isn't surprising. I don't involve myself in Parisian politics, and Leandre runs a tight ship. It's not like regular gossip leaks out about what's going on. Not reliable gossip anyhow.

'And what did you tell him?'

'Just that two of my Talented friends are coming to visit. I gave him your names. Nothing more.'

It's more than I'd have given him, but then I'm incredibly paranoid. With just cause, as has been previously established, but incredibly paranoid nonetheless.

It'll have to do though. We ring off with a promise to keep him updated in case of any delays and make our way into the train station.

Calling it a train station is a bit like calling a Ferrari a "nice car" or a politician "not totally honest". It's an understatement that doesn't really deliver on the sense of grandeur the building gives, both internally and externally.

With the prominent corner clock tower all twiddly Victorian Gothic detailing, I can well believe some tourists might think it to be Westminster itself and the clock Big Ben. Mainly because a lot of tourists shouldn't be allowed out of their front doors, let alone their home countries, but it's a striking building. Inside?

Inside, they've really gone to town. Steel and glass bind together in industrial chic, the curving arc of the structure nestling chic boutiques and stylised, over-priced takeaways and eateries, all designed to excavate money out of the passersby's pockets like a council-licensed Fagin. The entire building feels like a weird through-the-looking-glass version of me. Antiquated on the outside, bright and new on the inside. I'm the exact opposite. The outside is less tarnished than my soul though, obviously.

We get onto the train with little hassle. The metal detector causes Aicha to go into a weapons-grade sulk. I'm talking gamma-radiation driven "The Incredible Sulk" level sulk. It's because it reminds her that, as well as disintegrating her, De Montfort's energy bolt destroyed all of her favourite weapons.

I carry spares for her, of course, and gave some to her as soon as we left the secret room at the gatehouse. That doesn't mean she isn't going to mourn those lost. They were like her babies, extensions of her. She isn't talking about it, but I can sense she's still worried. I can't lie. So am I. That magic bolt has screwed with her regeneration. The question is – will it get better again? The flip-side to that is what if it doesn't? What if it gets worse?

Sadly, it's a question I feel sure we'll find out the answer to one way or the other before we get to the end of this particular yellow-shit-road we find ourselves marching down.

CHAPTER EIGHTEEN
SÖLL, AUSTRIA, 11 FEBRUARY 1939

I throw a hasty *don't look here* in the direction of Otto and the kids. It's not enough to fool any Talented seriously *looking*, but the idea is to keep the attention focused on me. Time to make myself a big old visible target. At least that's something that plays to my strengths.

I can feel the arriving Talented, and it doesn't feel good. There's almost a taste in the air, a smell like cold loam enriched by decaying flesh. If I'm any sort of judge, it's a nature spirit. A lot of people seem to always associate nature as a force for good, forgetting it'll just as happily freeze the marrow in your bones, then crack them open and crunch them down. Nature's a fine and wonderful thing. Just stop making the mistake of believing it's your friend. There's a reason we learned to bring fire to the night. To make the dark safer. Or at least to help us to believe it is.

I need to make sure its attention's all on me, and I reckon whatever's coming isn't going to want to sit down over a cup of tea and discuss how we can both walk away from here happy. Best way to get noticed, I've always found, is to piss people off.

Elemental magic's never been my forte, but it's still doable, and the expenditure of power is minimal compared to the impressive effect. Forming a fireball in the palm of my hand takes but a thought, and I fling it at the lower branches of a gnarled tree in the direction the Talented is coming from. The magical flames wrap around it like blankets binding up a lover on a lazy weekend morning, swathing it till every inch ignites, a golden crackling beacon to draw the eye.

That should get the message across.

It also acts as a torch, giving me a clearer view of the murk roiling down the path towards me. It's not a cloud exactly. More captured shadow. It's like the trees and branches move just *so*, forming and shaping shade. Natural darkness bound and carried. No easy trick. I've no idea if this is an ingrained ability of what's approaching or a casual demonstration of power. Neither answer is exactly comforting.

As I watch, the encroaching gloom halts and parts. A woman steps out — or a woman-shaped entity, at least. The anatomy is close enough to human for my brain to apply the label. It rethinks that description when she moves farther forward and is lit up by my tree-beacon.

Were she human, were this a fairy tale, we'd be into the realm of wizened crone or wise and wily hag. They've told fairy tales about her in these regions. Those tales are simple. Don't meet her. If you do? Run.

She's gnarled in every sense of the word. Bent up, she's almost wrapped around the walking stick she leans on. Except her hands are the same shape and shade, warped and whorled, twig-like fingers blending into the texture of the staff. Rags of grey and green, tattered and torn and patched with lichen cover her bulbous form. Her feet, sticking out the bottom, are green, bushed with moss-like slippers, though I can't tell you if it merely covers her feet or comprises them. So far, she looks like a nature spirit. It's the head that sets her apart and lets me know who I'm dealing with. What I'm dealing with.

At least I know she's not fae. It's a safe bet considering the red rust traces that carve lines into the iron surface of her face. There are no fae with metal skin as far as I know. The streak marks make age wrinkles out of the stains, marking her with rusted ancientry. Rheumy wide white eyes track back and forth between the tree in flames and me, saucer-like in the metallic face, half hidden behind curtains of filthy, tangled locks that cascade off her head and down to her waist. They're the colour that beige walls go when the owner smokes a couple of packets of cigarettes a day. They also move but not in the way of an actress', billowing, lustrous and gleaming. No, these move like there're living things burrowing in them. I've heard messy hair described as a bird's nest. This is more like bugs' nests. Wrought with infestations.

That matches what I've heard about the Buschgro'Bmutter, or Shrub Grandmother, though. Sadly for me, she chooses to demonstrate the truth to those rumours and legends. Her free hand jerks upwards to her grubby tresses, stiff stop-start movements reminiscent of a clockwork doll. Then she starts to scratch.

The screeching noise, like tearing metal, is almost terrible enough. It grows, reverberating through the trees, building like nails on a chalkboard but where more and more claws join in, screeching their way down the surface. Her hand flickers back and forth, shaking her hair. A snow-globe's worth of dandruff flakes scatter down, coating the floor around her.

Except, disgusting enough as that is on its own, it isn't dandruff. The flakes scuttle forward, growing as they do. I can see now they're not white but translucent, an opaque shell with half-obscured organs dark smirches beneath. By the time they near the tree, they're the size of large dogs with three legs on each side of their body. Sharp pincer jaws pop out of their head, perfectly designed to tear chunks out of a person's flesh. Not ideal when said person is me.

My sword's in my hand in a second, and I'm powering it up before I even realise. I've fought some monstrous creatures over the years, hellish chimeras concocted by mad alchemists and fae beasts that've haunted our collective nightmares since the worlds first touched. Fighting giant head lice might just take the trophy for most disgusting.

The first one makes a scurrying feint at my right side, and I'm relieved when my sword cleaves its head clean from its thorax. The substance is hard-looking, and I was worried whether my blade would penetrate. Whether because of how sharp I keep it or the magic encasing the edge, there's no problem. At least with killing that one. There're plenty of other problems. Hundreds of them.

Because that's how many of these fuckers there seems to be. I follow on from the strike with a half-spin, driving the blade point through the abdomen equivalent of another that's reared up, looking to decapitate me in revenge for its fallen brother. I'm able to keep the momentum going, tearing the blade sideways, freeing it. I can't turn it in time for another arriving at speed, so I bring the flat hammering down on its head. There's a popping squish that tells me I've crushed one of its eyes, and the creature goes still, at least for now. I don't know enough about lice's physiology to know if their brains are in their heads, but if they are, I reckon the odds are pretty good I've given it a severe concussion.

I don't have time to worry about that right now though. It might be out of action, but the rest of the arriving horde isn't. I hack and slash my way through the nightmare-fuel –all glistening grub-like bodies– spilling out their viscous juices to mix with the snow-drifts, forming slippery globs of slush just to make keeping my footing even more difficult. Holding my own is possible, but I'm aware that this is just the precursor for the main event. Out of the corner of my eye, as I slaughter the arriving in-sectoid herd, I can see the Buschgro'Bmutter closing the distance, her moon-shaped eyes locked on me. Each time I look away and then back, it's like she's flickered closer. I don't know what other magic she has in her arsenal, but considering giant pet lice are her starting foray, I'm not in any hurry to find out.

Except, I might not get to anyhow because my attention's been too fixed on her and not enough on my feet and the battle at hand. One of the lice has slipped behind me, and suddenly, lancing red hot pain rips through my hamstring as it tears a chunk out. The impact shoves my foot forward, splaying out in the gunk underfoot, and I go sprawling. I throw up a shield in time just as the bugs swarm over me. The magic keeps them from ripping me to pieces, but it does nothing about the weight, and their suffocating presence makes it hard to breathe in more ways than one.

Through the occasional gaps in the wiggling masses, I can see the Buschgro'Bmutter, covering the distance between eye blinks. Her mouth, which was little more than a crack before, is now opening, squealing wider, a rusted, snake-like unhinging, juddering open. *Click-click-click-click*. It's fair to say it's fucking terrifying.

The wound in the back of my leg is pissing blood, soaking into the snow beneath me. I'm pushing magic into it, trying to stem the flow but to little effect. Lice bites don't heal, apparently. Part of my brain keeps trying to insist what a good title for a pulp fiction detective novel that'd make. I'm assuming that means either fevered infection is setting in, or I'm getting light-headed from blood loss. Or both. Neither are good options, and that's before the demonic hag brings her special brand of metal-face doom on me.

Basically, time to cut and run. I *push* outwards, scattering the giant nits left, right, and centre. A few land on their backs, their stubby legs wriggling in the air, but wind gusts right them again, and they skitter back in my direction. Looks like these parasites don't give up once they've tasted blood. They're worse than lawyers.

I have time to get to my feet though, and I am more than ready to demonstrate that discretion is the better part of valour by hightailing it out of here. The Buschgro'Bmutter is still jerkily closing the distance between us, so I turn and run. I'm pleased to see that both the kids and Rahn have disappeared. One goal achieved. Now to get some breathing space to make a new plan of attack.

I'm used to running across mountainous terrain, pursued by monsters. Which tells you exactly how shitty my life is. That's not the issue right now. Problem is the gaping hole in my leg. There's a reason we use the phrase "hamstringing" someone. It's not easy to pound your way over uneven terrain at the best of times, with roots and fallen branches half-hidden in the drifts snatching at your feet. When you're slowly bleeding out from your left hams and an agonised hurried limp is the best your right leg can manage, you're not about to set any land speed records.

I throw a glance over my shoulder, pushing a bit, trying to find the maximum plotted point on the graph curve with speed versus pain on each axis. My vision's greying at the peripheries, which tells me I'm probably at it, if not over it. A glance backwards tells me the decision to run is working, at least for now. Despite the horror of how they move, the short limbs mean the gigantic lice aren't that quick, and they're even more encumbered by the obstacles on the floor than I am. The hag's still pursuant, crossing distance with sudden jerks every time I blink. She's not closing yet. I'm not sure how long I can keep this pace up though. At least she's still chasing me rather than hunting out the kids or pursuing Otto. For now, I'm winning.

Which is precisely the moment when the tree in front of me pivots a branch to face me, and I run straight into it, impaling myself through the stomach like a shish kebab, ready to get grilled.

And judging by the *click-click-click-click* closing in from behind me...

The Buschgroßmutter might not wait till I'm cooked. She might just eat me alive.

Chapter Nineteen
PARIS, 7 JUNE, PRESENT DAY

Good God, it feels great to be back in France. I wonder how long that feeling will last.

The train journey, at least, is painless — a word I seem to be running out of opportunities to use as a descriptor except sarcastically. I message an update to Isaac, using the private communication to fill him in more accurately on the situation with Aicha and her regenerating. If it doesn't improve, if it goes the other way, then fuck the De Montfort situation. I'll take the risk and get her back over to the East, Lebanon as a starter. Find the Druze and make her go back to the Well of Life, drink the Aab-al-Hayaat all over again. As far as I'm aware, she's still its official guardian. I'm sure they won't mind her getting a do-over. It might seem selfish that I'd consider risking the world to save Aicha. You know what? I don't give a flying fuck. She's worth it. Of course, she won't let me, which is part of the reason why she's worth it. I'll find a way to cross that bridge without her blowing it up with sticks of dynamite when we get to it.

By the time we pull into the Gare du Nord, evening is falling fast, especially with us regaining the hour that those thieving bastard timezones stole from us when we headed to England. Fine. I'm still a long way from needing to sleep. Push comes to shove, I can keep going for another twenty-four hours before I start looking really crazy. I can get down with Thorin and Company's approach. Dark for dark business.

The station itself feels more like a repurposed hangar than the slick modernity we left behind in London. There are still adjacent cafés and food stalls, but it doesn't carry that polished-up capitalist dream clutched quite so tight to its heart. Prices are still exorbitant, maybe more so; this is Paris after all, but there's a Gallic nonchalance about it, a wearied shrug at the inevitability that you'll end up separated from the contents of your wallet without the need for gleaming window displays.

The outside is Napoleonic elegance. I wonder if perhaps this place is more of a fitting image for my current state — stunningly beautiful on the exterior, empty and hollow inside. Man, maybe I should have joined up with those Goth vampires after all.

In the square outside, you'll definitely get separated from the contents of your wallet. And your wallet itself. And the shirt off your back if you aren't careful. It's a central arrival point for starry-eyed tourists and, as such, a fertile ground for pickpockets and muggers. As with many capitals and major cities, getting distracted at a terminus can be terminal.

I'm not worried about that. We ping as major threats on any petty criminal's radar. The streets either give you honed instincts or a honed blade in your belly. Bothering us is likely to lead to the second. Easier pickings surround us on all sides.

The interior of the station, the square outside, and the neighbouring cafés are neutral territory. No matter which way you come into the city, you can make it to the Gare du Nord without setting foot outside of the metro system. I've only had to parley once with Leandre's people officially, but here's where it happened. It makes sense as a meeting place. Just a pain in the arse that we aren't meeting Al-Ruhban here directly. I can't help wondering what has happened in the city to cause the lockdown. It makes me distinctly uneasy. Surely we've disrupted De Montfort's plans with our unexpected appearance at least slightly? Could this really be his doing? It's added more unknowns in just when I felt we were finally getting our hands on a few puzzle pieces.

Our guide is easy to spot. Anyone not Talented who looks will see a man who's apparently watched one too many detective movies. A tan trench coat and trilby with a scarf carelessly tossed over one shoulder can be a tough look to pull off. It helps, of course, when it's only an illusion. The man most people see would give Humphrey Bogart a run for his money, and I notice more than a few ladies giving him appreciative looks.

The actual creature himself wouldn't have the same success with the style. Mostly because he would look ridiculous with the trench coat billowing out behind him like a bridal train. He only comes up to the illusion's waist. Humanoid features don't disguise the fact that he clearly isn't human. You don't need to catch a glimpse of his razor-sharp teeth to know that. His nose takes up half his face — a rounded beak, almost a snout, and his eyes are cat-like slits. Clad in felt trousers and a billowy top closer to a smock than a shirt, he tops off the ensemble with a hat that looks like Pharrell Williams pimped out Robin Hood's bycoket, complete with a peacock feather protruding high enough as to tickle the glamour's nose. Basically, we're looking at the anthropomorphic embodiment of Little Man Syndrome.

We stroll over. He turns, picking up on our movement. On seeing me, his eyes widen, only highlighting further their strange inhuman quality, and he falls forward, prostrating himself in front of me. He's clearly panicking too because he forgets to throw up a *don't look here* glamour before doing so. The sight of this Jake Gittes wannabe suddenly hurling himself at the feet of two beautiful women would be hilarious, as would the enraged haughty regards some of the ladies checking him out throw our way, were we not aiming for discretion. I wrap us in the breeze, dancing a discarded coffee cup across the square, and blow the attention away from us. Looks like I'm getting the hang of my fae magic. Slowly but surely.

Now that we aren't Paris' latest piece of street theatre, I bend closer to the little creature. 'I'm not Maeve. Relax.'

I don't know what he finds weirder. The Winter Queen suddenly turning up in the centre of Paris or the Winter Queen turning up in the centre of Paris and not actually being the Winter Queen. His expression holds a thousand and one questions. I try to focus on that rather than the large lump of snot half-protruding out of one of his considerable nostrils. Questions are easier to handle.

He draws himself up, scrabbling back to his feet before issuing a bow and striking what would be an elegant pose were it not for the leaking bodily gunk clinging to his proboscis for dear life.

'*As Helios' chariot charts the growth*
Of arcing hope and dark deposed
So your visage sets our heart aglow
Thy humble servant art Scarbo.'

Oh. My. God. I force a smile onto my face. 'Delighted to meet you, Scarbo, and my thanks for coming to meet us. Can you give us just a second?'

I grab Aicha's arm and get to a safe distance before the laughter I felt bubbling up bursts out of my mouth. She trembles with the effort of restraining hers, her lips quivering. She's always had better self-control than I.

'Jesus Christ, that was the worst poetry I've ever heard.'

She nods. 'Less Moliere, more Moil-nah.'

Ooh, good classics joke. 'He's like a shitter Etrigan.'

'He's no Jack Kirby, that's for sure.'

I force myself to sober. 'Do you know anything about this Scarbo? The name's been ringing a vague bell since Al-Ruhban mentioned him, but I can't remember.' I could go hunting through my mind palace, but we don't have time for that.

She goes to shake her head and then pauses. 'Didn't someone write a piece of music about him?'

I snap my fingers. 'Ravel! Maurice Ravel. The *Scarbo Suite*. I knew I recognised the name.' I look back over my shoulder at where our host stands watching us, still standing in a pose like he expects someone to pop up and carve a statue out of him from a block of marble. 'What do you make of him?'

Aicha's brow furrows. 'Odd. Pompous. Pretentious. Not the sort I'd expect Al-Ruhban to be friends with.'

I nod. 'My thoughts exactly. I'll go talk to him again. Keep him busy. Can you give Al-Ruhban a call, just confirm this is the guy we expected to have meet us? There can't be many others like him in the local area.'

'Hope there aren't any others like him. Anywhere.' A momentary look of horror spreads across her face. 'Could you imagine if there were two of them, and they *held a conversation*?'

She shudders. I don't blame her. That's nightmare fuel right there.

Leaving her to make the call, I wander back to the weird little poet. 'Sorry about that. Just needed to sort a few bits and bobs out. Right, so you're going to take us...'

It's not the most subtle of tests, but it's been a long day, travelling to another country and back and battling the undead alongside a perma-stoned Hob King. My tact and tolerance for weirdness are both in free fall at this precise moment.

'As time creeps forth 'pon moving hands,
And all must pay who choose to dance,
As pawn in chess, all move to plan
Pursue our route to Al-Ruhban.'

This isn't going to get old quickly; it's been born ancient, a wizened little baby already in need of a walking stick. The only small blessing is I expect we'll be on public transport for a good part of the way to Al-Ruhban's. That should make avoiding having to speak to him easier.

Aicha rejoins us. Her inclination of her chin as she walks past me, half-way to a nod, is enough to tell me she got hold of Al-Ruhban and Florid Hood checks out.

'Shall we go?' Aicha asks. I see our guide draw breath, but I cut in before he can murder the French language any further.

'Absolutely!' I keep my tone bright and bouncy to minimise any insult by not letting him drop any more shit rhymes. 'Please do lead the way.' Before he can answer, I turn back to Aicha. 'Have you been to Paris before? It's been a long time since I've wandered through these streets.'

There's a dark truth to that statement. I can't help mulling it over in my mind while I chatter inanely at Aicha, not allowing Scarbo space to bust out any more doggerel. Last time I roamed through Paris, I wasn't interested in the ornate architecture, the avenues Napoleon had driven through the city, forcing the poorer inhabitants out to the banlieues (a word that literally means "banished" — in this case from the city centre, now handed over to the wealthy). The fads and fashions, the constructions and conversations were pale ghosts to me then, the roads wisps and the traffic wights. Only two things were real. The pain of my family's death — Susane's and my unborn child's, and the smoky lights of the opium den I made my way towards.

I realise I've lapsed into silence. Luckily, between my hangdog expression lost up in squalid, painful memories and Aicha's closed-faced glare, our host hasn't been struck by the muse. I feel pretty confident it's the same muse that inspires every fourteen year old to craft earnest, angsty poems about love and death. I'd probably prefer to listen to those, in all honesty.

We take the metro. It isn't until we find ourselves on the Ligne 5 that I realise we're heading south. Jostled between a mother's harassed attempts to tend to the squalling of her baby, who's furious with the incomprehensibility of the world around it, and a portly man whose carefully pressed suit speaks of money and privilege but whose breath and demeanour speak of a steady flow of different alcohols, it's hard to get a word with Scarbo. Talking to him would involve a rubbish choice. Should I talk to his illusion, where the chances he'll be able to hear me over the hubbub are slim to none? Or should I bend down and talk into his actual ears, which... Well, let's say it will probably make a lot of people in the carriage uncomfortable.

In the end, I wait until we get out of the cramped interior and onto the platform. The sign informs me we're at the Place D'Italie, centre point of the thirteenth arrondissement, or district. Scarbo's home territory. Also, the furthest district directly south before crossing the ring-road into the banlieues, like Kremlin-Bicetre. Or, to put it another way, as far away as we can possibly be from Al-Ruhban without leaving Paris entirely.

Aicha clocks it too. 'Right, poetical Professor Frink,' she says, looking about ready to knock the creature's stupid oversized hat off. Possibly with Scarbo's head still attached. 'Can you explain why the fuck we're in entirely the wrong place? Preferably without all the "whys" and the "wherefores", and the "oh, the poetry, it burns my soul", okay?'

The little creature looks grumpy as hell. I guess getting called out for your spiel is bad enough; being threatened with high-level violence on top adds insult to probably fatal injury. Sadly, the threat isn't enough to get him to stop himself.

'*From there to here, a simple hop.*

But e'en for me, the rules don't stop.

An emissary I am not

If Leandre's letter I've not got.'

Well, it's significantly more simple than any of his other recent verses. I can't help wondering if he's under some form of curse. Either that or he's just really pretentious. Which is a curse of its own, I guess.

Anyhow, we clock the gist of what he's saying. Apparently, he can travel between the neutral territory of Gare du Nord and his home turf with no concern, but to take us any farther, he needs his official credentials. I want to ask him why he doesn't already have them on him. That would involve him replying though, so I decide I don't want to know that much. He's not as annoying as the fucking Tarrasque, but then nothing is. That doesn't stop him from being pretty bloody irritating.

We come out of the metro next to an oversized glass box, with bustling escalators and prominent advertising screaming shopping mall. We're on the south side of a massive roundabout large enough to host a small park replete with a fountain in the middle. Around it crowd five- or six-storey Parisian buildings – all intricate metal-work on the black iron balconies, all counterposing colours making up the brickwork, which is different between the main walls and the delicate picking out around the floor-high windows. It's all very lovely, but I'm not really concentrating on the scenery. Honestly, I'm more bothered by the *people* crowding us than the buildings.

I know I just came from London but still. That was a momentary visit with us heading towards a clear destination in a foreign country. Now I'm home. I'm on my turf. So it's weird just how uncomfortable I feel.

Toulouse can get busy, especially in the summer months. It's a tourist destination, so while Paris empties in August – when France grinds entirely to a halt and just shuts down for a month – Toulouse can rapidly fill. But that's *my* city. The pavements guide my feet where I need to go. Plus, you develop a certain instinct for which bits to avoid and when.

I don't get the feeling that you can avoid the bustle anywhere in Paris. It surrounds us like an invading horde, like a wave of vaguely irritated noise and hassled movement crashing in all directions while we cling to the rocks. Aicha's stance is constantly changing, minute shifts in posture and position as she re-aligns herself each time a new potential threat enters our vicinity. It's like the world's most tightly contained HIIT routine.

Everybody looks pissed off. It takes me a moment to realise why and then I get it. We're not moving. We've stopped, stock-still while we adjust to this perpetual motion surrounding us, and as such, we're clogging up the machine. Other people have stopped, but they're to the sides, up on the steps of the shopping centre, out of the immediate tide of bodies. We're just gawping, somewhat overwhelmed by the entire experience. A terrible, horrible thought occurs to me. I tap Aicha on the shoulder, which is a spectacularly stupid idea considering how tightly wound she is right now. I don't lose a finger, but it's a close call.

'Are *we* the tourists here?' I'm aghast, and by the micro-expression that crosses her face, her equivalent of doing an impression of the famous 'Scream' painting by Edvard Munch, she feels similarly.

Fortunately for our sense of self-esteem, our host has obviously decided that we've gawped enough. He scurries towards the nearest boulevard. The one heading south. Because of course we're heading even farther in the wrong direction. What else would we possibly do?

Scurrying is definitely the right word for Scarbo's movements. There's something mouse-like about him...if you stretched out a mouse's hind legs and forced it to be bipedal. Which, incidentally, if you do, you're only one step away from going full-on Doctor Moreau, and you need to check yourself before you wreck yourself. It's amazing how much ground he can cover, weaving through the crush of pedestrians, round obstacles like bollards and beggars, trash cans and trees, their bases sealed in concrete to keep them under control, without breaking stride or a sweat, so that we have to work hard to keep up with him.

It's only been about five minutes, but I can feel my misanthropy growing with every step. Why do I want to save humanity again? Perhaps we should just call it a bad idea and hand over the keys to the cockroaches as we switch the lights off on our way out. I'd probably be feeling agoraphobic if my recent imprisonment in Faerie hadn't left me with borderline claustrophobia. You'd think the two would balance each other out. My life doesn't work that way. I suspect I'm just going to end up not feeling happy or content anywhere. Good God. After centuries of not really considering myself of any real nation or nationality, have I finally become truly French?

'I hate this.' There's a distinct whine to my voice. It sets my teeth on edge. By the muscle I see practically strobing in Aicha's jawline, it does the same to her.

'Paul. You're a twat. Shut up.' I guess it's hard enough work being on high alert constantly with the crush of bodies in all directions without having to support my moaning. I decide discretion is the better part of valour when the homicidal, highly trained rage machine next to me is in a hyper-aware state. This body is too useful to lose due to poking the Aicha bear.

We're far enough down the Avenue D'Italie (naming the road connecting the Porte D'Italie and Place D'Italie must have taken the town-planners *ages*) when Scarbo ducks into a fairly nondescript building off to the side. I expected we'd be in the sort of Parisian townhouse ringing the Place itself.

Instead, it's a concrete block seven storeys high, with a car-repair garage situated underneath it. Not what I expected from the ostentatious fellow. Not until we get inside, at least.

Inside, we are in another world. As soon as the door clicks shut back into its electronic lock, silence reigns, and it's a blessed relief.

Whichever interior designer got let loose in here had a penchant for marble and a budget as unrestrained as their taste. Gold filigree is worked into every gap where the marble isn't, and the ceilings are coffered to within an inch of their lives. Each spotlight has Fleur de Lys moulding surrounding them, and there's an electric chandelier hanging in the middle of the lobby because of course there is.

Scarbo isn't looking to give us time to *ooh* and *ahh* over it all. He scuttles across to the elevator to summon it. I don't even need to exchange a look with Aicha for this one.

'Which floor?' she says, then adds, 'Use your fingers,' when he opens his mouth.

He flushes, and I can see he's pissed, but common sense wins out in the end, and he holds up five fingers.

'We'll meet you up there,' I say, waving cheerily as we head for the stairs.

Maeve's body is in reasonably good shape considering between her mind-fuckingly powerful magic and her position as supreme ruler of Winter, she didn't need to do anything ever. We trot up the staircase, which is, of course, just as ornately wrought as the lobby even though, I imagine, it's not in regular usage. I wonder if there's a room somewhere in the building that operates like Dorian Gray's portrait; plasterboard walls covered in grimy woodchip and cheap, badly fitting laminate. All the dust and spiderwebs get banished there, progressively becoming insta-death for any allergy sufferer who stumbles into it while the rest of the building gleams like it's just been constructed. I wonder if I can come up with that spell.

Then I wonder if I can apply it to my own house so I never have to think about cleaning it again. Then I think about how long it's been since I was at my house to clean it. It's not the cheeriest train of thought, more a train of thought filled with half-cut French nihilists all ready to expound on their latest reasons about why life is pointless.

We come out into another hallway that is apparently just a block of marble that's been hollowed out. I swear to the Good God, there's even marble on the ceiling. This place could make Nero declare it to be trying too hard. It fits with our host though, who is waiting impatiently by an apartment door. He's not actively tapping his foot and pointing at a wristwatch, mainly because he's not wearing a wristwatch, and if he did that with Aicha, he'd not be wearing his wrist for very long, but his exasperation is clear. Considering he's the one who's dragged us in entirely the wrong direction, I think that's a bit rich. In the same way Bill Gates is a bit rich.

He leads us into an apartment that catches me off guard. Painted walls are a relief to my marble-overloaded senses. I can see a lounge at the far end through thrown-open double doors. There's not a lot in it, but I suspect what there is probably costs as much as the apartment itself. Which, as we're in Paris, is the same price as a small chateau in the Toulouse region. There's a table and chairs, mixing industrial flourishes of metal with glass and wood. If you stuck it in an art gallery, I'd not hesitate to make the appropriate coos of attention over it. On the other side of the room is what looks like the Holy Grail of sofas – painfully hip cubes that look like they might actually be comfortable as well.

A landline phone, something I thought had ceased to exist, sits on a small wall-mounted plinth and starts to ring. Scarbo swoops over to it. When we don't instantly move far enough away for him to get some privacy, he gesticulates wildly at the lounge on the other end of the corridor and turns his back to us. We head for the next room. Whoever said I can't read subtext?

Sadly, this is one time I could have done with being utterly, pigheadedly ignorant of it. The moment we step over the threshold, I feel the wards snap into place. A quick *look* around shows they're everywhere. The walls glow, every inch covered in murky green workings the colour of pond scum. There's a barrier extending across the doorway behind us, and the windows are so heavy with sigils, I can't even see out of them. The floor, the ceilings — all fluorescent with the same damn magic. We spin around to see Scarbo hanging up the landline and pulling the mobile phone he used to call himself out of his ruffled pocket.

The sneaky little shit-head. We've been set up.

CHAPTER TWENTY

PARIS, 7 JUNE, PRESENT DAY

Double-crossed again. Just goes to show, never trust a poet. Although Scarbo's so shit, he hardly counts as one. Someone should revoke his poetic license.

The little fucker is grinning wildly, his pointy dentures on display like he's been awarded them as medals for treachery and terrible poetry. He jigs on the spot, jumping and clicking his heels together.

'Calm it down, Rumpelshitstain.' Aicha's eyes are so damn narrow, I'm amazed any light can squeeze its way in. 'Won't hold us forever. Then we're going to kill you. Oh yeah, and your "poetry"? Lepre-corny.'

Scarbo stops capering. I guess the fairy tale character resemblance is a sore subject based on his expression. The dig at his lyrical prowess? I think that's pushed him over the edge. He advances up the corridor, his teeth still showing but this time bared. To be honest, he looks like he'd like to take a bite out of us. Good. Come on through and show us what big teeth you've got, little man. I'll show you how snugly my size-eleven boots fit up your anal cavity.

No such luck. Clearly deciding we haven't suffered enough in being captured, he decides to torture us as well. Through the medium of spoken word.

'*Afore these forms were ere begat,*
And these four walls were ere intact,
Scarbo was known, the merry man
Who ere could lay a clever trap.'

'Well, if I were you, I'd "*ere*" on the side of caution, and let us out "*afore*" I shatter your teeth with a jack hammer and merrily scrape your face off with a cheese grater.' Bored indolence is what I'm aiming for. Based on how pissed off he looks and how much he's gnashing his teeth, I reckon I'm about there.

Aicha is even more direct. 'I'd say you're a dead man or whatever, but thing is, considering your attempts at poetry, you're already dead. Inside.'

Oof. The little creature turns a scarlet shade of utter fury. It genuinely wouldn't surprise me if steam starts shooting out of his ears.

'*Positions change, oh how they've switched,*
The lions fed the mouse's gift.
A poisoned cheese to gouge the lips
I'll see you chained...'

The wretched fucker leans forward, his eyes locked with Aicha's, his lips pulled back in a snarl.

'*...you mouthy bitch.*'

Her hand flies forward. I assume her idea is to slap it into the barrier, to force a way through. It's a strong point of her magic. Aicha's excellent at heavy duty destruction, hard as I know that must be to believe. Problem is, her hand doesn't stop when it touches the barrier. It passes through. Or rather, she keeps moving forward. Just nothing comes out on the other side.

It takes me a moment to realise what's happening, and another moment to realise it's caught her so off-guard that she's off balance, unable to stop herself moving forward. I leap towards her, grabbing the collar of her coat, and heave her back into the centre of the room, away from the doorway. By the time I get her, she's lost her right arm to halfway up her bicep. It's cauterised, like the barrier just burnt it away. Perhaps that's how it works. I've no idea. Her face is rigid with fury, and the hiss of agony that escapes her lips is so low, so controlled, I know only I can hear it. She's not going to give him the satisfaction of showing him what excruciating pain she must be in.

Not that he really cares. I think he might have taken more time to gloat, but seeing Aicha maim herself seems to satisfy him enough, and he turns and leaves. I'm torn about that. On the one hand, it means we can't find out why he's double-crossed us, whether it's him or Al-Ruhban, whether De Montfort is involved. On the other hand, it means we don't have to listen to any more of his mangling of the French language. It was enough to make me start resenting my own eardrums. Not a healthy relationship to have with one of your senses.

Once I'm sure he's gone, I sweep Aicha up and lay her on the cubist sofa. She tries to protest, but I can see her arm isn't growing back, not nearly quick enough, at least. The pain is clear, knowing her as well as I do. I don't want her to suffer.

'Rest. Get it together. You're supposed to be the one who thinks us out of tight spots. I'm the one who's supposed to get myself disintegrated charging into lethal spells. Stop stealing my glory.'

She manages a snort, which reassures me slightly. There's a paleness to her face. I wonder just how deeply she's paying for taking that energy bolt to the chest. A trip to Lebanon is looking more and more appealing.

Meanwhile, I take a tour around the room. It's a brilliant trap, really. The sigils were sufficiently dormant; we would've had to *look* really hard to see them, which of course we didn't. Complacency strikes again. With Scarbo being fae, I, at least, would have expected him to use natural materials to channel his magic. By using runes and sigils, he caught us completely off-guard.

The workings are simple. They make it impossible for us to break them, effectively turning the walls and windows into an adamantium prison. I pick up one of the expensive-looking chairs and hurl it at the glass front just to be sure, but it smashes to smithereens on contact. I felt sure it would, but it does my soul good to destroy something expensive, especially when it belongs to the treacherous scum-sucker who trapped us here. The doorway is a separate magic, some sort of particularly vicious fae warding he threw up as soon as we crossed the threshold. One ingress point. One way in and out, and he sealed it tightly shut the moment we walked into the trap. All the carefully inscribed magical sigils make sure breaking out anywhere else is equally impossible.

Next, I pull out my phone. No signal. No surprises there. This is a well-laid trap, and I'd have been astounded if he missed something so obvious, but better to check than kick myself for not having bothered if he did. I search each corner, every one of the nooks and crannies. It doesn't take me long, what with the minimalist interior décor vibe. My hope he might have missed a spot turns out to be as fruitless as the owner's desire to master rhyming.

I grab another chair, resisting the urge to pulverise this one too. Instead, I pull it over next to Aicha and perch on it, leaning on my hands. To my immense relief, I can see her arm is reforming. Slowly. Way, way too slowly. But reforming nonetheless.

I look at her mock-seriously. 'You know when we use the expression "give someone the finger", this isn't what it means, right?'

She shows she knows exactly what it means by demonstrating with the remaining hand. The fleeting grin that passes across her face makes it worth it.

It's time to get serious though. 'I don't see a way out, *laguna*. I've looked all round. Once you're healed, take a spin, see if I've missed anything, but it looks watertight to me.'

She nods. The fact she doesn't leap to her feet and immediately investigate speaks volumes. Her forearm is back now, but she still doesn't have her hand. I bite my lip and try to hide my concern. I obviously fail miserably.

'It's fine, *saabi*. Hurts like hell, but it's fine.'

Okay. Looks like we're discussing this now. 'It seems to be reforming even slower than last time.'

She shakes her head. 'Same speed. Promise. Not slowed down.'

I peer at her pensively. I'm worried she's just saying this to reassure me. Thing is, Aicha Kandicha has always been entirely honest. Brutally so. Ego-death-causingly so. She's my friend. I have to take her at her word. 'Okay. Promise you'll tell me if that changes?'

She nods. It'll have to do. She changes the subject. 'Why do you think Tiny Twat set us up?'

I know what she's really asking. I verbalise it for us both. 'You mean, do I think it's Al-Ruhban?'

I can see it. That momentary flicker of pain buried deep in her regard. Aicha doesn't have a lot of friends. She doesn't give those kind of bonds light-heartedly. If Al-Ruhban has betrayed us? I wouldn't want to be in his shoes when Aicha gets her hands on him. And hooks. And a variety of sharp cutting implements.

All I can do is shrug. 'I've no idea. It could be Al-Ruhban. Could be Scarbo working off his own back? Hell, maybe it's got nothing at all to do with De Montfort; though considering the timing, I find that hard to believe. My guess? One or both of them are agents of that bastard Simon.'

Aicha's hand has reformed at last. Her fingers flex almost gingerly, like she's worried they aren't really there, or like they'll fall off again if she does so. Reassured, she gets up and double checks everywhere, looking to see if I've missed something. I don't mind. I hope I have. Sadly, I hope in vain. She comes back and sits down, shaking her head slightly. Same result. Good God damn it. I'm getting sick to the back teeth of capable villains. Whatever happened to the Villain's Code, of leaving a fatal flaw in every carefully laid-out plan or monologuing long enough for someone to ride to the rescue? I suppose we got lucky that Ben was so desperate to explain his reasoning to me back in the whole Veil of Veronica saga. I can't believe that was only three months ago. Feels like three years.

Looks like we've got nothing but time on our hands for the moment. Might as well try to use it productively. 'What do you think he's after, De Montfort?'

Aicha looks at me. Looks like she's thinking super hard. I lean in closer. 'Bones,' she deadpans.

It's brilliant. Pitch-perfect delivery. Regardless of our predicament, of everything going on around us, I dissolve into a fit of hysterics. Nailed it, Kandicha. Nailed it.

Once I regain my ability to look at her without giggling, I try again. 'Okay, outside of the bones *he's obviously after*, why? What links them all together? *Don't say flesh and tendons.*'

I got there just before she did. One for me. This time, she gives it some proper thought. 'They all have the same feel. The same as your *talent*, as Almeric's skull does.'

I nod. It's that. It has to be. 'And apparently, there's enough of them to build two complete skeletons.'

'Apart from the shoulder bones.'

'Right. Apart from them, at least as far as we know at the moment. So why two? And what does he want with them once he has them?'

We both lapse into silence. I feel like we're almost there, like we're on the edge of unravelling the whole damn mystery that seems to have been central to everything since I got caught out and strung up by the shizzard all that time ago. It's like that word on the tip of your tongue, that memory stirring in the recesses of your grey matter. For a moment, I can almost grasp it and then it's gone like smoke through fingers, and I'm left shaking my head in frustration.

Aicha's not getting anywhere either based on her expression. I get up and pace the room. By the time I've done another exploration, searching for some magical equivalent of a thread I can pull on and then sit back and watch the trap unravel, she's fallen asleep. I guess the impact of today has been higher than I imagined. She looks wan, worn, and it hurts a little, deep inside the callous, shrivelled organ I call my heart. She's already paid so much, so many times for me. I can't stand to see her paying yet again.

Still, there's not a lot we can do. Not exactly a massive selection of options. We're trapped and being bone weary isn't going to change that fact. I sit back in the chair I dragged across, shuffling my legs forward to find a position that's comfortable. I fail miserably, but it doesn't matter. Approximately half a millisecond later, I fall asleep too.

CHAPTER TWENTY-ONE
PARIS, 8 JUNE, PRESENT DAY

Less than a day. That's how long the feeling of being glad to be back in France lasted. Although, to be fair, that's longer than a lot of my bodies last.

I t's amazing what the light of day can bring. For some, a walk of shame, the brightly lit streets only compounding realisations about decisions made in dark bars or clubs the night before. For vampires, it can bring death — or at least an excuse to indulge in your New Romantic face-painting tendencies. For me? It brings inspiration.

Not always, obviously. Good God, no. My normal reaction is closer to the shame-walkers clutching excessively heeled strappy shoes, hurrying homewards. Morning's normally the moment when I assess all the stupid things I did the night before and battle the overwhelming shame and regret that threatens to submerge me. This day though. This time I strike gold.

There's an important question I need to answer first though. I go over and study the doorway, examining the swirling magic that's a mix of Egyptian symbology and Nordic runes. Not surprising. If a fae is going to incorporate runic magic into their power, they might as well go all out, really amalgamate. I'm familiar with both though, obviously –thanks, Isaac– and it doesn't take me long to get the gist of them. The main thing I'm checking is that Scarbo configured the doorway differently to the rest of the protective barriers. Basically, I want to know if I can touch the other warded surfaces without burning my hand off. Like when the chair hit the window, it shattered instead of dissolving. I sigh with relief when I touch the wall without losing the tip of my finger.

When I turn round, Aicha's awake. She's looking better for a night's sleep too. She watches me, but she knows me. Her eyes already blaze with curiosity, yet still she keeps schtum. Inspiration is a gift from the gods; she knows better than to interrupt me when they've sent me a belated birthday present. Normally they forget I even exist unless it's time to break out the cruel twists of fate. Those always seem to end up arriving at my address rather than getting lost in the post.

I take a last turn around the room, a last curious look over everything. Looking for ways this might not work other than the glaringly obvious. Thing is, even if this fails, I'll end up outside the containment wards. I really don't want to lose this body, lose this fae *talent*, but if that's the only way out? So be it.

The fae aspect of the *talent* is the question, and boy, it's a doozy. I'm pretty confident this is going to work. The only time you should stake your life on "pretty confident" is when you reincarnate in the nearest dead body if you die or if you have no other options. So both in my case.

My tour of the walls doesn't reveal anything that changes my mind nor anything to confirm my guess either. At this point, I'm just stalling. I walk back over to Aicha.

'Can I borrow a knife, please?' I hold my hand out, and she slips a knife pommel into it, her head tilted on an angle, like a bird chick trying to work out if you're there to feed it or feed on it. I don't have time to explain what I'm up to. She might try to persuade me not to. Worse than that, she might succeed.

Sometimes, the best thing when you're committed to a possibly stupid, potentially lethal course of action is just to get it done. So that's what I do. I walk over to the wall, just next to the expansive bay window giving us a view of the morning brouhaha that is every street in Paris. I crouch, one foot forward like I'm going to tie my laces. Then I jab the knife straight into the plug socket in front of me.

I don't really understand the magic I've stolen along with Maeve's body. Not properly. What I've gleaned so far is that it's all about nature. All about working with the world around me. Working with the elements. Electricity is an element, right? Well, in one way, yeah, it's a human modernity, like the ever-present metal underpinning the entire city that is making me break out in metaphysical hives. In another way, though, electricity is ancient. It's not invented; it's just an elemental force that we've been wily enough to capture and harness to our will. Try telling lightning that it's a human construct. That's a rapid path to a good old-fashioned smiting.

So as I shove the blade tip farther into the prong point, I *push* my *talent* with it, feeling it flow outwards. Shit. It hits the blade guard and stops. The blade is metal. I didn't think this through. My *talent* doesn't work with steel or anything else born of iron.

Luckily, electricity works perfectly well with it. It passes straight through and into my hand, and now my *talent* can commune with it, shape it, make it conduct. The metal only strengthens the connection, and it creates a bridge, bypassing the blockage it forms for me. Okay, now I just need to control it before it overloads my internal organs and kills me. No problem.

I can feel it. The burning in my nerves. I don't know if you've ever picked up a static charge and then gone to open a door or shook hands with someone loaded up with that potential electricity without realising it. That weird, horrible momentary shock? Imagine that but continuous. And over every inch of your skin.

To say it's distracting is like saying, I don't know, jabbing a knife-blade into a power socket isn't generally a wonderful idea. I need to focus, need to pull my *power* and the electricity in and bind them together, but it's hard to concentrate, and I can feel my nerve endings overloading. One by one, they blink out, going numb — all of this happening in a matter of milliseconds. I don't doubt that soon that sensation of blinking out is going to be happening in my chest. Then it's game over.

The threat of death is a powerful motivator to learn, in that you only fail once. Unless you're me, of course. Then you fail to learn however many times you die. Normally. Not this time though.

This time, it clicks. I feel the surging current, and I can see how it moves like a wild torrent of water, how it swirls like a churning column of air, how it shifts like the earth's inexorable tectonics, how it burns through my body like fire's insatiable appetite, and I get it, I really get it. I see how it works on an elemental level, and I bind it to me. It bucks like a wild stallion trying to throw off a foolhardy stable hand, but I cling on, clutch it with all my desperate desire to escape, to win, to live, and slowly it calms. I've broken electricity and tamed it to my will. Badass.

I must look a right state – my hair sticking out in all directions like in a cartoon, probably a few wisps of smoke coming off me too, but I'm not bothered about that right now. I'm more interested in the options that have just opened up to me.

What I have now is a conduit – literally. Sure, I can start flinging lightning bolts around, but as there's only Aicha and I in the room, that would end with us either getting stuck inside a raging inferno or me hitting Aicha with one by accident. Which would cause me to wish I was just stuck inside a raging inferno.

What conduits can also do, as well as supply, is conduct. The clue is in the name. And now? Now I can talk to the electricity. I can shape it. I can make it carry my will. More than that, it can hold my power, allowing me to piggy-back on it, dive out through it, and most importantly, bypass the wards. At least magically.

Once I'm out on the other side, outside the building, I let my *talent* sink out into the earth, travelling through the compact soil, looping around stones and dead bugs already half-way on their journey to sinking deeper into the depths and carbonising. I've got an idea, and my power follows my thought process, traipsing through worm-tunnels to find...that.

A root. The inverted fingers of a tree digging deep into the ground, soaking up the moisture and nutrients that rain and tiny deaths bring to the soil even underneath an imposed concrete skin. Now, though, it's my *talent* travelling up those spindly tendrils as they thicken, enjoin, and interweave into more considerable, hardier stems, racing along to reach the trunk itself.

But the *talent* isn't just a neuron firing across the tree's pathways. It's leaving a trace as it goes. It's taking control of the tree, like that zombie fungus that hijacks caterpillars and makes them do its bidding, a helpless passenger in its own body. I'm not doing anything that malevolent though. All I want is to make one specific part of the tree do one specific thing. I want to make a certain branch grow. And so it does.

The ringing tinkle of glass smashing inside the room brings me back to myself as the pieces falling from the window hit the floor. It's a mess. Good. I hope Scarbo has to tap dance through here barefoot before he clears it up. Actually, when I get my hands on him, I might just make it so.

The runes the little scumsucker laid made all the surfaces impenetrable. But only from this side. After all, with our phones cut off and our *talent* blocked, how were we going to get outside assistance?

I put up a *don't look here* over the bough itself as I coaxed it out of the ground. Even the most blasé, world-weary Parisian might be shaken from their black coffee and packet of Gauloise by trees attacking building windows. Now I persuade the branch to thicken up so we can walk along it. I bow, letting my leading hand continue outwards to indicate the exit.

'Your carriage awaits, milady,' I say to Aicha. Not going to lie, I'm more than a little pleased with myself.

She looks at me and arches an eyebrow. 'If this leads to a tree village full of dancing Ewoks, I'm setting it, then you, on fire. Fair?'

'Fair.' Can't argue with that. I think that's her way of saying well done. I'll take it as that, anyhow.

We balance across the limb. Shimmying down the trunk is easy enough; we're both highly trained warriors; plus, we've got our magic back at our disposal. I may slip slightly about halfway down, but the tree shoots out a protrusion to catch my momentarily flailing foot, letting me get my groove back on. I think I got away with it without Aicha noticing.

'You're as shit at tree-climbing as you are at risk assessment, dickhead.' Nope. Apparently not.

Now we're on the ground, I get the tree to curl back down through the concrete, pulling the branch away from the building. It'll blossom like a motherfucker in a couple of days. The rest of the trees on the avenue are going to be jealous as all hell. Least I can do after it staged such a daring rescue.

Thanks, good budding buddy. Thanks indeed.

Chapter Twenty-Two
PARIS, 8 JUNE, PRESENT DAY

Our daring escape? Tree-rific.
And definitely very fir-tive.

We saunter off down the street. Scarbo runs the Thirteenth District. Doesn't mean he's the only Talented being in it. It sounds like a job description straight out of Dante's imagination, but he might have other lesser powers working for him. If the apartment itself was under observation? Then they know we're out and free, no question. On the other hand, if they're just loitering around the quarter with an instruction to keep an eye out, then nonchalance in our movements might keep us off their radar. Most people, when trying to move inconspicuously, might as well wrap themselves in flashing neon garlands. Looking at you here, Isaac. Their movements become tense, jerky, their eyes whipping back and forth, trying to take everything in. Everything is too deliberate. It draws the eye, almost subconsciously. And for anyone looking for someone, they hone in real quick.

We just walk like we don't give a fuck. Back to normal operations for us. We pull off the Avenue D'Italie to the left, onto Rue Tolbiac. Almost immediately the bustle dims somewhat. Enough I feel I can breathe properly again. We take the next right, and suddenly we're not being constantly crushed every step we take. White stone walls and charming little red-brick houses – actual, proper houses, not just buildings subdivided into multiple apartments – make it feel like we've stepped into a different city, a different world. There's still people, but there's space. It's a relief.

But there's something else I'm seriously worried about. Something we haven't discussed and that needs to be said. However much Aicha won't want to hear it.

'Do we need to abort on this?' I keep my words gentle as we make our way through the city. I don't want her to feel there's any pressure or recrimination in what I'm saying.

Her head shoots to me. 'What do you mean?'

I hope she takes this the right way. 'We can get on the train. Get up to Charles De Gaulle. Pick up flights for Lebanon or the next closest option. If you need to go...' I mime drinking, with accompanying glugs.

'Get acting lessons? Definitely not from you.' She's being deliberately obtuse, but she's also not punching me in the face for suggesting we quit the mission. That shows she's taking the suggestion seriously. Worrying in and of itself. She shakes her head. 'It's not getting worse. Promise, Paul. Will tell you if it does.'

I'm not her keeper. I can't force her. All I can do is worry silently and keep a damn good eye on her regenerative abilities when they get tested. I'm pretty sure we're going to see that happening again real soon.

I move the subject on to our other areas of discussion. 'What the ever-loving fuck do we do now then?'

There're no obvious options, no simple answers. There's also a whole world of subtext tied up in what I've said. Did Al-Ruhban betray us? Why? To who or for what? Is De Montfort mixed up in this or is it a separate power play?

Aicha sighs. 'We pay Al-Ruhban a visit. Either let him know he's been stitched up. Or else stitch him up. You know the skit from the Wutang album, *36 Chambers*, where Method Man is describing how he'll sew someone's arsehole closed and keep feeding them and feeding them?' She nods, happy with what she obviously considers appropriate imagery. 'Like that.'

Yeah. Makes sense. 'I take it we're not going to give him a courtesy call first?'

She shakes her head.

Nah. Of course. No way we're going to tip him off we're on our way in case he has done us over. I prefer to pop up unexpectedly, like a bad penny.

'Is he still up in Saint-Ouen?' I ask.

She nods. This is hard for her. I can understand. I'm also really hoping Al-Ruhban hasn't set us up. When I met him, I liked him. I don't really want to kick his teeth down his throat. Won't stop me from doing it if he's set us up, and I know it won't stop Aicha either. If anything, their friendship will only focus her, push her to even more extreme ass-kicking for him having betrayed her.

A thought springs to mind. 'Remember what Al-Ruhban said about the pirate radio station and how they use that to broadcast information? Any idea what frequency it is?'

Of course Aicha knows – or remembers; it's entirely possible Al-Ruhban told it to us when we spoke and I just dumped it out of my short-term memory. Luckily with Aich around, I don't need to go rummaging around in my mind palace.

It's a simple enough task to download an app on my phone that mimics a transistor radio. We tune up the right frequency and get the dulcet yet unquestionably powerful tones of Aretha Franklin singing 'Respect'. A few people look at us funny as we walk past them. I wonder what they can hear? Static and white noise maybe. Either way, the music on the radio winds down, and the presenter comes on.

'And that was The Queen of Soul herself reminding us all that a little respect goes a long way.' The presenter's deep, breathy voice fits beautifully to the song that's just gone. There's a touch of American accentuation to her French. I can't work out whether it's an affectation or because she's come over from across the pond.

'And a word from the Prince, just a little reminder to keep it clear in all our thoughts. No moving around. Keep your area tight, my people. There's word running of wolves among the sheep. The Last Cathar and the Druze Queen are supposed to be out and at large. The Prince has labelled them unwelcome guests. If they end up in your area...you know what to do. The same thing as this other Prince said doves are going to do...'

The Purple One's electric jamming comes out of the phone's hi-frequency rich speaker. I turn down the volume. My eyes meet Aicha's. Apparently Prince Leandre has declared us persona non grata, and all the Talented throughout Paris, rulers and servants, have been given our names and told to take care of us. Sadly, not in the "make them a nice cup of tea and give them a back rub" sense either.

'Well, fuck,' Aicha says.

"Well, fuck" sums it up pretty nicely, really.

Chapter Twenty-Three
SÖLL, AUSTRIA, 11 FEBRUARY 1939

The blood pooling around my feet in the pink-tinged snow looks suspiciously chunky. I wonder if I might have dropped a vital organ or two out of my gut wound. Avoiding looking at it is the order of the day. Seeing my own intestines never gets less nauseating.

The first of the giant lice reaches me, but now that I'm effectively restrained by the tree branch through my body, it seems happy to sit at my feet, like a beagle who's brought the hunt to a trapped fox. The clicking behind me tells me I've not got much time before the weird hag gets to me. When she does, I think being torn to pieces by oversized parasites might be the better option.

So I plunge my sword back into my etheric storage, safe for next time. A second louse rocks up and reaches up the side of my body, its skittering legs making my skin crawl at the contact, then bites my arm off.

My time of useful consciousness now is severely limited. I'm fountaining blood out of the stump. Combined with my leg and stomach wounds, I'm about to pass out. Problem is, I want to be dead before she gets here, not unconscious. I've no idea what getting eaten alive by the Buschgro'Bmutter will do regarding my reincarnating, but I'm in no hurry to find out.

Luckily, I still have my left hand. They've not thought to render me armless yet. Heh. My fingers skirt my waistband and find the dagger, which is much more disposable than my sword, secured by my belt. The *click-click-click-click* is damnably close. I can almost feel the heat of her breath on the nape of my neck. I'm really hoping that's my overactive imagination, or I might be too late.

Whipping the blade out, I bury it into my chest, then twist and rip, wiping out my heart. An eerie screech like the squeak of a crypt gate amplified through a valley of piled-high bones emanates from mere metres behind me as another louse bites off my remaining arm at the bicep.

My last thought as it fades to black is that if she's enraged, killing myself was probably a damn good call.

My next thought is how fucking cold it is. I half-expected to come to back in Salzbourg. Instead, I snap upright inside a snow drift, my new body already setting into the teeth-chattering shivers that suggest hypothermia is nearby. Wet clothes, sodden from exposure to the elements, in freezing temperatures are a recipe for rapid death. Trust me, I'm an expert at dying rapidly.

I invest a small amount of *talent* to heat myself. With a minimal amount of scouting, judging by the position of the mountains and the lights twinkling through the trees, I'm not far from where I was killed. A kilometre, maybe two.

Reaching out, I search for the small amount of my essence I invested into the stone I gave to Otto. Honestly, I'm not expecting it to work, so when I feel the tug of it across the forest, I'm delighted. We've gotten lucky. He's only metres away, having fled in this direction. I'm happy to take a bit of luck for once. In fact, I can hear blundering cracks of broken twigs through the woods now that I'm listening. I'm less pleased about that. If I can hear it, so can the Buschgro'Bmutter.

Jumping up, I start to move towards the noises and immediately go sprawling, tripping over something else in the snow. Looking down, I realise it's not something else but someone else. A middle-aged man with receding hair lies under the bank. It's not his features so much as the bullet hole in his forehead that draws the attention. Looks like he was executed, though whether by German authorities or vengeful locals, I've no idea. Another set of feet peek under the white blanket, possibly two. Not my concern right now.

I set off loping through the trees, following the vague directions of the stone's location and the more precise auditory clues of the crashing and cracking. A few moments later, I catch up with the man.

Unsurprisingly, he practically leaps out of his skin when I hiss his name. I've no idea how much he saw of my last showdown with the Buschgro'B-mutter –presumably none based on the fact he got far enough away to stay alive– but he's well educated in the occult, with a powerful enough imagination to know nothing good is likely to come out of the dark undergrowth. When he sees my face, he visibly sags.

I press my finger to my lips and take his hand, pulling him back the way I came. I've wrapped air cushions around his feet so as to muffle the sound a little. It's clear he's not someone made for stealth missions if he's being this loud despite them.

When we return to the small clearing I came back to life in, I feel Otto rear back, alarmed. I whip my head around, expecting to see giant lice ploughing through the brush towards us, but I catch the direction of his gaze. Ah. It's the dead body that's alarmed him.

More than that, he's practically frozen. I tug at him, but he won't move. It's like Medusa just popped up into his eye-line.

'Come on, man!' I'm keeping my voice low, but it's an effort. We don't have time for this.

He seems to come back a little, but still he doesn't move. His face is as white as a sheet, like he's seen a ghost. Or maybe, perhaps, something else that haunts him.

'I can't.' He shakes his head, though whether to emphasise what he said or to deny the reality of the body in front of him, I can't say. 'It's...it's too much. The camps. Himmler said...the camps...'

It becomes a little clearer. We've heard tell about these so-called "concentration camps" at Auschwitz, Dachau, and many more besides. Stories have arrived about the terrible conditions, the practical slavery imposed on those shipped off there. Starvation. Torture. Rape. Murder. And I fear that may only be the tip of the iceberg.

Based on the trauma written across Otto's face, I may be right. I guess that was the straw that broke the camel's back and led to his suicidal resignations.

I definitely want to get all those details out of him later. Not least what Himmler said, that fat fuck. But right now, I don't have time to mollycoddle Rahn. I need him over by the dead body.

I pull his hand up, intertwining my fingers through his like carefree lovers lost in Spring's fields and feels. 'Do you trust me?' I ask him, drawing a sword from my storage.

He looks up at me, confusion furrowing his brow, knotting his eyebrows. 'Not really. I only just met you.' I suppose it's a weird question to ask, especially in such a strange clinch in the middle of a wintery mountainside while fleeing for our lives.

I hear a distant *click-click-click* back towards the houses. We're out of time. 'Doesn't matter,' I say and then swing my sword, chopping his arm off at the wrist.

To his credit, he doesn't instantly faint, although I think it's mainly the disbelief that keeps him standing. Guess he didn't expect that.

This isn't going to last. Any second now, he's either going to squeal like a stuck pig or pass out clean, probably straight through a load of loudly snapping branches. What I've got planned is going to take most of the rest of my magic. I need a second to focus. We have one chance for this to work, or I'm going to be as much defensive use as a wall made of mashed potato.

I'm seeking to understand on the fly an aspect of my magic that happens instinctively — Grail-gifted *talent* rather than my natural one. So this may not work. In which case, I've probably just done the Ahnenerbe's work for them because Otto Rahn's going to bleed out pretty quickly.

I also need to make a precise assessment by eye. Luckily, after being hung, drawn, quartered, tortured, butchered, blasted, burnt, torn limb from limb, eaten, guillotined, stabbed, shot, blown up, and everything in between...I have a reasonable grasp of human anatomy. Before I can think it through too much, I bring the blade down through the dead arm poking out of the disturbed snow.

The newly dismembered limb is the same length or close enough as the one I just chopped off Rahn. Seizing it, I slap it over the gushing stump Rahn's still staring at in pale-faced disbelief. Then I reach down inside myself and pour my *talent* into it.

Sealing the flesh and bones together is a real struggle. I don't often use healing magic due to just dying and instantly reincarnating in a new body, but my own *talent* has been intertwined with my reincarnating magic for over seven hundred years now. I'm working on the principle that a touch of the knowledge must have rubbed off on it by osmosis at some point. I try to think about how I feel when I snap back awake, when the magic floods through a corpse and pours life back into lifeless meat, teaching it to move and be again. Don't get me wrong, I'm no necromancer (thank the Good God); I can't raise the dead. Well, I won't, anyway. Same difference.

But bringing back a dead limb, connecting it to a living system? That I think I can do. It's just a case of fusing it to the life force already there, coaxing it into understanding what it means to be animated again, to sense and feel. As I discharge my power into the connection between the alive and the expired, I try to persuade the arm to sense, to join, to move.

Honestly, I think I get lucky. The fact the corpse has, in effect, been kept on ice has stopped any real decomposition from setting in, making the whole thing easier. When I see the first sign of the little finger twitching, I sigh in relief. Otto's looking at me with baffled horror, his eyes flicking from me to the dead hand becoming one with the rest of his nervous system. I get it must be weird, looking down and seeing a hand that isn't yours. If there's anyone in the world who's going to understand that sensation, it's me. But I don't have time to handhold him through the disassociation.

There's a tiny dribble of power left in the hand I just chopped off. Not much but enough. I fall to my knees and slap his arm into place where I hacked off the corpse's one. Making dead meld with dead is a piece of cake.

I look up at the shell-shocked German and smile brightly.

'Back in a second!' I give him a cheery wave and then impale myself on my sword.

CHAPTER TWENTY-FOUR
PARIS, 8 JUNE, PRESENT DAY

There's nothing like having to cross hostile enemy territory packed full of Talented to really ruin your day. Except, perhaps, having to negotiate with traffic wardens.

'Only you,' Aicha's eyes nonchalantly scan the entire street, clocking every single potential threat without anyone but me noticing, 'could end up dragging me into a fucking Walter Hill film about 1970's New York when popping into Paris.'

I can see the parallels with *The Warriors*, but that's a touch unfair. It's hardly like I dragged her here. We both agreed this was the most sensible course of action to take.

'Incidentally, if any vampires turn up in that ridiculous face-paint again, dressed like the New York Knicks, and packing baseball clubs, I'm going to shove the wood straight through their hearts. Without sharpening them into stakes first.'

On that we're in agreement.

While we might not have a solid plan, one thing is certain. We need to get out of the Thirteenth District. Heading for Place D'Italie, where we came in, seems like the most likely way to walk smack bang into any ambush that might be waiting. Instead, we head north, picking our way towards the Corvisart Metro Station. It nestles under the tracks elevated up above the road. With a basketball court tucked in between the two sides of the road underneath, it feels like how I imagine the Five Boroughs of New York must have looked back in those halcyon days of hip-hop and the crack rock epidemic. I hope that's not a bad omen. I really don't want to find hordes of magically charged gangs blocking our path between here and the northern suburbs. Of course, with magic users, you don't need a gang. One sufficiently badass mage can totally fuck up your day – your last day if they're powerful enough. And there're plenty of magical people and beings in Paris who are powerful enough. And all of them serve Leandre.

We head up the concrete steps, the walls tattooed with spray-paint as tags muscle against each other for the prime real estate. Aicha takes the phone off me and pulls a set of in-ear headphones from somewhere. One gets nestled in her ear like some sort of security detail protecting a high-profile celebrity or politician. No doubt she's keeping an ear on what the Talented radio station is spewing out. If they get wind of our location, we want to know about it. Luckily, I studied the metro map on the last ride down here with Scab-bro once I realised we were heading the wrong way. This trainline takes us over to Bercy. Switching there to the Line 14 should take us straight to Saint-Ouen. Simple, right?

I try to distract myself from the sense of impending doom that thought gives me — considering how it's never ever going to be that simple — and concentrate instead on the actual impending doom surrounding us throughout the entire compact metropolis we're currently traversing. Specifically, where said doom has come from.

'Was it Al-Ruhban?' Best to get straight to the point. It's not a pleasant thought that he might have betrayed us. Doesn't mean that Aicha will shy away from it for one single second.

Her gaze is everywhere, moving constantly, everywhere but meeting mine. She knows I'm no threat. She also knows everyone and everything else might be. 'Not looking good for him.'

I sigh. She's right. That whole first phone call was shady as fuck. The whole "can't come meet you" malarkey, and then sending us Scabby Brow instead? The odds of him being innocent aren't zero, but they're in single digits by my calculations.

'What are you going to do –' I start to say but break off when she shakes her head.

'Wrong question. Wrong time. Whatever needs to be done, obviously. First question is how do we get to him?'

She's right.

The metro and Saint-Ouen is a good starting plan, but we both know the odds of us getting a peaceful little train ride all the way to our destination, feet-up-and-read-the-newspaper style, is even less than him being innocent. I run the options through in my head.

'Give him a call? Draw him out?' I know we already discussed ringing him, but that was to ask questions. This would be some sort of cunning trick to lure him into a trap. Bring him to us. Save us running the gauntlet of all the hellish shit that Paris and Leandre might be able to throw at us.

Aicha purses her lips, contemplating it. Finally she gives another small headshake. 'No. If he's innocent, that's just going to complicate matters. If he's guilty? Too easy for him to lead us straight into a trap.'

Which leaves us with no other option but to head to Saint-Ouen. There's only one additional problem. 'What if he's not home?'

'If he's not home, he's travelling.' Her eyes are embers still holding a fire's fury in a night-time hearth. 'Not supposed to be travelling, is he? Means at best, he's heard the radio and not reached out. If he's not home, he's guilty. We'll leave Paris and lay a Plan B. A way to contact Leandre. Explain what the fuck's happened. Convince him of our innocence. Make sure he's guarding the bones.' That burning intensity in the depths of her gaze intensifies. 'Then we hunt them down.'

I don't need to ask who they are. As for the rest? She's right, of course. We don't *need* to get to the bones themselves, useful though it might be to study them. Even for that, Isaac's the expert we'd want on the case. What we do need to do is make sure De Montfort can't get anywhere near those bones while we track him down and then break all of his bones instead. If we can convince Leandre we're on the same side, get him to up the security levels, make him be on guard against the threat posed by Scarbo – and Al-Ruhban if he's guilty – it'll give us some breathing space. The Good God knows I could use some right now. Then we can get to making sure both of them break their bad habit of continuing to breathe.

So all roads lead to Saint-Ouen. Or all the metro lines.

Except, sadly, that isn't true, and we need to change onto one that actually does. We jump out through the metal doors that whoosh open long before the train stops moving – surely a lawsuit waiting to happen – and head up one set of stairs, planning to head back down another and grab the next arriving subway train heading our way.

That plan lasts as long as it takes us to get up the first flight of steps. The entrance to Line 14 absolutely reeks of Talent. I hardly even need to *look* to know there's someone with serious power waiting for us down on that platform.

Aicha and I exchange glances, then without a word, we make for the exit. I'm *looking* at everything now, overlaying the magical and the mundane, waiting for the assault I'm sure is going to come. Nothing. Maybe we got lucky?

Nope. My plan to now hit the streets and head north, to try to pick up the line a stop closer to our destination crashes to a halt as soon as I feel Aicha stiffen. She strides purposefully in the opposite direction, having picked up on something I haven't.

Or hadn't. Because now I feel it. That prickling of hairs along the back of my neck, each strand leaping to attention in its follicle, straining like individual dowsing rods pulling at my awareness.

Someone's watching us. Someone who knows who we are. Someone with a shitload of *talent*.

I let Aicha lead the way. Our target destination's changed. We're not looking for a way out; we're looking for an arena. Somewhere we can throw down with whoever's on our tail. Ideally, somewhere we can hold the advantage. For me, that would mean wide open green spaces, but that's not an option. Paris isn't short of parks, but we're rapidly approaching midday; they're all going to be ram-jammed with locals grabbing a bite to eat and a breath of comparatively cleaner air. Not to mention the ever-present tourists. No. Best I let Aicha choose the battleground.

She steers us back out onto a major boulevard; the traffic seeming to run twice as hard for having been forced around the pedestrian shopping area we just skipped through. I can see she wants to turn right; it's radiating in her posture, the way her eyes dart towards the alley we're passing — but instead we pull left. Her frustration is apparent. We're being hounded. That rarely works out well. If you don't believe me, ask a fox.

She swears suddenly, and I feel it too. The Talented that's chasing us? They're up in front now. Problem is, a second ago they were behind us. Either they can move extremely fast, or we're dealing with more than one being.

Aicha doesn't hesitate. There's a gate to the side, set in a higher white stone arch. It's locked, but Aich hits it shoulder-first, and it bursts open. There's a red sign over it that says "The Bercy Pavillions" and something else, but I can't read the rest. I just have time to note the creepy-looking statue of what looks like a top-hat-wearing centaur looming out from the top of the arch before we rush inside. Probably not a good omen.

The look on Aicha's face speaks volumes. She's seriously pissed off. We've been caught in a pincer manoeuvre, completely outplayed. They cut our options off one by one, so now we're going to make our stand here. Wherever here is.

We're in a courtyard, and I start spooling in power quickly because luckily, it's absolutely abloom with flowers and trees, strong and anchored despite the surrounding cobbles. There's a gate at the other end, a way out. Aicha doesn't head that way, and I don't know whether it's because she can sense more danger outside, or she's tired of running. Either way, before I know what's going on, she pulls me behind her, busting through some red double doors next to us. They're gaudy, brightly coloured with gold-trimmed portholes at head height, and they smash open like they're made of paper when she makes contact with them. Oops. Apologies to whoever owns the place. Still, better collateral property damage than people.

It's dark in here. Seriously dark. Even the light from the courtyard that penetrates in our wake is quickly subsumed in the gathered gloom. I kick a bit of my *talent* up into my eyes so I can see what's going on. The walls on either side are display cabinets. I'm not seeing well enough to identify all the things inside; I don't want to burn through all the power just to know what said cabinets are displaying, but it looks like plates or cut-out pictures. I'm more drawn to what's ahead of us.

As the room opens up, I can see what looks like a kitsch elephant statue about chest-high. Strapped to its back appears to be a hot-air balloon, although I can tell by the lack of movement, the way it doesn't billow despite the draft we've brought in by obliterating the front doors, that it's not made of fabric. I don't have time to make sense of it before Aicha's leading me off to the side, into another enormous space.

It takes my brain a moment to compute as we rush through the huge first hall, made of the same stone-built walls as the outside. My first thought is, *Huh, not every day you see a carousel inside a building.* My second is, *Or even two carousels.* It's weird and only adds to my sense of dislocation, of not really knowing where I am or what's going on. It brings up a sensation akin to panic. Logically, I know it's a kickback to my recent trauma. Dark rooms full of unexpected things while feeling trapped aren't comfortable places for me right now. Sadly, knowing that does precisely diddly squat regarding helping me keep calm. Only Aicha's presence, reassuring in its deadliness, does that.

We come out into another vast chamber. This one has garish booths lined up along each side as far as I can see, all reminiscent of visiting distractions that rolled through Toulouse at the end of the nineteenth century and the start of the twentieth. I realise where we are now. This is the Museum of Fairground Arts. I've heard of it but never had a chance to visit. Having a day out at a museum in another city becomes considerably harder when the locals are likely to think you're plotting a hostile takeover.

The central space is fairly empty. At the other end, one of the carousel horses has had its head knocked off. I'm wondering if careless tourists or poor workmanship are to blame when all the lights come on, blinding me.

If the place seemed garish before, now it's next level lurid. It's also sending my already triggered nerves into hyperdrive. Lights flash on all the booths, various parts of them dancing and twirling in time to tinny, cranked-out tunes from their sound-boxes. It's like a group of phantoms has decided to run their own fairground forever, and it's creepy as fuck. Not to mention massively distracting. Enough so that I only realise the horse isn't a discarded prop when it moves.

There are some things I got wrong when I first looked at it. It's not made of plaster but flesh; real muscles bunch and bulge as it walks forward, hoof clops ringing out even over the fairground din. It's an understandable mistake to make. For one, because it's decked out in drapery so flamboyant you could easily believe it painted on, like a carousel horse. For two, because I didn't make a mistake when I said it has no head.

Now unless I'm gravely mistaken, it tends to only be chickens that continue moving around once you chop their heads off. And as a general rule of thumb, they don't then advance on you menacingly like they're going to neck you to death. Plus, it isn't as though the head was just freshly chopped off. I'm not staring down its trachea. I can't play waste-bin basketball with sugar cubes down a gaping neck hole. The top is sealed with skin, like it's quite normal for horses to rock about without important things, like heads and all the accoutrements — mouths, nostrils, *brains*.

It says something about how easily I am distracted by bizarre illogicalities that the most pressing thought in my mind is how it can stalk towards us without one of its own. The second is that this makes it a stalking horse. Heh.

I want to turn and run this one past Aicha, but one look at her face tells me it's not the moment. She's looking seriously concerned but not by the headless horse. Her eyes flick left and right. She's searching for someone. Presumably the rider of the headless horse. I wonder if it's like a reverse Dullahan, the headless horseman we successfully humiliated back at the Winter Court, or if the owner is cranially challenged as well. I *pull* a grain of splintered wood from one of the gorgeously painted panels of a sideshow booth and fling it in front of us, knitting the memory of its time long ago as a tree into a barrier to hold the creature back while I try to work out what the fuck is going on and who we're facing off against.

'La Guillaneu,' Aicha hisses through gritted teeth, never breaking her scan, and now I understand why she's looking so worried.

La Guillaneu. Well, fuck me sideways with a candyfloss stick. That counts as bad news. In the same way as receiving a letter bearing the news you've got two weeks to live is. When it's arrived a fortnight late.

La Guillaneu is a hag. I don't mean that in the disparaging sense. A lot of the words thrown as abuse against old women — hag, crone, witch — are an age-old habit. Only difference is, when they used to be thrown at them back in the day, it was shortly before the old women themselves got thrown. Into a lake or onto a bonfire. Now an insult, then a legal accusation.

No, a hag is a major Power, defined by strange abilities that don't seem to obey the already illogical rules of how *talent* works. There's few of them around, which is a good thing, because that level of magic and weirdness combined isn't something one wants to be encountering on a daily basis. They're the sort who tend to live in houses with legs complete with flying cauldrons. Eating children is an optional extra but definitely seems to be on trend in hag circles.

I don't know much about La Guillaneu. She's from the Vendee region, where in some legends she plays the role of a post-Christmas Krampus, in others a clean broom, sweeping out the old and ringing in the New Year. Without her brushing away the restraining memories of the past twelve months – so the story goes – time itself will seize up, choked by all the grief and suffering. Or, in another tale, it might be her who does the choking down. Of body parts from those who make it onto her naughty list.

'How fucking powerful is Leandre that La Guillaneu is subservient to him?' I look wildly around now, not even pretending to keep it under wraps like Aicha. The horse is a distraction, an opening act to get us warmed up. I'm on the lookout for the main event.

'How utterly fucking stupid are you that you're focused on that question right now? More pressing matters, dickhead.'

Ouch. I don't take offence. See my recent comment about being easily distracted. I'm basically the cybernetically enhanced dog from Pixar's *Up*. Only considerably less charming, sadly.

A cackle drawn straight from the Disney playbook of "announcing exactly how spectacularly evil you are" echoes out around the rafters. It runs up and down an off-key sorceress laugh, starting at "ha", ranging up to "hee", and then descending back down to "ha" again. Well, at least somebody's having a good time, I guess.

A cloud of smoke billows out from the archway we came in from. Not like a pellet from Batman's utility belt to allow a dramatic entrance or exit. This is more like a creeping fog when you're lost in the woods, filling every gap that might lead to a way home and promising a dreadful night is about to get a lot worse. Much like, I suspect, our day is about to.

There's no mistaking a hag for a normal old-age pensioner or "easy target"as they were known by the Inquisition. When the smoke skulks back out of the room like someone's just hit rewind, it leaves La Guillaneu standing there. Guess she has some temporal-style magic at her disposal. She's dressed in what might be tattered black rags or might just be part of her flesh, like the Wicked Witch of the West got frozen mid-melt. Her green skin only adds to the effect. She's carrying a broom. Whether it's a weapon, a form of transport, or she just has terrible OCD isn't immediately clear, but I'm betting on the first one as a minimum. Probably the other two as well. Her face is that of a wizened old crone, at least from the nose down. But her forehead is ridged bone like a skinned Klingon. It might be a mask, but I think it's part of her face. Maybe she's part dinosaur or something.

Either way, two spurs come off the bone and elongate back over her head into horn-like points.

She cackles again, a terrible smile on her lips that sends shivers down my spine. 'Hello, my poppets, my cutie pies. I've no woods these days for you to lose your way in or wander from the path. Still...' Her eyes gleam like polished coal under her bony forehead. 'They call the city the urban jungle. Just a fancy name for a forest, that, isn't it, my loveys, my sweet things?'

I'm trying to keep my attention fixed on her, but it's hard. Her horse is chomping through my barrier on the other side, which is majorly distracting when it doesn't have any teeth. Plus, it shouldn't be possible. Looks like her ride packs more than a little punch in the *talent* department itself. That explains how they boxed us in, at least. Unless there's someone else involved, in which case, we're totally and utterly fucked as opposed to merely fucked like we are now.

'What do you want, La Guillaneu? Bit early in the year for you, isn't it?' I can break down the etymology. *Au gui l'an neuf* – mistletoe for new year. Mind you, I doubt she'd get many kisses even if you hung a whole goddamn mistletoe shrub from the ceiling.

She gives that grating laugh again and claps her hands together. 'Oh, aren't they a clever poppet; aren't they precious? Wonderful to see them taking an interest in words so young, isn't it? Still, some silly, sloppy logic too though, my butterball, my snookums. Thinking I'm only allowed out and about at the end of the year. I'm here all year, my little loves, my bunnykins. I just like to start the new year in style with a little hunt.'

Based on the way she's herded us into this trap, she enjoys it the rest of the time, too. 'Why are you hunting us, La Guillaneu? We've done you no harm, and have been wrongly accused of ill intent.'

Her eyes narrow, and she raises her broom ever so slightly, a movement that is tiny but still definitely threatening. It's a weapon then. 'All just words, those are, my darling ducklings, my pumpkin pies, and not ones I can be trusting. We all have our roles to play. For those who'd bring harm against my sovereign liege, good Prince Leandre, I can sniffle out their tasty sweetmeats and take a teeny taste, my poor little lambs, my little lost sheep.'

Well, that answers another question – she's sworn fealty by choice to Leandre. I just have time to wonder what he might have done that would've gained the loyalty of such a strange force as La Guillaneu before my priorities are otherwise engaged.

Having unbelievably deadly hag magic flung at you has an uncanny effectiveness regarding focusing the mind.

CHAPTER TWENTY-FIVE

PARIS, 8 JUNE, PRESENT DAY

Trying to avoid getting turned into blood and cooked intestines inside a tight-fitting skin. Turned into a haggis by the magic a hag is.

The magic that comes roaring out of the bristles of her broom isn't like any I've ever seen or felt before. It doesn't smell of nature, no fresh-cut grass nor rotting bog, like fae magic does. It doesn't carry an odour of death to it, as those who mess in the necromantic arts find lingers on everything they cast. It doesn't even have a clear colour, my synaesthetic way of identifying individual magics since my first battle of will and power with Papa Nicetas.

This power swirls with every colour and none, an absence of colour and the presence of ones I've never seen before, ones I don't think even exist. It moves equally strangely, arrhythmic — one moment flowing out like ripples, then in static leaping advances like it's teleporting from spot to spot. It's so different, so totally and utterly bizarre, that it nearly hypnotises me. I almost forget to do anything – either move or try to counter the power. Then I feel Aicha ready herself, and I remember that she's already taken one uncanny magic blast to the chest for me this week and how she's been paying for it since. I'll not have her pay the price for me again this time.

So I need to move. I duck and roll sideways, leading with my shoulder, trying to keep an eye on the working the hag's cast. Unsurprisingly, it tracks my movement and swings in my new direction. What is surprising is when my roll reverses.

As I flip back to my feet, I watch the knife Aicha threw return to her hand, accompanied by vehement cursing from her. Looks like she took advantage of the hag's distraction of concentrating on me to try for a thrown attack. No doubt magically sped up. Apparently, it worked well enough to make La Guillaneu reverse time itself to keep the blade from hitting. Her own spell draws back closer to her too, giving me some breathing space. Not much, but I'll take any air pocket I can get in a situation like this.

The do-over has given me time to work out an idea to counter the spell. I search under the floor, under the foundations, and find what I'm looking for. A root from one of the trees thriving against the odds in the courtyard. I shove my *talent* into it and *push* the root straight up with a speed that would have Maverick and Goose applauding and high-fiving, probably in an unintentionally homoerotic manner.

The tip of it bursts through the concrete like a supersonic bullet, shattering the tile. It grows rapidly, branches forming out, limbs stretching until it's an approximation of myself in wood that would make most sculptors hand over their chisels and awls before heading off to sob into a pint.

A crash behind me tells me my barrier has gone down, letting Mr Ed-less through. Luckily, I have the best brawling wing person anyone could ever hope for. I'll let her deal with the cloppy bastard at my six. Right now, I need to stop that magic from hitting me. I don't think it's likely to just clear out my sinuses and freshen my breath.

I hurl a huge chunk of *talent* into the devastatingly handsome wooden sculpture I've formed so that it moves, dancing and waving on the spot. I'm not quite at the point of creating wooden versions of lungs –alveoli are a bit fiddly for me to knock up on the fly– but I throw my voice, getting "it" to shout, 'Over here!' at the weird magic bolt. I doubt even a hag can imbue a spell with that sort of level of independent thought. All I'm really trying to do is give it a more immediate and appealing target than the flesh-bag it was originally aiming for.

It works. There's enough of my *talent*, enough of my essence in the simulacrum, along with the movement, to draw the blast to the reformed root rather than me. The wyrd magic wraps around the effigy. I watch with a mixture of horror and artistic appreciation as the spell hits. The wood thins, retreats at a rate of knots, and the bark turns the fresh green of a new shoot. It isn't getting forced back underground. It's getting forced back in time.

It's a devastatingly clever spell to have used against me. If it had struck my body, I'd presumably have de-aged equally quickly, ending up as a squalling babe on the floor. It wouldn't be the first time I shat myself during a battle, but it'd probably be the most literal. Of course, keeping me tied up in a useless body rather than releasing me to go grab my next ride is a stroke of genius. Especially as the chances of her knowing I've had my own *talent* eaten and am only borrowing the fae power this body is capable of are slim to none, thankfully.

I can hear what sounds like a pack of bison stampeding through the hall, along with the whickering snicker of Aicha's blade cutting through the air itself. I'm not hearing a lot of flesh getting cut though. I risk a peek over my shoulder.

Hot damn, for not being able to see where the hell it's going, that horse is fast. It's practically doing a four-footed tap dance, seeming to match Aicha's implausible quickstep as she pivots around it, her blade a blurring glimmer. She spins around, back to me, and the horse turns too, allowing me to see its primary form of attack.

Where the creature's neck joins its body, it is now hinged open, and shark-like rows of teeth gleam briefly before it snaps shut where Aicha's right elbow was milliseconds before. It's the kind of thing some Japanese manga artist might have come up with in the 1980s, in between designing nightmarish tentacle porn to scar an entire generation. Basically, freaky as fuck. Doesn't explain how it can see where it's going, but it explains how it feeds, at least. Although "biology of those attacking us" isn't an important starter subject unless the question is, "Where can I poke them with this sharp pointy thing to make them stop attacking us?" That's always a valid question worth answering.

A rustling noise in front of me reminds me I've a battle of my own to deal with. I snap my head back to see the hag swinging her broom down at it. I perform a Neo-like lean back that Fat Joe would be proud of, as would I if she wasn't already twisting her wrists, twizzling the bristles back in my direction. Luckily, I don't waste time marvelling at the chances of me winning the next Limbo competition in this body but pull my sword from my etheric storage in time to meet the brush-head swinging at me, bringing myself back to an upright position by using my countering move to give me momentum.

That the bristles ring against my blade rather than get the equivalent of a quick trim confirms my suspicions that they aren't made of straw – or, at least, not normal straw. Some sort of magically enhanced super straw perhaps. The sort of straw that would have left the Big Bad Wolf wheezing like an asthmatic at the very first Little Pig's house. Strong enough to withstand a blade wrapped in the thorny *talent* of a fae is pretty impressive. Considering the noise it makes as it clashes with the edge of my blade, you could call our battle a *ringing* endorsement. Heh.

I've no time for dad jokes as we engage in a fever-pitch exchange, blade against broom. I'm slightly quicker than her, in this inhuman body at least, but it's like fighting when drunk...on the high seas...in the middle of a tempest. Every time I get inside her defences, time rewinds slightly, throwing me off kilter, leaving me lurching as I find myself back into the downswing of a moment previously rather than the clever little reversal upswing I believed myself to be performing. Each move that should catch her off balance leaves me reeling instead, and it's very fucking annoying. She's sweating, at least; using this sort of temporal magic can't be easy, and she clearly went with the "go big or go home" school of casting for that first power bolt she launched at me. I guess she doesn't have enough gas left in the tank to pull anything of that size out of the bag again, for now at least. I'm not confident enough of that to bank on it though. That caution is straining me. I'm trying to stay aware of what she's going to pull *talent*-wise and the natural materials I might use when she does.

It's a wise decision. She's not totally spent. She lunges, catching me on my cross-guard with a heavy downward sweep that makes me partially buckle, only just keeping from going on one knee. As I push back upwards, she surges back and then splits in two.

I can feel it. The Father-Time-fucking hoebag. This isn't just an illusion. She's pulled on a moment when time branched, when she could be in one place or the other, and then made them happen simultaneously so she's in both. Damn and blast. Holding my own against one has been hard. Against two? I have the feeling this isn't going to go well.

Now I'm solidly on the defensive. I don't know how long she can keep this up, but I don't think it'll have to be long. Every time I parry one, the other gets through my guard, and it's only my reflexes that are stopping me from being made to resemble a fine-tooth comb. As is, I'm picking up more red stripes than a sunburnt zebra. That's a lot less fun than it sounds. My T-shirt's cut to ribbons, as is my jacket, and I'm bleeding profusely. Also, fun fact I've never known before. Catching lacerations on your tits is mind-bogglingly painful. Unfortunately, as they're in front of me (and prominently so), I'm struggling to avoid it happening. Women – reason 9,567 why I admire you so much and believe whole-heartedly that you should run the world.

Not the woman I'm fighting though. Or women, rather. I wonder if they're capable of independent thought, if one of them realises they're going to cease to exist once the spell wears off. I suppose in the middle of fighting for your life isn't the time for such existential thinking. Unless you're a twat like me.

I need an assist, but by the sounds of it, Aicha's busy enough with Champing-on the Wonder Horse. Part of me thinks I have the raw end of the deal here, having to deal with the hag and her time magic. Then the other part of me remembers how fucking fast that horse moves and is quite happy to just have to deal with someone taking the piss out of the laws of temporal reality.

Thinking about the hag's nag (try saying that twenty times fast) gives me an idea. I try to keep up with the bushido-grade brush wielding the multiplied La Guillaneus are performing. Falling backwards, I let my *talent* surge out through the building, into the other rooms. It only takes me a moment and only costs me a cracked rib from a reversed poke from one broom to find what I'm looking for. Yes. Perfect.

From behind me comes the sound of my backup arriving. The two La Guillaneu's heads pop up, and I can see the surprise writ large on them.

From the archway behind me, a crack commando team of carousel horses comes galloping out of the darkness.

Now, look. I know what you're thinking. Compared to a time-manipulating hag and a fevered-dream demon horse thing, a bunch of wooden fairground rides aren't particularly menacing. And you know what? You'd be right most of the time. Thing is, I've got a particularly deadly weapon in my arsenal. It's called my imagination.

The horses are wooden, and however dead that wood is now, it remembers what it was to be alive. It's easy to coax it into growing or splitting or splintering. I can imbue the dead wood with the memory of what it was to be a bough, to bend without breaking. So the legs are working, driving them forward to my aid. And the teeth are working now too. I've snapped them open along the painted lines and left the jagged edges, ready to grab and tear. Plus, there's the rest of their forms.

These are fairground attractions imagined by Lord Humungus from *Mad Max 2*. I've made all the natural knobs and whorls of the wood that were sanded down and painted ever so beautifully regrow, pushing them outwards into multicoloured spikes. The only thing you could say for riding one of them on the carousel now is that you wouldn't be likely to fall off no matter how fast the thing turned.

There's eight of them, and it's enough to temporarily even the odds. I don't fancy my chances of defeating La Guillaneu one-on-one as is. I'm really just stalling, hoping Aicha can get the win over Hwin and then we can double team the hag. In a fight, obviously. Jesus. Mind out of the gutter, please.

The hag on the left breaks off from attempting to sweep me off my feet or, at least, sweep my feet off me and turns her attention to the stampeding murder-horses behind me. Right-hand hag keeps right on swinging. It means the fight's bearable again; although considering the variety of depth and locations of cuts I'm now sporting across my body, she definitely still has the advantage.

The blood slicking up the floor is making it harder to keep my footing. My body's trying to heal –apparently fae physiology doesn't enjoy bleeding out and subconsciously tries to do something about it– but all that's doing is tiring out both my power and my energy levels even more rapidly. Left-hand hag lowers her head so her bone-antlers point straight at my arrayed wooden horses of hurt and charges past me for all the world like an enraged stag. By the sound of splintering wood behind me, their body spikes aren't doing much to help them against the hag's frenzied assault. Still, they were never meant to be more than a distraction. *Buy me time with your gallop into sawdust, my little wooden stallions.*

It's not going to be enough. I'm tiring, burning through my power to keep the chargers charging. Burning through my energy trying to heal. Burning through this body, I reckon. Good God damn it, I'm not ready to go back to being unTalented again. Not now. Not yet.

The brush is getting through more often than I'm stopping it now. My hag (*My hag! Talkin' bout my hag – my hag!*) swings it in lazy sweeping arcs that are deceptively quick. A screech escapes my lips when she rakes it across my midriff. The upper bristles feel like they've cut between my ribs, while the lower ones may well just have given me an unnecessary caesarean. I drop to one knee. I can't help it. I'm used to pain – hell, I've been through enough of it in my life to make me an honorary woman even when not wearing this body, but it's just too much. On top of the exhaustion, the constant pressure of the surrounding metal, the trauma I'm still lugging about like my own personalised shithead of a monkey clinging to my back, I'm done. My sword comes up, horizontal to the floor, but my hand's wobbling, the blade mirroring it, like that optical illusion of making a pencil bend that kids always do. La Guillaneu knows it too. I can see the triumph in her eyes, a flash of victory. Perhaps a little look of mercy too, of appreciation of a valiant opponent, and I know right then she's going to do me what she thinks is a favour but is actually going to shaft me right royally.

She's going to be merciful. She's going to kill me. Shit.

CHAPTER TWENTY-SIX
PARIS, 8 JUNE, PRESENT DAY

Oh. So this is how it feels, not wanting to die. How do normal people ever get anything done?

I can see it in the angle she's holding the broom at. When it comes sweeping back down again, it's going to tear out my throat, rip out my oesophagus entirely. I can tell you from personal experience that makes continuing to live quite a challenge even under the best of circumstances. Kneeling, almost burnt out in a pool of my own blood definitely isn't the best of circumstances.

I'm not a quitter, but I'm a realist. This fight has about two or three moves left before it's finished, even ignoring the noises of breakages quieting down behind me. It's about to be two-on-one again. More like two-on-about-a-half as I reckon I'm half-dead already.

But just as I'm playing through the potential moves like a chess grandmaster who can already see the only way out is his king toppling, the hag freezes. I hear a *poof* behind me, and Thing Two pops out of existence. I can feel it. My wooden horses fall too. They'll do me no good now. No point burning through any more of my depleted stores of *talent*.

Aicha's lazy drawl carries across the room. 'Who wants to bet I can make this death even more traumatic than Artax? And let's be clear, that fucked me right up.'

La Guillaneu's attention is no longer on me at all, so I risk turning to see what's going on. Man, it's a shame I've been so busy fighting for my life. It looks like I've missed a treat of a show.

They've trashed the other side of the vast chamber. Huge segments of the faux marble floor have been ripped out, so I can see the concrete underneath. One of Aicha's swords, her katana, is buried into the foundation handle first, its blade poking straight up. That's major-league impressive strength. Even the ceiling has sections that have fallen down, and through the holes they've punched in the walls, I can see the next room, some kind of Cabinet of Curiosities. I feel sorry for a moment for the owner. Some of this stuff is priceless. Or was until, for example, I turned it into an army of spike-covered warhorses. Sorry, antiquity fans.

Aicha has the upper hand though. No surprises there. Headless horse demon or the Druze Queen? It was only ever a matter of time.

She has her wakizashi to the creature's throat-slash-mouth-mashup combination, just a little lower down than where it was opening, trying to take chunks out of her.

'Reckon Buttercup here isn't just a construct. They're an independent creature. And they're not a spirit. So they have to have a brain in there somewhere. Got me thinking; I reckon the thing's head? Must be on the inside.'

I feel it. Feel the moment La Guillaneu triggers her chronomancy. Before I know it, I'm back up on my feet, and my intestines no longer feel like they're about to pop out of my abdomen. Several of the horses are back intact – although, considering what I've done to them, the owner would probably disagree, and they're all connected to me magically again. Hag Thing 2 hasn't popped back into existence though, which is interesting.

I whip around and see just what a clever fucker my good friend is. Because, sure, the hag's locally reversed time a good couple of minutes. That is some seriously brain-exploding amount of power to be throwing about. She's gone all out, and I don't doubt she's running pretty close to empty herself now. Except Aicha accounted for it. Clever, clever fucker.

La Guillaneu's horsey friend is still in Aicha's grip. Still threatened with evisceration. Only this time, he's suspended over the blade Aicha wedged into the floor. Reckon it freaked him out enough, finding himself in this position, that he became too panicked to reach out to the hag by whatever mental connection they have. Either that or Aicha threatened him effectively enough he didn't dare.

Whatever the reason, she held him under constant threat of death while I kept the hag occupied. Then, when it all came to the crunch? She just switched position. Enough that the hag saw the movement from the corner of her eye when Aicha called out. Enough for her to think it was Aicha just getting the upper hand rather than having held it for long enough that the hag doesn't have enough magic to wind back that far.

Now it's La Guillaneu's turn to look defeated. Her broom is held in a half-threatening pose, like she's trying to menace me in return, but my stomach's closed up, and my wounds are slowly healing. There's only one of her, and if she moves a muscle, her companion dies. The headless horse may not be a construct, but I'm willing to bet there's a real strong psychic link between them. She's invested in their relationship.

She sags. 'Wait, my poppets, my little diddle-dumplings! There's no real problem between us here. I'm just looking after my liege lord, my snuggle-bums, my sweetikins. You said before, you weren't here to kill him like we've been told?'

Oh good. Now she wants to talk. Funny how it's only now, when there's a sword pressed against her familiar's throat, that she recognises words are the answer. I'm feeling pretty vindictive right now, and part of me wants to tell Aicha to cap the mofo, and we'll finish her off together. Except...

Except she's right. She's not doing anything anyone wouldn't expect her to do. For the hag to have sworn fealty to Leandre, he's either seriously impressed her or else befriended her.

If I called Isaac up right now and told him someone was up in Toulouse, looking to kill me, he'd be on them like a ton of bricks. I mean, being as it's Isaac and he makes John Lennon look like a bloodthirsty steroid freak, I'm sure he'd try to find a peaceful solution first or restrain them with Nith's help. But if all that failed, and he really couldn't do anything to stop them other than by killing them? If he really thought my life was on the line, he wouldn't hesitate.

So as much as I want to curse her out, to tell her to go to hell and bring the pain, I don't. I let out a long-suffering sigh, which I instantly regret because an immediate agonising burning sensation reminds me just how much grief my chest section has suffered. Still, I bring my sword down, its point resting on the floor.

'Right. Let's talk.' I sit cross-legged on the floor, my sword in front of me. It's a helluva vulnerable position to take, but Aicha has the horse firmly pinned down, and I'm exhausted. I still fancy my chances of getting into a defensive position if the hag suddenly comes at me, but either she's wasting her time as a chronomancing wyrd witch-thing and should go straight for a starring role in Broadway, or she's not acting and the fight's gone out of her. We might not have officially raised a white flag, but I reckon there's a truce, for the moment at least.

'So if you're not here to harm the Prince, my little dumplings, my dreamykins, then why are you here?' she asks, and finally we have space to tell our side of the story. Heavily redacted, of course. I believe La Guillaneu is loyal to Leandre, but I'm not about to test that by telling her about all the crazy powerful bones kicking around or tempt her to go have a bit of a parley with De Montfort instead. I tell her we've news of a threat to the Lutin Prince, that it corresponds with our own aims –because she's never going to believe we came here just out of a philanthropic sense of duty– and that Scarbo set us up. She narrows her eyes at the mention of Sir Doggerel.

'He's a nasty little sod, that one, isn't he, my snuffle-bunnies, my coochicoos? And so annoying with his endless appalling poetry. It's a terrible affliction to have such a verbal tick, isn't it, my angels, my sweetums?'

I don't snort with laughter. Look at me, all growing up over here. I can feel Aicha's amusement radiating off her, but she's too occupied keeping our hostage under control to risk taking the piss out of the hag, however tempted she must be. As long as she avoids calling us "my preciouses", I can probably just about hold it together.

Instead, I nod in agreement. Terribly annoying, indeed. I look askance at La Guillaneu. 'So we find ourselves in a bit of a pickle. All we want to do is have a sit-down chat with Leandre –'

'After Al-Ruhban...' The threat is obvious in Aicha's voice. She's really pissed off about even the thought that he's set us up.

'...after him, yep. Instead, we find ourselves –' I make an expansive gesture, indicating both the place, the museum, the room, the stand-off itself, the whole damn mess. 'Here. So how do we get out of this without everyone ending up dead?'

I can see she's thinking. I don't doubt primarily to make sure that, whatever agreement we strike, it's going to protect her and her interests first and foremost. To wield time-altering magic, you have to be whip-smart. And also probably certifiably insane, but as long as we get the right promise out of her, that's somebody else's problem. Not for the first time, the thought occurs to me that, considering the mental health issues and the undeniable trauma present throughout the Talented, some sort of professional confidential counselling might just result in a lot fewer deaths inside the community. Happy, well-balanced magic-users? I shake the thought from my head. Nah, impossible.

'How about this, my sweet-peas, my buggaboos? I'll make a promise to let you leave and not pursue you upon my power. In exchange, I'll have the same from you, not to pursue me once this is all completed nor to hold a grudge against me, my cherubs, my chickadees.'

I'm just thinking it sounds like a reasonable offer when Aicha pipes up. 'And not to set anyone else after us either. Keep where we are and where we're going secret. My Little Pony here gets included too.'

Another effective demonstration by Aicha of how razor-sharp her mind is. Almost as sharp as her collection of actual razors. The hag purses her lips. 'I'll need your oath in that case not to bring harm to Leandre as well.'

That's not an oath I'm ready to make, at least not in that form. 'How about we swear an oath that we intend him no harm as long as he brings none to us once this mess is cleared up?'

We're deep into the haggling over the precise terms of the accord. Now it's La Guillaneu's turn. 'In which case, I reserve the right to inform Leandre of your presence and your purposes, my petals, my cupcakes, hmm?'

There's a big potential risk there, a possible get-out clause for her. 'Acceptable, but only if you inform him and no one else. No messengers or intermediaries.' Otherwise, she could just tell Scarbo himself. After all, he's officially one of Leandre's messengers.

A wide grin spreads across La Guillaneu's face. I don't think she was planning to stitch us up like that, but she sees the potential loophole herself now. It's the smile of someone appreciating a clever move in a board game or a well-executed strategy employed in sport. 'Very wise, my doveys, my dearies. Very wise, indeed.'

So we strike the deal and seal it with a promise on our respective powers. We put away our various weapons and take a much-needed momentary breather. Looking around the museum, the pause allows me to feel sorry for the owners. Putting together a collection like this, of antique fairground rides and attractions must have been next to impossible. We've destroyed something whimsical and beautiful. Admittedly, to keep ourselves alive, but it won't make the proprietor feel any better when they discover it.

I look at La Guillaneu. 'Can you do anything about this mess?' It's a stretch, but, hey, if you have a hag who's willing to mess with forces no mortal being should ever meddle in, might as well try to use that to make things right.

She sighs. 'I need to get my energy back after our back and forth, my chickadee, my boo-boo-bear.' She looks around at all the wanton destruction – holes punched in walls, shattered rides, deformed carousel gallopers. 'Still, I lured you here, and I do love this place.' No surprises there considering how she's decked out her steed. 'I'll do what I can, then go make a call to my Prince, my snufkin, my little love.'

Even better. If she fails to convince Leandre or if he decides eradicating us just to be sure is still the safest course, it'll give us a head start before he sends more after us. I nod my thanks to La Guillaneu, too tired to thank her properly, and Aicha and I head outside.

I take a moment in the courtyard to breathe in the fresh air and pull in some power from the flora in the pretty borders. I notice one tree has disappeared though. A thought strikes me, and I dig into the soil where it's conspicuously absent. Twenty or thirty centimetres down into the already disturbed ground, I find what I'm looking for. The nut that was a tree.

The one that took the hit for me when La Guillaneu threw that first spell. It having lived a whole life, then been reversed back to this state, packed full of potential, it thrums with power. For me, as a fae, it's like a portable battery, something I can draw on if I find myself too far away from Nature's helping hand to deal with a major threat. I pop it into my pocket rather than my storage. I want to keep it at hand. Beating La Guillaneu doesn't mean it's going to be plain sailing from here on in.

That's another thing I don't want to mention but can't help myself thinking about. Aicha looks exhausted. Various holes where the horse-monster thing got its teeth into her are still filling in. My own lumps and lacerations are healing too, thanks to the nearby greenery, but that's only the outside. Inside, I'm on my knees. The fight has taken it out of me in a big way. And we're nowhere near in the clear yet. The next train should take us straight to Saint-Ouen. There's only one problem with that.

First, it's going to take us straight through the heart of Paris. Through the first arrondissement.

Straight through Leandre's own territory.

CHAPTER TWENTY-SEVEN
PARIS, 8 JUNE, PRESENT DAY
That's quite enough "timey-wimey" magic for one lifetime.

We trudge back through the pedestrian zone towards Bercy Park, our eyes peeled. Just because La Guillaneu's granted us safe passage doesn't mean there won't be any other Talented around with entirely different opinions on the matter. I just have to desperately hope that Al-Ruhban turns out to be on our side after all, and we're heading towards a safe haven instead of a potential trap. I suspect Scarbo will have discovered we've escaped by now. If he or they or whoever is arrayed against us at the moment have any sense, they'll be anticipating our attempt to head for Saint-Ouen. That means either en-route or at the destination itself, we'll probably get bushwhacked. The thought does nothing to improve my already gloomy mood.

We enter Cour Saint-Émilion without any further problems, hop on the train, and pass through a couple more stations. The line's getting progressively busier. Passing the Gare de Lyon, we dump out as many as we take on, but Chatelet is a heaving monstrosity of a stop. The bodies are packed so deep getting on and off the train, I don't know how anyone can move through the crush without becoming incorporeal or perhaps changing from a solid into a liquid or gas. And as the doors slide shut, Aicha's fingers press down firmly on my arm. A warning. Shit.

My eyes scanning, I try to spot what she's seen.

'Look down.' Her voice is low, and I obligingly bring my gaze down, searching the floor.

I still don't see what she's seen. Everyone, everything looks normal. Then I notice something that sets alarm bells ringing like fucking air raid sirens.

The passengers, cramped and crowded all the way down, are moving peculiarly further along the carriage. It's like an oscillation, like they're all tied on a piece of string that's being waved back and forth. One passenger doing it could just be them shuffling, trying to get comfortable. All the passengers doing it in a transmitted rhythm with no one noticing? That's magic in action.

This peculiar wave is about ten metres from us when we get to our feet and head in the opposite direction. By Aicha telling me to look down, I assume it's some sort of small creature, probably fae, making their way down the train, looking for us. The only advantage is if they're only waist or knee high, they'll have trouble spotting us at a distance. The problem is they're making good progress. The wave is coming closer, only six or seven metres back now.

'Did you see them? What are we dealing with?' I keep my voice low. Luckily, the unwritten rule of public transport is "mind your business" and apart from exasperated glances at us for daring to force our way through the crowd, everyone is doing their best to studiously ignore us.

'Jetins,' is the answer I didn't want but should have expected.

Despite how the name sounds, jetins aren't actually lutins with jet-packs (which would be totally fucking cool and something I now need to make happen). They're lutins all right, but the subspecies name is from the verb *jeter*, to throw. They come from the northeast French coast in Brittany where, despite them being proper wee folk, their favourite pastime is hurling menhirs, those huge rocks Obelix from *Asterix* had a fashion penchant for carting about, out to sea like humans skip stones. You know what garden gnomes look like? All flowing white beards, rosy cheeks, and cheeky grins? Strip off the beard and any sense of humour, then jack them up on steroids, and that's a jetin. They're basically like normal small fae but who've bathed in a cauldron of Asterix's magic potion. Or to put it another way, they're the ants of the magic world regarding their physical strength comparative to their size. They're very literal too. If one of them says they're going to rip the piss out of you, they don't mean they're going to tease you. They mean they're going to tear out your urethra.

It makes sense they're here, what with the ruler of Paris having the convenient title of the Lutin Prince. Their serving him is logical, but it's another headache I could do without, especially on a crowded train.

They're the perfect agents for Leandre to have sent searching for us. Tiny as they are, they can easily weave through busy crowds, and they have the natural lutin resistance to magic. In a brawl, they're incredibly difficult to hit, whereas you present an easy target for them. Plus, there're loads of the little fuckers. Dealing with a swarm of miniature beings who'll tear your toes off just because someone once told them, 'This little piggy went to market,' is about as fun as it sounds.

Aicha hisses, and I turn my attention ahead. Ah, fucksticks. There's a similar wave coming towards us from the other direction. We're about to get caught between two groups of vicious mini-Hulks, where I've not got room to swing a cat, let alone a sword. Actually, swinging a cat in this kind of enclosed environment would probably be more effective. Launching an enraged feline down the carriage at the arriving tiny bastards might distract them long enough for us to get past. Or they'll end up saddling it and then we'll be facing mounted tiny bastards. All academic because of the lack of readily available moggies on the Paris metro. Poor forward planning, if you ask me. Instead of paw forward planning.

I'm close to paralysed with indecision. There's no way out of this I can see that doesn't involve either us or a bunch of civilians getting done over. All the jetins have to do is restrain us till the passenger numbers reduce, then hustle us off the train. And then probably onto the train tracks.

Just at that moment, the train starts to slow down, and I glimpse the first signs for "Pyramides" ornately painted on tiles outside the windows. At first I panic. We're literally in the heart of Leandre's territory. Then suddenly an idea comes to me. A cunning plan, as Baldrick would say.

Although I hope this one has a better chance of success than his do.

Chapter Twenty-Eight
PARIS, 8 JUNE, PRESENT DAY

I'd like to send the little fuckers "jetin" off into space. By firing them out of a catapult. Maybe a circus clown cannon.

I dart towards the escalators, trusting Aicha to follow my lead. The Good God love her, she doesn't even hesitate, though I bet she's burning up wanting to ask me what the hell I'm playing at. We're right in the heart of Paris, racing full-speed out into Leandre's territory. If we were actually here to assassinate him and were a pair of clumsy bastards, it might look exactly like this.

We run up the moving steps, into a shining metallic lobby, and damn it, there's just too much metal everywhere. It's like blasting a bat with sonar, totally fucking with me. I know where we need to go, so I weave a small *don't look here,* not enough to make us properly invisible, just less interesting despite being two stunningly beautiful women running full pelt from some invisible monsters only we can see.

Aicha flicks a hand out, and the plastic shields of the ticket turnstile pop open and stay like that. She's likely just wrecked the motor, but as I was going to burst through them like the Kool-Aid Man, she's probably saved the Paris Transport Authority some money. Then we're up the next set of steps so fast, it's like we're almost flying, which is good because we've definitely been spotted.

The jetins that must have been standing in the metro station at the top of the stairs, waiting to see if we came up on the Line 7 or the Line 14 erupt into tiny chittering cries as we advance. Luckily, they expected us to employ stealth rather than bursting out at full pelt, doing everything short of screaming, 'Look at me; I'm going to assassinate Prince Leandre!' at the top of our lungs to grab their attention. The incomprehensibility of it has granted us a moment's leeway.

We hurtle out of the mouth of the steps and into the most entirely Parisian landscape possible unless you somehow picked up the Tour Eiffel and balanced it on top of the Arc de Triomphe. The buildings are that Napoleonic design, epic in grandeur, gorgeous in detailing, unaffordable for mere mortals in pricing. In the distance, I can see just a glimpse of the Louvre, the tip of the pyramid the metro stop is named after. That's the direction they expect us to head in, of course. Towards Leandre's seat of power. I love wrong-footing people. Especially foot-high people.

Because instead, we bound round the corner and head north, away from the Louvre. I'm glad I have the *don't look here* spell in place because we must look manic. Nobody runs in Paris; it's far too un-chic, and running like you have the hounds of hell snapping at your heels isn't the done thing. I'm laughing too – a little of that nervous energy bubbling up and bursting out whether or not I want it to. Running for your life is a good way to help you remember just how valuable said life is.

Aicha has to be worried about me. This isn't my normal behaviour. All right, recklessly acting without apparently thinking is entirely my normal way of behaving, but the slightly mental laughter's a new and probably unwelcome addition. But Aicha keeps pace with me, trusting me implicitly because she rocks harder than sedimentary strata. Good friends are hard to find. The best friends? You don't need to find them. They always find you when you need them.

It's a quick dash to our destination, a right off down a side street that connects to the Rue des Petits Champs, then hell for leather down that road. The high-pitched chittering nobody but us can hear gets closer and closer. It's not far, but I'm not sure we're going to make it; based on the level of noise gaining on us, there're way too many jetins for us to take out in a straight street brawl. The only way is onwards; I just hope we can outpace them.

The Rue Vivienne comes up on our left, and I screech round the corner like fucking Road Runner. I swear I kick up a cloud of dust behind me. I think I can even hear a couple of the little fuckers coughing on it. I'd be delighted by that –*choke on my exhaust fumes, you wee shits*– except it would mean they're far, far closer than I want them to be.

We're nearly there. I can see the palm trees, their fronds waving above the black metal railings, and I pull in a little power from them to push it into my tired legs for a last spurt of speed just as someone snatches at the hem of my raised leg. They miss, sending only a rush of air brushing past my ankle and saving me from a spectacular face-plant. I motor forward, bursting through the doorway of what looks like a palace. Mainly because it was once. Not of the king but of the prime minister and priest, Cardinal Mazarin. Because that is what Jesus wants his followers to do. Amass wealth and live in palaces. Pretty sure that was one of his key lessons on the Mount.

Now it's full of a whole different kind of riches and home to a different type of acolyte too, but it doesn't matter because we're in their territory now, and I'm screaming, 'Sanctuary! Sanctuary!' at the top of my lungs, which is totally not the done thing in a building like this...

Because it's a library and not just any library. It's part of the French National Library. And I've just invoked sanctuary.

Good God, I really hope it works.

Then it happens. I feel it as much as see it. I hear it too because a jetin just behind us bounces backwards, doing an impressive roly-poly into a nearby bush. I turn to give the creature a middle finger salute, which gets it gibbering with rage as it picks itself back out of the flowerbed. Then I flop down for a moment myself, exhausted.

The horde of jetins accumulate at the doorway, poking at the barrier with bared teeth, howling their frustration at their quarry being so close and yet inaccessible. Aicha's trying to hide it, but I can see she's impressed.

'So you've managed to get us trapped in a building with multiple entrances and a horde of jetins outside. Have you never seen a zombie movie, dickhead?'

See, majorly impressed. Told you so.

'Actually,' I start, unable to help myself, 'if this was a movie, it'd be less *Night of the Living Dead* and more *Evil Dead*. And not even *Evil Dead 2*, with some laughs thrown in to mellow out the horror.'

Her eyes narrow. 'What have you done?'

I consider hemming and hawing, but Aicha's still running on adrenaline after our chase through the streets of Paris. Too much chance of getting myself stabbed. 'Well, you've heard of the Agrippa, right?'

The small intake of breath she gives is well deserved. The Agrippa is the stuff of nightmares. A book as tall as a man and apparently bound in the skin of one, it's supposedly a sentient being packed full of secrets that can give almost limitless magic to anyone able to parse the words contained inside it. Many a power-hungry idiot has attempted to wrest control of it, only to find themselves getting eaten away line by line of their being until there is nothing left but blank pages in the place of a human life. Horrible.

The Agrippa is the book that reads you when you try to read it. And eats up all your words.

Aicha is now giving me a look. That patented Aicha look that promises violence in the very near future. 'Tell me we are nowhere near the fucking Agrippa.'

I shrug, trying for nonchalant and failing badly. 'Define near?'

'In this building.'

'Then, um, yep. According to Isaac anyway. Nobody else knows. Apparently Leandre got his hands on the Agrippa. But being not a total fucking idiot, he didn't read it. Instead he locked it away here.'

I can see precisely what she thinks of my plan, getting us locked inside a building with a demonic book that eats the Talented for breakfast. Before she can properly tear into me though, there's a gentle *clip-clopping* behind us. She tenses as we turn away from the frenzied jetins to see...

'Is that Mister Tumnus?' Aicha asks unbelievingly because yes, it sure as hell looks like a reddish-skinned faun with bumpy horns on his forehead and a little pointy beard.

'It only *looks* like Mister Tumnus. Please, please don't headbutt him. They're the ones keeping us alive,' I hiss through clenched teeth. 'Urluthes!'

I see the moment of realisation switch on in Aicha's expression.

The friendly looking and entirely illusory creature trots forward and peers up at us. He's only just bigger than a child – only just bigger than Lucy when she first meets him in *The Chronicles of Narnia*, if I remember correctly, and there's a kindly expression on his face – the same expression he wore in the movie right before he went and sold her out to Jadis, the White Queen herself. I can't help wondering if that's why this urluthe is presenting himself like this – they've not yet decided if they're going to help or hinder us.

Urluthes are strange creatures. As nobody's ever seen what one looks like in reality, only their illusions, no one really knows what they are. Some believe them to be fae, others some sort of offspring of the Muses themselves. Regardless, they're my kind of creature because they live to inspire the imagination, especially through the magic of reading.

Mister Tumnus – or the image of him tilts his head slightly. 'You requested sanctuary?'

I nod. 'We're being chased for wrongdoings that are not our own.' I'm gabbling, as if getting the words out quicker will increase the chances of him agreeing to help us. I take a deep, calming breath and try again. 'They're trying to cut our story short without due cause.'

And this is it. The point where we find out if my gamble pays off. The moment hangs on a knife's edge because there is every possibility the urluthe is just going to throw us back outside to be torn limb from limb by a group of miniaturised Hulks who are definitely very, very angry right now.

The creature that looks like Mister Tumnus purses his lips, his shaggy goatee (no pun intended) rustling at the movement. Then he nods and says, 'Follow me!' before turning and heading deeper into the library.

It's jaw-dropping. We're hustled past every conceivable style of luxuriant interior design covering the last five hundred years, right up to the modern with a twirling steel staircase that I can appreciate artistically even if it turns my sensitive faerie stomach. There's marble and works of art likely worth millions. They've built it partially into a museum, so we're hurrying past exhibits as well. Rococo flourishes give way to gold-filigree wood panelling, and as we cross the main reading room, I fight the urge to just throw my head back and gape. The ceiling is all rounded panels, like pagodas supported on fine stone pillars. The mixture of gold gleaming under the channelled daylight curves and arches; it is stunningly beautiful. Our host is clearly used to it because he doesn't slow at all. And as I'm hoping he's going to keep us alive, therefore, neither do I. I can always come back and gawp later on.

'Sanctuary...' the urluthe says. It's a struggle to keep pace with the creature, but as our lives are in his hands, I make the effort. Surprising how motivating that can be. 'No one has ever requested that before.'

'Never?' I can hear the razored edge to Aicha's voice, ready to flay the flesh from my bones.

'Stories are sacred to the urluthes, right?' I flash her a grin that falls apart, sliced in half by a stare just as sharp as her tone. 'It paid off, didn't it?'

'I don't believe' –there's a goat-like bleat to the urluthe's calm voice– 'I agreed to your request.'

Ah. Fuck. I turn my attention back to the creature clipping along at a pace – and indeed clopping along at a pace thanks to his hoofed feet. Better to concentrate on him than the rage-storm building at my terrible excuse for a plan. 'I assumed the whole "follow me" thing was a tacit agreement to it?'

'Well, yes,' he says gently, never slowing. 'And Lucy assumed it was perfectly fine to head to tea with me, and that nearly didn't work out too well, did it? At least not till she convinced me to be on her side.'

Oof. He has a point. 'Are you saying you're going to hand us over to the White Witch?'

The thing that looks like Mister Tumnus stops abruptly and turns round, his eyes wide. 'Of course not!' There's a look of shock on his face, the kind that's slightly tinged with disgust, as if I've just spoken lewdly about his elderly mother. 'That story is told. This one is still being written.'

Oh, good. That's a relief. Or it is until he keeps speaking.

'No, we cannot get involved mid-tale. So we shall hand you over to a neutral party to act as arbiter. If you can persuade him as to your need for sanctuary, then so shall it be written. Otherwise, I'm afraid your story will have to be unwoven.'

A sneaking suspicion starts to form in my head. 'What do you mean, unwoven?'

Mister Tumnus treats me to a charming smile full of wonder and whimsy, and it's quite clear how he got a small schoolgirl to trust him despite the fact he was a treacherous snitch. 'Why, in that case, we'll feed you to the Agrippa, won't we? It's always hungry for tellings as fascinating as yours must be!'

And with that absolute bombshell, he turns and trots back off down the corridor.

The violent clip to the back of my head as Aicha goes past is almost welcome. The pain certainly is. It is pain that is highly deserved. 'Trapped. Surrounded. In an indefensible position. If you get us fed to a magical soul-swallowing book as well, I'm going to be more than peeved, dickhead. Whatever story you tell to get us out of here? Better be a gripper.'

Ha. A gripper. Agrippa. Humour in the face of terror. I'd probably find the situation funnier if I didn't roll these particular dice recently and end up getting my magic chewed down by a bogeywoman of the Talented community. Having my *talent* munched up as a main course was bad enough. I've no wish to have my soul served up as dessert.

Swallowing hard, I pick up the pace to keep up with the cantering faun and my absolutely furious best friend.

CHAPTER TWENTY-NINE
SÖLL, AUSTRIA, 11 FEBRUARY 1939

When I sit up in the dead body I just stuck the hand back onto, Otto Rahn can't help himself. He gives a little half-skip, half-jump, his feet pedalling for a moment in the air, and shrieks. Considering all the blood and battlefield surgery done to himself and the corpse I'm now inhabiting, I'm amazed he's still conscious. Especially when I remember he didn't know about my reincarnating, so he just watched me kill myself right before a disfigured dead body reanimated. Slightly unsettling, I'd have thought.

'Otto, it's me!' I can feel the shimmering change as I take my own form back. The man's mouth flaps open and closed soundlessly, and he flops down onto his arse in the snow. Understandable. The whole day has been a lot to take in even for someone who knows something of the Talented world. And the day's not done.

I look down at the previously dead arm and clench my fist in delight at what I see swirling inside it. The curse marker has stayed. I was worried it might go back to Rahn given it's woven with a part of his soul, but it has held to me. I'm cursed! Hooray!

And just in time for the first of the oversized head lice to skid over a patch of icy snow into the clearing.

'In a minute, run,' I say out the side of my mouth to Otto, 'but not till I say so.'

If he was aghast before, the arrival of the gigantic insect is just the cherry on the cake. He looks about ready to drop dead of a heart attack, but luckily, my words make it through, and he stays put. I need to be sure of something before he heads off.

Click-click-click. Suddenly the Buschgro'Bmutter is in the clearing with us, her burnished face still all rust and wide, dead staring eyes. Her head clacks back and forth, snapping between me and Rahn, who's close to a mental collapse. Only paralysing fear is holding him still now. When the fight-or-flight kicks in properly, there's only going to be one possible option.

I hold up the left hand, showing the swirling curse, and as I hoped, the metallic visage clunks around to fix on me. The jaw starts to click open once more, and the wolf-sized lice scutter in my direction.

Pulling my sword from storage, I throw the last of my magic at Rahn, coating him in a *don't look here*. If the Buschgro'Bmutter wants to find him, it'll do nothing, but it should keep the lice off his trail.

'Now! Run!' I shout as I switch the sword pommel into my left hand to get her to focus on it as I pull a little surprise from my storage with my right, then spring forward.

It is time to become death for these damned oversized bugs. I'm more reckless now, heading straight for her, cutting my way though as I go. Mandibles snap at me from left and right, but I sever them where I can, and the beasts squeal in agony and rage. They're not made for jumping, but they'll climb me if they can and bite my head off. I manage to stomp down hard, my foot carrying through a louse's carapace. Bits of its juices run down the inside of my boot, which would be a concern if I expected to still be wearing this body in a few more seconds.

Now I'm almost at the Buschgro'Bmutter, or she's nearly beside me. The way she moves, those flickering movements, there-then-gone-then-there, a flip book staccato quickstep across the white enveloped ground. It's going to be all about judging this, watching that pattern, learning it, assessing the right moment...

There. I lunge forward, my sword-point straight out. Straight through the back of the Buschgro'Bmutter's mouth.

Or it should be. The blade should be protruding about half a metre out of the back of her head. But it isn't.

Instead, the mouth snaps shut like a mouse trap, biting down. A millisecond later, it clunks back open, and the blade's gone. Then blink, and the mouth has moved forward, engulfing my arm up to the elbow, impossibly deep compared to what can be seen from the outside.

Snap. I can't see it yet, can't even feel it. But I know the arm's gone. The lice are swarming around my feet, and the only reason they haven't devoured me whole is that they know that's what their mistress is going to do instead.

Perfect.

The *clink-clink-clink* that comes now isn't from her jaw even as it snaps back open with that heavy-set clunk. Instead...

Instead, it's the sound of the grenade pin as it bounces off the shells of one, two, three lice underneath my right arm. I pull the surprise present close to my chest and release the safety lever. The white-saucer eyes, now mere inches from mine, click back and forth between the grenade and me.

'Otto Rahn says hello,' I say before the world erupts in fire and pain and noise.

And I'm gone once more, escaping away from the deafening inferno's engulfment.

But not far.

My eyes fly open, but I hold my body stiff as a board. I don't let my *talent* flood through the corpse, reanimating it, remaking it. Instead, I cling tight to it, wrapping it up, bundling it up with my life force and making the two as small and as insignificant as possible.

Because I'm not foolish enough to believe that a hand grenade can kill a nature spirit as powerful and as twisted as the Buschgro'Bmutter. This body's slightly propped up, enough I can see the scene in front of me. Smoking blackened lice corpses litter the clearing, some still ablaze, some embedded onto tree stumps and branches, like the trees are getting revenge for the first death the hag devised for me. The Buschgro'Bmutter herself is standing where she was. Black smudges and tarnish marks cover her iron head, and judging by the tiny plumes of smoke coming off both her clothes and arms, parts of her either are — or were — on fire as well.

I hold my breath. This is it. This is where we find out if my ruse worked. Will she *click-click* over to me and swallow me whole? Will she *flit-flit-flit* in disjointed blinks after Otto till she devours him?

The creature stands stock-still for some time, till I can feel my lungs starting to burn, desperate to heave a gasp, whether it'll betray me or not. Then...

She turns like a pockmarked, hunchbacked, clockwork ballerina in a music box, stop-start spinning on the spot to face the way she came. Then in rhythm with each blink, she's gone, back off into the forest and away to wherever she came from.

Between eating the curse and seeing me die, the Buschgro'Bmutter believes the contract completed.

I don't know whether she's really fooled no more than I know the details of her pact with the Nazis nor whether it's willing or forced. Perhaps she knew perfectly well I wasn't Rahn. Perhaps she felt me come to, heard my stifled breathing mere metres away, understood that my death was only ever temporary. Maybe she's happy to go along with fulfilling the letter of the instructions given, ignoring the meaning underneath, and leaving us alive as a result.

Or perhaps I'm a master of cunning and subterfuge. Yeah, you know what? Let's go with that.

I let the *talent* I've been clasping to my breast go and stagger unsteadily to my feet as they regain the ability to stand. Once I manage to shake some life back into them, I set off at a half-run after Otto Rahn.

I don't have to go far to find him. He only made it about two hundred metres before slumping against a tree, shaking. Shock's kicked in. The whole thing's been way too much for him. When he sees me, his relief is palpable. I'm pretty sure he thought the next face he would see would be iron-clad rather than flesh.

'Is she...is she dead?' The tremble in his voice matches his hands. He's close to collapse, both physically and mentally.

'No, but she's gone. And she thinks you're gone too.' It's not necessarily true, but it's close enough and as much detail as he needs to know.

He nods, his Adam's apple bobbing up and down like he's trying to swallow the truth, to consume it so as to make his overloaded brain know it to be true. I take his hand and pull him to his feet. I know he wants to go, but there's one more thing I need to do to give him a proper chance at getting away.

'Come on.' I pull him in the direction of the clearing. He's understandably resistant at first, but I gently insist. Despite the terror coursing through his system, he knows I've kept him alive so far, that I could have thrown him to the wolves to save my skin any number of times and haven't. In the end, that's enough to coax him into action, so he follows me at a halting stumble.

We get back, and I sweep at the snow bank where I came to twice so far. With a small amount of cleaning, I uncover the last of the feet I saw. A young male this time, late twenties at a guess. I'm massively relieved it's a man. That's going to make the next part easier.

What I want to do isn't going to take a huge amount of *talent*. Problem is, I'm running on empty, and I'm too whacked to meditate or perform any of the rites and rituals that might draw it back in more quickly. The only option is to do it slowly, letting the power trickle back in and then out again. I place my hands on either side of the corpse's face and look back up at Otto Rahn for two reasons. One, because I'm going to tell him what I'm doing and I want to make sure he understands. Two, so I can study what he looks like and transmit it through my touch.

'Before we go, I'm going to remake this corpse, change it to look like you.' Remodelling dead flesh isn't difficult. It's frozen solid, so warming it to make it pliable, putty for my intent, is the first step. 'Facing down the Buschgro'Bmutter has taken a lot out of me, a huge amount. This might take a while.'

Rahn stares at me, but he doesn't respond, and his eyes slide away to the dead body. We've some time before I'm done, and the corpse isn't going to get any more alive unless things go terribly, horribly wrong. I decide to deal with the elephant in the room.

'You mentioned the camps, Otto.' His head snaps back in my direction. Now he's focused. I keep my voice calm but firm. I doubt he's had the opportunity to speak about this before, but bottling it up will have done him no favours. 'What happened?'

He opens and closes his mouth a few times, but no words come. Instead, his eyes shut, and pain pinches his face tight. After a few moments, he tries again. 'I was so proud,' he says. 'I was so proud when Himmler noticed my research. When he requested to meet me, he told me my work would change the world, that I was the catalyst for a glorious new Arthurian age. I felt valued, justified in my obsessions that had driven me to Montsegur to chase the Grail and the Cathars. I felt...seen.'

Otto's eyes open, but the pain doesn't leave. It's magnified in that intense regard now fixed on me, all that shame and guilt and anguish pouring out. 'He made me feel so special. Inducting me into the SS. At first, I played it down to my academic friends. Me, a liberal researcher, dressed in a military uniform! I insisted it was just to pay the bills. But deep down?'

He sighs, a remorse-filled exhalation, the sound made when we come face to face with our own failures. 'Deep down, a part of me loved it. To be one of the strong ones, you know? One of the bully boys instead of those pushed around. I'd always mocked those drawn towards authority, but suddenly I understood the pull.'

I nod, understanding, if not sympathetic. It's easy to walk the wrong path, harder to own it. I'll give him that even if I don't entirely forgive him for willingly aiding the Nazi bastards. 'So what happened?'

He laughs and waves a hand at his somewhat spindly frame. 'I did. I'm not one for sport or fighting or shooting. Never have been, but suddenly I'm an SS officer, and there are expectations. Himmler couldn't keep me from all of those even if he wanted to. It was felt by many, probably by all, that I needed to toughen up. So they sent me for a tour of duty at Dachau.'

Tears run down his face, and I understand the horror isn't for those he loved who've paid the price but for those he watched pay on his behalf and did nothing to save. 'I watched what happened. The starving, the torture. The rape and murder. I thought to myself, *Himmler can't know! He can't know what's happening!* I found an excuse, pleaded ill health and fled back to Wewelsburg. When I saw him, it all came flooding out, a stuttered list of the horrors I'd witnessed. And Himmler, my patron?' A shudder runs through Otto as he thinks back. 'Himmler just looked at me, puzzled. "Of course, Herr Rahn," he said. "And this is just the start. If the Aryan race is to rise, we must purge all the impurities." Then he shuffled his papers, and I was dismissed.'

The flesh under my hand is warming, becoming malleable. My eyes haven't left Rahn's face, and now I can start to mould it into his likeness. I think he's done, that he'll lapse into silence now he's poured out his tale of horrors he stood by and allowed. But he's not. Not quite.

'Then I got the form they required I fill out, to provide documentation proving my pure blood. It didn't worry me until I went to speak to my mother. Until she showed me her birth certificate with her religion and race listed. She'd never believed, so had never mentioned our heritage. Turns out I was made for the camps after all.' He laughs, sharp and bitter. 'Just as an inmate rather than a guard.'

I look at him askance. 'Your mother was...'

He nods. 'Jewish. So am I.'

Of course. Judaism is passed through the maternal line. For a bunch of racist arsewipes like the German National Socialists, it's more than enough to send him off to those terrible camps for the rest of the war. Or as long as he survives.

A high-ranking SS officer and Ahnernebe occultist who's secretly a gay Jew? Yeah, I can't see that going down well with the rank and file. I can't imagine Himmler being delighted about it either. It doesn't excuse Rahn's actions or lack thereof regarding the regime, but at least he's being honest about them, and it does explain why he quit. It looks like learning to live with what he's done or hasn't is going to be the work of a lifetime.

The conversation's been cathartic. I can see he's calmed down. Perhaps expressing some of the horrors he saw before has helped him come to terms with the ones he's just lived. Or perhaps he just feels these ones were deserved. Either way, I think I'll change the subject.

'So what now then, Otto?' The material under my fingertips is starting to listen, to hear what I want it to do. I weave in wounds as I go, cuts and blows and bite-marks, like over-sized insectile teeth have made a meal of the dead flesh. The features change slowly, taking on the visage of the strange man whose life I'm trying to save. A little while more and I can leave Otto's dead doppelgänger for any determined search party to find. I doubt the Buschgroßmutter is going to give them a blow-by-blow report of our encounter. Better they find a dead body and write him off for good.

A little of that peculiar fire comes back into his gaze. 'What I've always intended to do. Find the Grail. Though not for that swine Himmler or any of the rest of his bastard friends. What?'

I can't help myself. The chuckle escapes my lips before I can bite down, and a second later I'm practically roaring with laughter. Perhaps it's my form of processing what just happened. Either way, it takes me a second to calm down, although seeing the affronted look on Rahn's face nearly sets me off again.

Eventually, I calm down and wonder how much to tell him, how to let him down gently. 'You saw how I came back?'

He nods, his eyes widening at the memory.

'Well, let's just say I've been around for a while. A long while. Mainly in Occitanie and the Languedoc.'

He leans forward, breathless. 'The Grail! Have you seen it?'

I nod, searching for how to phrase what I need to say next. 'It's gone, Otto. Destroyed. It doesn't exist anymore. Hasn't for hundreds of years,' I say it as softly as is possible but also make sure the words are run through with steel. He needs to know the truth.

Otto Rahn looks at me, searching my face, his eyes burrowing into mine like my fingers are doing to the dead man beneath them. A twitch runs from a mouth corner, up to his eye, then another, little micro-spasms as he tries to digest what I've told him. Seconds pass, then the corner of his mouth turns up.

'It's a joke.' He smiles, grinning irrepressibly. 'A joke. The Grail cannot be destroyed, not by mortal hands.'

'Seven hundred years mean I probably don't count as mortal anymore,' I remind him, but it doesn't make a dent in his grin.

'Bah! Either you joke or you lie. Perhaps to protect the Grail, no? To keep it safe?' Suddenly he's all business again, the intensity ratcheted up even higher. 'Please! Tell me. I'll keep the secret. Just let me see it one time.'

I insist again that it's gone, destroyed, and he falls silent, withdrawn. I can see he doesn't believe me, and when I ask where we're heading, he simply mutters, 'France' and leaves it at that. As we pick our way through the Alps over the next few days, his temper thaws, and he engages me in fascinating discussions on esoteric theory. He fills me in on some of the terrible workings attempted by the Ahnenerbe, but each time I try to talk once again about the Cathars, about the Holy Grail, he falls silent or switches the subject. After a time, I give up, letting it drop.

I accompany him as far as Toulouse, where we part; he continues onwards to the other mountains, the ones far more home to me than the perilous Alpine peaks. There's no question as to his initial destination. He's heading for Montsegur, no doubt seeking his mentor Antoine Gadal.

Years later, when the war's ended, and I find myself back in the area, I cross paths with Monsieur Gadal, a man who talks a big game of magic for one who is entirely unTalented. He's not half the intellectual that Rahn was. Suspicion engraves itself into the lines of his face, and he's insistent that he's not seen Rahn since he left the region in the early thirties. Other enquiries meet with equally blank expressions. Nobody knows where he went or what became of him.

Once more, just as he did with my help in the Alps in the winter of 1939, Otto Rahn disappeared from the face of existence, without a single word or clue as to his whereabouts.

The strange, conflicted, gay, Jewish, liberal SS Nazi officer and esoteric scholar — gone without a trace.

CHAPTER THIRTY

PARIS, 8 JUNE, PRESENT DAY

I wonder if the Agrippa was named after Marcus Vipsanius Agrippa, the famous Roman general and constructor of the Pantheon. Or whether, just maybe, it was made out of him instead.

This is, it would be fair to say, starting to look like a bad plan. Actually, it's starting to look like the latest staging point in a series of consecutively terrible plans that commenced with me deciding to go to Leicester first rather than stopping off in Paris en route and has only continued since with us asking Al-Ruhban for help and getting palmed off straight into the treacherous hands of Scabster himself. De Montfort knows I'm back in the game, and whatever his own — doubtless, far more competent — plan was, he seems to have stepped up the time frame. Or if he hasn't but the shitty little ditty prick is working for him, now he'll know where we are, and he will surely do so.

So instead of being ahead of the game, sitting down for a nice single malt with the Prince and discussing his defences, maybe organising a visit by Isakob to study the bones, we've got ourselves trapped inside a building, right in the heart of Leandre's power, about a five minute trot from his headquarters, with our hope of survival hanging by a thread and being dependent upon known allies of the Lutin Prince.

Okay, *I. I've* got us trapped. Honesty may be the best policy, but honestly? Feeling even more guilty isn't helping me right now.

Maybe try a different tack... 'What about,' I say as I hustle up next to our host, 'if we forget the idea of sanctuary, okay? What about if...'

I search for the right words, the right way to phrase it. 'If we call this neutral ground instead? We... We could give Leandre a call under a flag of parley and have a sit-down meeting, sort all this out.'

It's far from ideal; he has no real reason to listen to us and every reason to make our brains melt and dribble out of our tear ducts, but I'm holding on to what Isaac said. About him being the most reasonable fae he's ever met. If that's the case, surely I, with my dazzling wit and charm, can persuade him as to our innocence.

Okay, the odds are long. But I still fancy them more than I do trying to get into a read-off with the demonic book in the basement.

Mister Tumnus pauses and frowns that specialised severe look that librarians have mastered over the ages. For a moment I assume it's because I'm speaking too loudly. It'd be ironic to get thrown out for such a simple disrespect before we even get to the point where I start being sardonic at everyone in sight. Instead, he points upwards at a sign. It's a picture of a chunky flip-phone straight from the late Noughties inside a red circle, a diagonal line barring across it.

The urluthe shakes its head in disbelief at the very idea of what I've suggested and then once more heads down the winding corridor, the shelves narrowing in as we pass from the proud touristic displays, into the building's bibliophile heart.

I look at Aicha, confused. She tuts and mutters, 'No phones in the library, you fucking idiot. Another plan. Now.'

Oh, right. Except that blows my plan B — which is actually the same shitty plan we originally dismissed, of calling Al-Ruhban up, trying to set some cunning verbal trap that gets him to the library where we can find out exactly which side he's on — out of the water too. If we can't use phones, I'm fresh out of ideas. And of course, I don't doubt that De Montfort is full of them. Probably nearly as much as he's full of himself and full of shit, but every second that goes by allows him the luxury of moments where he knows I'm free, moments he can use to make more twisted, fucked up plans packed full of his own special brand of devious evil, the utter jizzpossum.

Telling Aicha this does not improve her mood. I can see her casting about, looking for a better plan. Through the windows we pass —becoming fewer and fewer as we progress deeper in— we catch glimpses of jetins baring fierce teeth and shaking furious fists at us. Giving them the finger doesn't seem to calm them down either. Makes me feel better though.

What it means is that smashing our way out of the nearest destructible exit: fire door, window, brick wall is only going to lead us smack bang into more trouble. And that's before we get into what the urluthes might do to us for damaging their home. Hell, what may be, for all we know, their temple.

The urluthes are a riddle wrapped up in an enigma, then placed inside the Hellraiser puzzle box. On the one hand, as, at least as far as we can tell, the inspiration behind human imagination and storytelling, there's never been a greater force of good. On the other, if you know exactly how dangerous the power of narrative is when wielded in alternative manners, nobody has ever, *ever* wanted to fuck with the urluthes. Even if they could find them.

I've never seen one before. I don't know anyone who ever has. Not even Isaac, and I don't doubt he's tried his absolute damnedest. If we ever resolve this whole misunderstanding with Leandre, and I confirm the truth in the story about the Lutin Prince persuading the urluthes to act as guardians of the Agrippa, I'm sure he'll be writing beautifully elegant begging letters to the Lord of Paris, asking permission to visit the library post-haste. And there's still no guarantee he'll see one.

Because even when we know the urluthes must be somewhere, when we see the effect of their inspiring touch, they remain unseen. I've no idea how we first found out about them. I've even less idea how Leandre managed to parley with them. All that means is I'm even less keen to fuck with them — or him — than I already was.

I often wonder what they did before books were published. Did they hang around just outside the reach of campfires and fill children's heads with images of the adventures they'd heard, as the storyteller recited the voyage of Odysseus or the tricks of Anansi or the treachery of the Rainbow Serpent? I can only imagine their delight when Guttenberg had his moment of engineering genius. When the written word became widespread and stories perhaps lost something of their communal sharing but gained an intense private aspect. One that offered stimulation, education, and escape to so many when they discovered the magic a book could hold. Oftentimes when they do, when their heads fill with images of flying boats or greedy dragons or boy wizards plucked from misery and given more than they could ever dream of, it's an urluthe that's worked their spell, either over the book or the child themselves.

It's impossible to know because the urluthes don't socialise with other creatures or readily give up their secrets. We don't know how many of them there are or where they come from. There could be millions, billions of them. Considering the inspiration that books still bring to young and old, the worlds they carry them away to every single day, I think it is entirely plausible that there are more of them than humans.

And there's another question related to that, which I try very hard not to let haunt my own dreams, knowing the urluthes exist.

What if, one day, they decide we aren't worthy of their gifts anymore? What if they decide to inspire a different species instead?

I can't help wondering if it was the death of their imagination that finished off the dinosaurs — the loss of their stories and songs and all the inspiration that was carried with them rather than a flaming meteorite from the sky. If we only walk as the lords of the earth because the urluthes allow us to do so.

Our arrival at our destination shakes me from such maudlin and frankly terrifying thoughts. It's a quiet reading room, the sort loaned out to visiting scholars to allow them to study texts too precious to be checked out. The décor's equally muted, simple plain wood panelling, replacing the intricacies worked into all the fixtures we've seen so far. Basic desks arranged in rows are the main motif, each with an individual light source. One can imagine a researcher lost in the thralls of their book pile clicking it on, ready to hunt on through the night. This is still a place of adventure. Just of a different kind.

We're not alone in here. A man sits, another urluthe I assume, although I can't work out what character he's supposed to be. Maybe they don't all take on the guises of fictional beings. Or else, maybe I'm just not as widely read as I think I am. Considering how many books there are in existence, how many come flooding into the world every single day, it's a touch cocky to think I'll recognise every single cultural or literary reference I come across.

This individual is more easy to mistake for human than our Mister Tumnus. No goat legs or horns on him. He's dressed like a dapper fellow from the middle classes might have prior to the Second World War — black coat-tails matched with a waistcoat, a washed-out muted turquoise, and a top hat jaunting off so far to one side of his head that were a breeze to move one of his pale blond locks, it'd surely tumble to the floor. The giveaway that he's not human is his skin. Silvery-grey's not a normal colour unless you've been chugging back mercury; a cure-all that we realised was actually a kill-all a few centuries ago, thankfully.

He has a book spread out in front of him, but he's not reading. Instead, his gaze is transfixed by whatever he can see through the thin slit windows perched up high on the wall to the side of him. Mister Tumnus coughs, clearing his throat, and the character jumps, genuinely startled. He looks across at us with a slightly bashful, entirely bemused expression on his face.

'Oh, hello!' A smile that somehow looks like a question spreads across his face. 'How can I help you?'

Before we can answer, our guide does instead. 'Pierrot, I must be gone. They've requested sanctuary. I leave the decision to you.'

Pierrot, as the seated individual is apparently called, waves a hand vaguely at the urluthe. 'Of course, fine fellow, of course. Leave it to me!'

I turn to say goodbye, to ask who this is, why they are to be considered as neutral arbiter if they're an urluthe as well, but he's already gone. I think he stayed much longer already than he wanted to.

When I look back at Pierrot, he's staring out of the window again, almost seeming oblivious to our presence. I shift back and forth a bit, waiting in case he's just gathering his thoughts before our conversation starts. After a couple of minutes, it's clear he's not; he's lost in them instead.

Never let it be said I'm daunted by a lack of attention. I normally resolve that by blowing something up or setting it on fire. However, as we're in a converted palace full of priceless books and we're asking for sanctuary, I decide just to kick off the conversation instead.

'Hi!' Good God, I'm truly so shit at this, I can make an informal greeting sound awkward. My attempt to sound bright and breezy instead makes me sound like I want to talk to him about my personal murder cult and how much he really, really wants to join it.

It startles him back to focusing on us, at least. 'Oh, yes! Hello!' That same confused smile is on his face. His eyebrows are both bunched and raised at the same time, as though he's trying to force himself to see us while simultaneously doubting we are here. It's an impressively paradoxical effect.

I have to admit, I sort of expect him to take up the conversation from here, but he just looks at me with a polite sort of bafflement.

Okay, let's go for super polite. Effusively so. I can kiss arse if it gets us out of here so we can reach Leandre. Get to those goddamn bones before Demon Fart comes up with some genius stroke to lay his grubby mitts on them instead. 'Let me kick off by saying thank you to you and all the urluthes for...'

He startles as if I shocked him with a cattle prod, and I get the feeling he phased out again despite looking straight at us. 'Sorry, I might have misheard there. Did you say you think I'm an urluthe?'

He chuckles when I nod. 'Oh no, sad to say. I'm not one of them.' A wistful look travels to his eyes. 'I'd dearly love to be. Marvellous existence, marvellous.' He sighs, and I watch his gaze drift... drift... drift away towards the ceiling. Annnnnd he's gone.

There's a saying in French that someone is "in the moon", meaning their head is in the clouds. This chap's not just in the moon; he's created an Airbnb there, with guided tours of the moon's core. I resist the urge to snap my fingers. Primarily because it'd be rude, and I don't actually want to end up either scrapping with a crew of miniature Schwarzenegger-style lutins or being put next on the Agrippa's TBR list. I settle for clearing my throat. Loudly and pointedly.

Pierrot's attention snaps back, and he smiles apologetically. 'I'm terribly sorry. What were we saying?'

'You were telling us what you are if you're not an urluthe.'

Pierrot smiles again, although he looks as though he's not entirely sure he knows what he's smiling about. Or even if it is actually a smile. He only looks middle-aged, and he certainly doesn't appear human, but I can't help wondering if early-onset dementia can affect magical beings. It certainly seems possible based on the evidence at hand.

'Yes,' he says, and I can see it's taking an actual conscious effort of will to keep talking, to stay concentrated on holding a conversation. 'I'm not an urluthe, no, dear me, not at all. I'm a lorialet. Pierrot of the Moon, as they call me.'

I smile and introduce us by name, practically on fire with curiosity now. Why? I have literally never even heard of a lorialet.

'What's a lorialet?' I can hear the barely controlled frustration in Aicha's voice. Getting direct to the heart of the matter is close to a religion to her. Failing that, getting direct to the heart. With a rusty spoon.

Pierrot blinks owlishly. 'Oh, right, yes. Sorry. We're a rare breed. I suppose you might call us moon-touched. Certainly, that's how Moliere thought of me. The truth is, we aren't. Well we are, actually, but that's not the point.' The point seems to be something Pierrot takes a long time talking around and rarely actually getting to. 'More than anything though, we're urluthe-touched.'

Well, that's a huge amount of information to digest simultaneously. I start working through it bit by bit. The part about Moliere, France's equivalent to Shakespeare, gets my gears turning, thinking back to watching his firebrand —decidedly risqué by the standards of the time— theatre pieces when they came out. Then what that led to.

I click my fingers, though it's an instinctive, sympathetic action to my mind clicking onto the bit of information I'm searching for. 'The play "Dom Juan"! You're Pierrot the Clown.'

Oops. It has been suggested to me on more than one occasion that I should sometimes engage my brain fully before speaking. That perhaps just blurting out whatever is running through my head is not always the best way to interact with other people. Seeing Pierrot wince like I slapped him across the face when I mentioned Dom Juan and then again like I kicked him straight in the family jewels with the 'Clown' denominative says that perhaps I should have held onto that thought for a moment rather than just feeding it straight into my voice box.

Aicha looks blank at the Moliere reference (where Pierrot is a simple peasant whose fiancé gets stolen by the lecherous Dom Juan) but gets the second one. 'The Commedia dell'arte?'

Pierrot sighs dejectedly, a sigh that carries with it the weight of centuries of being wronged. 'Indeed, although neither are the most flattering portrayals of me... For Moliere, a dreamer must be a lover, and anyone as easily, umm....'

I can see him searching for the word. Initially, at least. Then it's almost like I can watch him progress from that to another thought and then another, and he's getting further and further away from us and more and more lost in his own head. There's no time for him to go meandering, though. Not with the mind-and-soul-eating threat of the Agrippa hanging over us on one hand, and the constant threat of De Montfort's fuckeries on the other. I decide to lend a hand. 'Easily distracted?'

He bangs his hand on the table, half in agreement and half as a reflex action at snapping back to the matter at hand. 'Quite. Yes, for him, anyone as easily distracted is a victim in the making, and what better victim than at love?'

I can sympathise. It's easy to get stereotyped. 'So neither Charlotte nor Columbina existed then?' Charlotte was the woman stolen by Dom Juan. Columbina — his wife seduced away by Harlequin in the commedias.

He sighs again, a deep, powerful sigh that suggests he's sighed in just such a way over just such a subject many, many times. 'No, they both existed. I made the mistake of telling my story to Moliere. He told them onwards, both when writing and when in his cups, and lo, a mooncalf I am made into.'

Ouch. Now it's my turn to wince for him. We've all had disastrous relationships — see my recent woes and imprisonment as a prime example. We don't all get said disasters immortalised in the two most dominant forms of Parisian theatre of the seventeenth century, theatre that has remained ingrained in the culture. It's basically like having photos of your hideous break-up waved in your face over and over by random members of the public. Forever. Grim.

I want to get onto the other part of what he said though. Firstly, because understanding it might just keep us from getting fed to a man-eating book, but secondly because my natural inquisitive bent is absolutely desperate to learn anything about our mysterious and enigmatic hosts. Also, fascinating though his history is, I don't think it's going to get us out of here and back on our way towards securing that rib cage.

I suspect he's not going to object to a change of subject. 'You said that the lorialet were urluthe-touched?'

'Do we need to break out the anatomically correct doll so he can show us where the urluthe touched him?' Aicha's voice is low enough that it only carries to my ears, and I suppress the snigger by choking on my own breathing. Luckily, Pierrot is entirely oblivious. To most things in life, I suspect.

'Indeed. Wonderful, wondrous even, creatures, the urluthes. Without them, I wonder if we would even exist. Whether when we still huddled in the backs of caves, hiding from things with quicker legs and sharper teeth than us, whether it wasn't them who got us telling stories to make sense of death and the dark. The secret ingredient in human evolution, if you will. The flint that sparked our imagination, which gave us our creativity too. Imagine if, instead of us, they'd given that gift to, I don't know, the giraffes or something. Just imagine...'

Silence. Stretching silence that tells me his last few words aren't just a turn of phrase. Nope, his eyes are glazed over, and I have no doubt he's imagining exactly that. The whole of human history but rewritten with giraffes. Like *Planet of the Apes* but with more reach.

I wave my hand in front of his face, and he starts, back with us once again. 'Yes, well, quite.' He harrumphs, clearly embarrassed. 'One to consider later.' He sighs, and his gaze creeps back to the window, but he forces himself to meet my eyes. 'The thing is, I don't just consider them. I *see* them. All my thoughts, all my dreams. All the things I read or imagine. I watch them play out for my entertainment.'

Pierrot rubs at his forehead, kneading worry lines that are probably more puzzlement lines for him each time he's pulled back to reality. 'You see, the urluthes give us such a gift, such a blessing. It's their touch that allows a child to escape into their dreams, to build whole worlds and universes in their heads so vivid they can touch them. They give us freedom, inspiration. It fades as we age, but those fleeting ghostlike flashes of the memory linger like will-o'-the-wisps to light our footsteps through our lifetimes. Well...' He shares that bashful smile again. 'It fades for most of us.'

I can see where he's going with this. 'It never faded for you, did it?'

He shakes his head. 'No. The urluthes tell me that their magic didn't just flow through me and dissipate as it normally does. Instead, it stayed, swirling, building, stronger and stronger. I tried to live a normal life — to take over the bit of land my parents owned and till the soil, take a wife. But it's hard to work from dawn until dusk when, just beyond the plough, you can see Troy falling, the walls ablaze as Helen weeps. And when you spend your evenings watching Sir Roland adventuring, his trusty sword Durendal by his side, well...perhaps you don't pay your wife the attention you should. Perhaps she's wooed away.' I can see a pain in his eyes. 'Perhaps a second one too. Love...' He sighs. 'It's the most inspirational of all the stories. I am an incurable romantic, ma'am, but I cannot give myself truly when I am far too lost.'

He looks desperately sad, his silver skin greying so that he looks wan, wearied by the thought. Doesn't seem like a good mood to be in when deciding our fate. Rushing his story doesn't seem like the best idea either though. I decide to try to move him onto what might, hopefully, be happier memories. 'So how did you end up here?'

He brightens up at this. 'As time went on, I found I no longer needed to eat nor sleep, which was luck, really, because I kept forgetting to do both. My skin changed though, marked me out, and I risked wandering into the path of those whose inquisitiveness bent more turned towards red-hot pokers and thumbscrews.'

I can't say he's wrong. If the Inquisition had got their hands on him, I don't doubt he'd have been sent to the pyre or the gallows. 'What happened?'

'The urluthes took me in.' Again, that half-apologetic expression fills his face. 'I can't tell you where, before here, but once Leandre gifted them this place, I took up residence. They give me the title of chief librarian. An honour, especially for one like me, but honestly? Chief dreamer would be more truthful. I do little but sit in this room and read and voyage away where my mind's eye takes me.'

Compared to the madness that is my life, constantly fighting and dying, it sounds idyllic. In fact, I make a mental note not to mention it to Isaac. He'd be here in a heartbeat, trying to sell his soul to the urluthes to become a lorialet.

Then he smiles warmly. 'Now, enough of me. What about you? Why are you here and asking for sanctuary?'

My first instinct is to skip to the end. Just tell him the bare bones. The Good God knows I just want sanctuary long enough for the jetins to leave, then to get out of here and back on the hunt. Back to being the predator rather than the prey, chasing that bastard Demon Fart to ground. And then tearing his fucking throat out.

But I pause as I draw breath and look at the man in front of me. The man so consumed by stories he lost his connection to the so-called "real" world. Who lives in the imagination. A man in whose hands our fate rests, and who is so wrapped up in all the tales ever told, he can hardly focus on us for longer than a moment at a time. And we really need to keep his attention.

I exchange a glance with Aicha, see the same thought written in her eyes. So we tell him. Enough, at least. We tell him of De Montfort and the bones. Of our coming to Paris to warn Leandre, to make sure the rib cage is secure while we hunt the rest. Of Scarbo's double-cross and our need to find Al-Ruhban, to see if he too is involved or an innocent party.

'From here?' I finish up, feeling the need for an enormous glass of water, followed by an even bigger glass of whisky. I'm parched. Aicha let me do the heavy lifting storywise, only interrupting to correct or insult me. 'Ideally, we'll get to an unsuspecting Al-Ruhban. Confirm his betrayal or his innocence. Get ourselves outside of Paris and the immediate threat contained in it. Then find a way to contact Leandre and persuade him of our innocence. At least put him on guard as to the risk posed by De Montfort to the rib cage.'

Pierrot has been leaning forward, his fingers steepled, his eyes wide and shining, devouring the tale. 'Fascinating!' He's exuberant now, as if energised by the twists and turns of our journey to get here. As I watch his eyes lose focus again, I can feel there's something different this time. I glance across at Aicha, and she gives me a slight nod. She sees it too. He's not just disappeared off into a flight of fancy. At a guess? He's talking through our situation with the urluthes through some sort of psychic connection.

As he's basically discussing us with the ethereal beings who hold the key to our survival, I don't disturb him. I don't doubt that if the urluthes wish it so, we'll be banished from this building in a heartbeat, finding ourselves back outside with a gang of bloodthirsty jetins for company or being fed to a man-eating book. It's a nerve-wracking wait.

It's easy to see when Pierrot rejoins us. He blinks, and his focus is back on us, his smile as gentle, albeit slightly bewildered, as ever. 'Well,' he says and stands up. He paces the room, his hands behind his back. There's a strange rolling gait to his walk, as if we are on a boat with a gentle tide making us bob up and down. Perhaps for him, in his waking dreamworld, there is.

He looks back at us. 'The urluthe greatly enjoyed your story, greatly so.' He nods fervently, still walking back and forth. 'I've passed my verdict, and they agree. They are prepared to help you. Or rather, they are prepared for me to help you.'

He stops pacing, and a serious look replaces that uncertain smile. 'Of course, there is a cost to it.'

Of course there is. Just as the Mother told me over and over.

There's always a price to pay.

Chapter Thirty-One
PARIS, 8 JUNE, PRESENT DAY
Trying to avoid telling Pierrot that "lorialet" sounds like an Irish truck rental company.

Now we're getting into the nitty-gritty. 'Right, so what do they want? A temple built in their honour? A fattened calf? My first-born? 'Cos I've got to warn you, you really don't want him.' Then I remember that even the body De Montfort wears isn't really my child, and a strange mixture of guilt and rage rumbles up in my stomach, like I might vomit up a shame demon to tear me and De Montfort to pieces. Rage for what he did to Susane, for all the things he did. Guilt because it's a relief that it's not my child he wears, a feeling I can't help even though it is awful, a dark part of my psyche I wish didn't exist.

Pierrot doesn't seem to witness the war of emotions going on behind my expression, thankfully. No, he's loading up to drop his own bombshell on us. 'The terms for their help are very simple. When this whole *adventure*' —he says the word so wistfully that I wonder if I haven't actually got the better end of the deal, living my adventures rather than being lost in dreams of them— 'is done, the urluthes want you to write it all down for them. They want you to write them a book.'

My stomach sinks. Write it down? A book? 'Do I look like a masochist?' That's what authors are, after all — torturing themselves with their attempts to twist tales out of thin air, poor shades of the urluthe-given inspiration that apparently makes our species what it is today. As for "a book"? Jeez. With everything I'd need to get down, we'd be at more than a trilogy, at least. Probably a pentalogy. I shudder at the very thought.

Aicha's grinning like the fucking Cheshire Cat, of course. 'Perfect, *saabi*. You can wear a beret and smoke a pipe. It's just the excuse you need to be even more pretentious than you already are.'

I know how to answer that. 'You realise I'll have to tell your story too?'

Her look doesn't change. Damn it. 'Of course. You know I'm going to read the first draft and force-feed you your limbs one by one if you don't present me in a flattering light?'

She always has a better answer than me. There's a reason she's the smart one. And the violent one. And the scary one. I'm actually pretty redundant, truth be told. I wonder if I should just give up taking a lead role and become her personal chronicler instead.

Pierrot smiles, understanding in his sad eyes. 'It's okay. You don't ever have to publish it. Just send a copy to the urluthes. A private addition to the stories they hold. I might have a peek, but that's about it.'

Oh good. Only Pierrot and an uncountable number of the very species that endowed us with stories themselves will get to read what I write. That's no pressure at all then.

Thing is, I'm far from confident that this is ever going to end — or rather, that it'll end when I die the ultimate death. That's sort of the whole point of life, isn't it? We all feel like we're the hero, whether tragic, comic, or epic. Or all three, in my case. The epic tragedy of a clown. An appropriate image considering our current company. Doesn't matter who you are, our ego demands that we must be the star of the show. Thing is, no one gave life the memo, so when we make our last bows, with no encore possible, the show just goes on. Turns out we're all just bit players, and only Death is a recurring guest star.

That being the case, I think I can accept the offer. I seriously doubt I'm going to get a chance to sit down and write a whole series of books before I kick the bucket. Who could ever find the time to do that? So I agree. There's a shaking of hands, and I suddenly realise I've been so hung up on the idea of having to jot my story down that I don't actually know what help they're agreeing to give.

'So you'll grant us sanctuary, maybe pursuade the jetins to fuck right off?' It might be a bit of a case of shutting the barn doors after the horse has bolted, but I'd like to know how much temporary safety I've actually gained us with that handshake.

'Oh no!' Pierrot brightens as my heart sinks. We're not even getting sanctuary? After all that?

He continues. 'You'll get much more than that. I'm going to get you to Al-Ruhban.'

'How?'

'By the moon-roads, of course.'

Damn it. 'So we have to wait until night-time then?' I can't quite keep the moroseness from my tone. It makes me feel like a petulant child. We only hoped for sanctuary until either Leandre could talk to us directly or the jetins were told to go by the urluthes, so a direct path to Al-Ruhban is beyond my wildest expectations. Now that we know it exists though, I want it to be *now*, like Veruca Salt stamping her foot for a golden goose.

Pierrot looks out of the window, and there's a wistfulness there even stronger than his normal expression. 'Oh, no,' he says, shaking his head softly, those bone-bleached curls bouncing across his eyes. If he were anyone else, they'd be annoying him, but I'm not entirely sure he even sees them. 'The world is always lit by moonlight for me.'

He stretches out a hand to each of us, and Good God damn it if I don't feel like Wendy getting whisked away out of my room by Peter Pan. I suppose in some ways that's exactly what Pierrot is. The boy who never grew up. The one who never lost his sense of childlike wonder and whimsy. And the only price he had to pay for that was the rest of his life.

We both take his hand without hesitation, and for a moment, I see what he sees. The world ripples outwards from the empty air like the line on an Etch A Sketch. Everything is highlighted in a silvery glow, but I can see more, so much more. I see hobbits and hobgoblins, moomins and misunderstood monsters, adventures I've ridden shotgun on a million times when I've opened a book's pages, all mapped out for me to see better than any Hollywood director could ever hope to capture. This is the real Silver Screen, moonlight-made moving images that fill my heart with an inexplicable yearning. I can feel the tears forming at the corners of my eyes, and for the life of me, I can't say why. There are times when language fails. Perhaps that's why it's so precious.

And over it all, the hoary luminescence of a daytime moon streams through the window — Diana hunting down Helios on his own turf, seizing dominance. It pours through the opening, and as I watch, it seems to pool at the feet of Pierrot like a quicksilver puddle. I wonder if it's as likely to drive you mad. Maybe all that innocence is just a form of insanity. I don't mind. It's all right. We're all mad here.

The rakish clown steps forward, and his feet find solid ground where my eyes tell me there is nothing but moonlight. In the middle of the day.

Apparently, one impossible thing isn't enough to convince them of the viability of another because my brain's still in solid denial even as he walks up and out, through the unfeasibly narrow window, drawing us up behind him.

We walk across a Paris evening-sky-turned-witching-hour by a magic older, perhaps, than humanity itself. The skyline is picked out like a storm-cloud, framed by the sun it shrouds, the lining we all hold on to when life's thunder rumbles. We're walking on air, and I'll be damned if I don't feel like the kid in *The Snowman*, seeing a world slumbering underneath us even though it's awake.

It's more than gorgeous. It's indescribable. It's as if Michelangelo possessed a spider and set out to weave his greatest ever masterpiece out of moonbeams. Paris, picked out in silver thread provided by Ariadne herself. A single line drawing made of molten white gold to design the most famous city vista in the world, a place of dreams highlighted by the fantastic, more real in this marvellous ethereality than it could ever be when faced with truths of faults and failings. I've lived for centuries, and this is still something else, something beyond the miracles and marvels I've seen across my existence. It's a moment of pure, distilled beauty, and damn, I owe Pierrot and the urluthes for this.

Trust me. Travelling by moonlight is the only way to travel.

CHAPTER THIRTY-TWO

PARIS, 8 JUNE, PRESENT DAY

Drinking in sights drenched in molten moonlight. This is one memory I'll revisit many times.

We pass straight over the top of Sacre-Coeur. It's a view of Paris I once would have considered impossible to beat, but, well — Mike Oldfield knew what he was talking about. The moonlight shadows are more than just a pathway. They're carrying us to where we need to go.

It's over too quickly. Not much past Montmartre, we're already descending. Coming down at a rate of knots. Pierrot is still just walking through the air, following the bridge built of lunar radiance, for all the world looking like he's just out for a midnight stroll. Through the air. In the late afternoon. It's totally mad, but a madness that is brilliant as well — an insanity I can embrace and just enjoy as opposed to most of the lunatic things life throws at me and just expects me to soak up.

As I step off the lightbeams, I stumble, finding the sense of solidity under my feet utterly off-putting after our Neverland moonwalk. Aicha dismounts with considerably more grace, of course, not even breaking stride. We each let go of his hands, and suddenly, we're back in the brightness of a June early evening. The sun struts, asserting his dominance, refusing to acknowledge he was even temporarily overshadowed by his night-time counterpoint.

'Tripping the light fantastic, *saabi?*' she says, giving me a nudge in the ribs with her elbow that comes dangerously close to putting me on my arse.

I'm too busy trying not to show my disappointment at being grounded. It's not the first time I've flown, whether mechanically or magically, but walking the lunar pathways is something else entirely. I look at Pierrot with newfound respect. Forget about Isaac. I'm giving serious thought to converting to the ways of the lorialet myself if that's one of the perks.

'Thank you so much.' I feel pretty safe expressing my gratitude. He was human once, and I can't see the fae rules — that thanking them lays you in contractual debt — applying to him. And I am genuinely grateful. I don't know how long I'll end up living — probably not much longer the way things have been going recently — but even if my lifespan's measured in millennia rather than centuries, that's a memory I won't need my mind palace to hold on to.

The lorialet tips his hat with a touch to the brim, but his eyes are already drifting off, and I can feel he wants to get away. No doubt the silver is calling him, the road back to the library, to get lost in a thousand worlds all over again. Moon-touched, indeed. The real origin of the word "lunatic" — lunar-tic, moon madness. But if what Pierrot has is madness, who would wish to be sane? A little more of his brand of crazy might make the world a gentler, more magical place without the need for *talent* or the power struggles that come with it.

We've come to ground on a nondescript road, definitely outside Paris proper. There's the odd building from the eighteenth or nineteenth century, but mostly it's late twentieth — plenty of tower blocks or their little cousins, the six- or seven-storey brick houses converted into flats. We're outside a nondescript white residence, unusual for having just a single buzzer. Of course, we're only just outside the ring-road, so a small house still means big money.

By the fact Aicha's currently burning holes in the wood with her glare, I guess this is the place. I turn back to Pierrot...but he's already gone. All that's left is a strange ache in my chest — that feeling when you finish a series and have to say goodbye to all those friends you made along the way. It's no wonder the lorialet looked melancholic. As frustrating as keeping him concentrated on the matter at hand was, I hope our paths cross again someday. Not least because I want to cadge another sky-stroll out of him if possible.

Aicha isn't wasting time. She's not just staring burning destruction at the door. Nope. She's assessing the warding as well to make sure it's not us who will suffer burning destruction when we go through. Whatever she sees obviously isn't cause for concern because she rears her foot back, and without a word, she launches it at the lock. The wood splinters. So do the three metal locks, including the deadbolt holding it in place. And the plank of wood securing it from the inside. And the hinges and half the plaster of the wall, plus a decent section of the door frame as the whole thing comes clean off and smashes into the wall opposite, about six metres back. Apparently, Aicha wants to make a statement. I'm entirely fine with that.

Aicha strides in. 'Knock, knock, motherfucker,' she yells and man, it's like Omar coming knocking at the stash houses, sawn-off shotgun under his raincoat. Al-Ruhban better not be involved in this, for his own sake. You come at the queen? You best not miss.

As the dust settles down, I see the man himself standing in a nearby doorway. He's white as a sheet, and I don't think that's solely because of the plaster he's picking out of his hair.

'*Lalla? Saabi?* What are you doing here? I thought you were with Leandre? And why are you destroying my front door?' His frown grows deeper
by the minute. 'This is most improper, invading my personal space like
this.'

I'm honestly surprised that Aicha was able to just kick the door in like
that. If you tried that at my house, you'd end up losing your foot. Either
Al-Ruhban is massively lackadaisical in his protective wards, or they're not
possible for a half-djinn. Or Aicha has another secret trick up her sleeve
that nullifies his ones in particular. I wonder if he's invited her in before, if
that's what has allowed her to get around whatever protections he put up.
They don't seem to try to fry me as I step over the threshold, so obliterating
the door clearly erased any that were there in the first place.

Aicha crosses the distance to him quick enough to make The Flash
whistle in appreciation. He's up by his throat against what's left of the wall
before he even realises it, her blade pressed to his throat.

'Try to phase' —she bangs him slightly against the wall in rhythm with
each syllable to really drive the point home— 'and I'll make living just a
phase you were going through. Am I clear?'

If I thought he was pale before, now he makes chalk look like it's been
hitting the tanning booth twice a week on the regular. 'Understood,' he
manages to stutter out. It's never easy to talk when you feel you're going
to open your own jugular if you so much as swallow.

'Good. Now. Convince me not to kill you. Quickly.' The monotone
menace in Aicha's voice is enough to convince anyone of the seriousness
of her deadly intent. The knife only underlines it.

'What? Why would you want to kill me?' His eyes roam over to me,
pleading. '*Saabi*, you know me...'

I hold up a hand to interrupt. 'Nope. Going to have to do better than
that. Recent events have involved people I mourned for centuries popping

up with the express intent of killing me or fucking me over, people who I loved with every inch of my soul. "Dude I once went on a jolly, chasing Nazi fuckwits around Saint-Ouen for twenty-four hours with" doesn't even come close to that category.' My eyes narrow. I'm nowhere near as bedwettingly terrifying as Aicha, but I'm still no slouch at intimidation. 'Try harder.'

Honestly, I'm pretty convinced Al-Ruhban doesn't know anything, but I'm not going to ease up just in case he's Pinocchio without the nose job. He's giving Pierrot a run for his money in the "entirely baffled" stakes right now though, and he's a Hollywood-grade leading man if he's faking that.

'Wait, please. I genuinely don't know what's going on.' I believe him. For starters, he didn't attack us the moment we blew in through his front door. You have to have cojones the size of the Elgin Marbles to brazen your way out after a double-cross like we've been through. He's never come across that way. Either he's running the longest of long cons — which, based on some of the long cons we're still currently reeling from running back centuries, isn't impossible — or he's innocent.

'Run us through what you think's been happening.' Aicha's voice is grating, like she's pushing the words out through a garlic press. I guess her throat's tight with the thought that a friend might have betrayed her, that she might have to kill him as retribution. Welcome to my world, *laguna*.

'I — I called Scarbo as I told you. He called me back yesterday evening, said he'd taken you straight to Leandre and that you were dealing with stuff together. Said he'd bring you here to see me once you completed your business with the Prince and to wait right here.'

'And you didn't listen to the radio at any point in the last twenty-four hours?' Looks like Aicha still needs more convincing than I do. The disbelief in her tone is evident. It's a fair point though. One I didn't think of.

'The radio... You mean the Prince's station?' He's not looking any less baffled. 'No. Why would I? I've not been out travelling, and you made it clear your meeting with Leandre was hush-hush. They were hardly going to be talking about you on the radio, were they!' He scoffs, then stops when he sees our faces. 'Were they?'

'Last question.' Aicha's tone is still ice cold. It'd give the Winter Court a run for its money in sub-zero. 'What have you been doing since we last spoke?'

Al-Ruhban's eyes flick to the doorway he came from. I peer through to see a huge TV set and recliner chair facing it. On the TV, a Persian man dressed in Ottoman Empire era clothing is discussing something in Turkish with a glamorous woman in harem garbs. There're a couple of empty pizza boxes and a discarded Ben & Jerry's ice-cream tub. It takes me a minute, but then I clock it. It's *Magnificent Century*, a hugely popular TV series in the Persian and Arabic world from 2011 about the longest ruling Ottoman Sultan, Suleiman The Magnificent.

'Well, either he was super relaxed about our set-up running perfectly according to plan despite the fact it hasn't, or he's innocent,' I tell Aicha, whose eyes don't leave the half-djinn she has pinned to the wall.

I'm convinced. No one is that casual.

Al-Ruhban's spent the last twenty-four hours binging his favourite soap opera.

Aicha releases her grip, though I notice her knife doesn't go back in its sheath. I see something else though too. Just for a moment, a flash of sheer, utter relief flickers across her, only for a micro-second before locking down into its normal impassive state. I wonder if Al-Ruhban will ever realise just how close she came to killing him or how glad she is that she didn't need to.

Of course, had it been necessary, I would've done everything possible to ensure I dealt with the matter instead. I don't think she'd have let me though. Honour matters to Aicha Kandicha. She takes it deadly serious. Emphasis on the deadly.

We go through to a neat, if plain, little kitchen. There's enough space for a small round table. We perch around while he sorts us out with some food and drink. Hospitality's important in Arabic culture, and guests need to be fed even if they've just exploded half your façade. I pick a chair that lets me keep an eye on him. Not getting poisoned is just as important to me as hospitality is to him. I'm mostly convinced he didn't set us up, but I'm not about to entirely lower my guard. Susane showed me how well that tends to work out for me.

We briefly recap our misadventures since arriving in the Gare Du Nord, leaving out some details — the scope of our agreement with La Guillaneu and the urluthes just in case. The skin tightens around his face as he fries up a load of peppers and onions. He's not happy. Rightly so. His "help" nearly cost us dearly.

By the time we finish, he's cracked some eggs into the shakshuka and is now carving slices of crusty bread. He already has a big pot of mint tea on the go, and Good God, it all smells so damn good, I'd almost forgive him even if he did set us up. The sweet, hot tea sets off against the rich, smoky tomato flavours of the shakshuka, and for a while, I'm too busy devouring it all to worry about anything else. Fleeing for your life is hungry work. I deserve the calories.

'I owe you both a debt. My misjudging of Scarbo's character is a burden to my conscience.' Sorrow is clear in Al-Ruhban's face. He obviously holds himself far more responsible than we do.

'I meant to ask — how did that happen? I mean, didn't you ever hear him *speak*?' I can't quite keep the incredulity out of my voice. 'Nobody who murders metric verse like that can possibly be anything but a villain.'

Al-Ruhban sighs. 'I felt sorry for him. It is a terrible curse to carry, to be forced to speak like that and to have no sense of rhythm or poetical finesse.'

He has a big heart, old Al-Ruhban. I can't imagine many people tolerate Scarbo's company for long. I certainly couldn't have even if he wasn't a backstabbing, treacherous snake.

There are other, more pressing matters at hand though. 'So what now?'

Al-Ruhban looks grave, tugging at his earlobe absent-mindedly, as if trying to jump-start his brain into action. 'Now we need to work out a way to contact Leandre, to get you a sit-down with him. Somehow. I cannot imagine a way it's possible, with his messengers compromised and the whole of Paris hunting after you. Yet, we'll work out a way; we must.'

'Love the idea, great blue-sky thinking. Let's circle back round to that though, okay, *kimosabe*? First, I want to drill down into why you're in the middle of a pow-wow with entities who are looking to activate a hostile takeover, hmm?'

We spin around. In the far corner — the one farthest away from the door — stands what, on first glance, looks like a daoine sidhe. Stunningly handsome but with a more courtly countenance than the wild ways of the Summer Court and with more warmth to his regard than the frozen wastes of Winter. He's dressed in a neat-fitting business suit, clearly individually tailored, with a pale-pink silk shirt worth more than my entire wardrobe casually worn under the jacket. His jaunty grey felt cap with two bright red and blue feathers poking out of the side should totally clash with the high-level exec wear but somehow doesn't. His eyes match the colour of his hat, light grey and not looking at all amused.

He also did something that should have been entirely impossible. Not getting past me without me noticing, though that definitely falls into the category of inconceivable. He's sneaked past a *highly alert, high-strung Aicha*. I didn't think even Solid Snake hiding in a cardboard box could manage that.

In fact, there's only one creature I've ever heard of who is supposedly capable of such a thing. Who can pass invisibly across any ward or barrier, travelling unlimited distances instantly — a result of his humanity burning away in the crucible of inconceivable magics, making him more and less than what he was before. A thing of myth, of inconceivable power but no longer human.

A creature now standing mere metres away from me. Who put a death warrant on our heads only a few hours ago.

Leandre. The Lutin Prince himself.

Chapter Thirty-Three

PARIS, 8 JUNE, PRESENT DAY

There's a reason Leandre uses magic to get into locked private properties without the proprietors realising. It's so he doesn't get shot for Lutin.

Aicha's up and armed in a second, and I'm not far behind her. Al-Ruhban's left gawping, his head swinging from us to his prince, back and forth like a goldfish watching a tennis game. Leandre doesn't look even slightly bothered about two hyper-powerful Talented pulling swords on him, which means he's either supremely confident in his ability to swat us like proverbial flies if we attack him, or he knows something we don't. Neither option fills me with joy.

He waves a lazy hand, indicating we should sit down. 'Okay, let's just stick a pin in that aggressive manoeuvring, okay? I'm not here to boil the ocean, yours or mine. I'm looking for some feedback on the optics. Honestly, all the insider info I've been getting is enough to make the markets jumpy, so I thought to myself, "Leandre, take this offline." Get to the heart of the matter, you know?'

I'm not entirely sure what he's trying to say, but I think he's suggesting we all calm down and talk things through. He doesn't seem to be about to try to melt our brains yet, so that's a good start. I raise a half-eyebrow at Aicha and get a headshake back. Problem is, I'm not sure if she's as confused by the business speak as I am or if she's saying she's not prepared to stand down. Possibly both.

'So.' Leandre spreads his hands wide, apparently unbothered by our remaining standing with our weapons drawn. 'What brings you to my little kingdom? And why am I hearing off the feedback loop that you're looking to relocate my crown onto your own heads?'

'Look, it's not that simple,' I start, but Aicha interrupts.

'Because Scarbo's a twat.'

I think that over for a moment. 'Okay, it is that simple, and Aicha's quite right. We came here to warn you someone's after the rib cage we helped Al-Ruhban get as a present for you a few decades ago. Because of the lockdown...'

Leandre interrupts this time. 'Ah, ah. I prefer the term geo-localised home working.'

I bet you do. There's no way I'm saying that though. 'Anyhow, he couldn't get to us, so he asked Scarbo to meet us and escort us here. Instead, he tried to lock us up —'

'Because he's a twat. Or a goal-alignment-misfunctioning, non-team player if you prefer.'

'Yes, thanks, Aicha; let's stick with "twat", shall we?' I waggle my eyebrows at her furiously to suggest that perhaps mocking the cranium-explodingly powerful ruler of Paris is perhaps not the best move. I probably just look like Gandalf after he's smoked way too much pipe-weed instead. 'Anyhow, he did a shitty job, although it took us a night to get free. Then we heard the all-points bulletin out for us, so we got here as quick as possible to find out if Al-Ruhban had been in on the grift or if he was just a shit judge of character. The latter, as it turns out.'

Leandre nods thoughtfully throughout all of this, his face super serious, trying to project that he's actively listening. 'Yes, I see. Gotcha. Goal-alignment-misfunctioning, non-team player, that's the new lingo, is it?' His head nods continue as he digests this. 'Roger, roger. That's locked and loaded in the old grey matter, if you know what I mean? Anyhow, sounds like you've been giving 110% the whole way round, real rockstar KPIs since you got here, and let me just say' —he presses his hands together and waggles them back and forth in a prayer-like movement— '*mea culpa* for ringing the opening bell on your stock devaluation, okay? My bad, there. But Scarbo's always been one of my top guys, a real closer, y'know? Still, every rising star has to come down to earth, I guess.' He sighs, tutting as though he's watching ticker tapes tell him that the universe is imploding, and it's absolutely wrecking the market value of his stocks and shares.

I have no idea what to make of this prince. On the one hand, you don't get to hold the capital city of France by being a buffoon, so I know, like categorically, one hundred percent knowledge in my heart of hearts, that this has to be an act. On the other, he genuinely seems to think he's Jordan Belfort on Wall Street in the 1980s. Then I remember De Montfort, the persona he created when playing my son, the carefree fop to disguise a core of steel and a heart full of hate. I wonder what else Leandre is hiding.

'What about the rib cage?' Aicha isn't letting his weird mannerisms —and I say that as someone who had to deal with Franc *and* Lou Carcoilh on the regular— derail her.

'Ah! Yes, champion. Good call.' He clicks his fingers at her. It's like the gun fingers we occasionally shoot but unironically. That's a gun finger misfire, in my opinion. Totally blows up in your face. 'Don't need to double-click on that. I have a high-energy, low-risk synergistic safe-option stock plan that keeps that away from any attempt to short me. Knew there were challenging headwinds on the horizon, regardless of our blue sky thinking. That's why I imposed a temporary non-relocation employee restriction across the whole business strata. The ribs are locked up tighter than Fort Knox. Only people who can get in and out are me and my lieutenants.'

I heave a sigh of relief. From what I can understand Leandre had the foresight — magical or mental — to know something bad was coming, which is why Paris was in lockdown. De Montfort wasn't banking on someone as well-prepared as the Lutin Prince. 'So your messengers can't get in? Scarbo can't get access? Thank fuck for that.'

I watch the change come over Leandre's face. Those grey eyes become chips of granite, and its emotionless state could give Aicha's resting stitch face (as in "talk to me and I'll give you something needing stitching up") a run for its money. Now we see just the tiniest glimpse of the Prince of Paris, and I'm glad I don't need the toilet at this precise moment. It makes bladder control a damn sight easier.

'Let's just put a pin in that for a mo, okay? BRB.' And like that, he's gone.

It's weird, not like any form of magical teleportation I've ever seen. No tearing open a portal across space and time, no dramatic clouds of smoke, no wobbly lines and accompanying teleporter noises. Just one moment he's there; the next he's not. And that, again, I suspect, is the real Prince. That he talks like a business bro to keep people thinking he's a fool, a liability. But that when he acts, it's instantaneous, precise, and, if you're in his way, almost certainly fatal.

And once, I might have believed that enough. I might have thought that enough to foil the plots and plans of any sneaky shit suicidal enough to try and steal off the ruler of Paris.

But this isn't just any sneaky shit. This is the fucker who got Jakob locked up in a skull for centuries. Who trapped me in a feedback loop of unending miserable death that would have broken my mind if Aicha hadn't saved me. Who slaughtered my wife and stole her unborn child without a second thought.

My heart is hammering away in my chest and my mouth is Sahara levels of dry, waiting for him to come back. Because I'm terrified that even Leandre himself might be no match for the sheer unbridled ruthless cunning of that walking stain on humanity's soul, Simon De Montfort.

He pops back a moment later, still with zero notification or fanfare, just one minute empty space, the next filled with Lutin Prince. His demeanour has not improved. In fact, he has a face like thunder...if thunder just discovered that its whole crypto portfolio has been wiped out. And I'm only just holding back. From shaking him and screaming at him to tell me the rib cage is still there. That De Montfort hasn't taken yet another impossible step towards whatever unimaginable evil he needs it for. That we haven't failed again. But as me dying in excruciating agony and losing this body would only be helping the fucker further, I restrain myself from physically assaulting Leandre, and wait to see what his next step will be. Because I'm pretty much a hundred percent sure the rib cage is gone.

'Right. Time for a little mano-a-mano chinwag, I think. Dot the i's and cross the t's, eh?' Again, there's no evidence of his *talent* at work, either prior, during, or after. Just one moment Scarbo's not with us, and the next he is. It might be unexpected for us, but it looks like it is for him too. He gawps at us. Before he has time to do anything else, Aicha sweeps his stubby legs out from under him and has her foot pressed to his throat. He's not going anywhere. Not willingly anyway. Probably not still breathing either.

Leandre watches all this with a sort of benign indifference. I think we're being humoured; he has questions to ask Scarbo, but based on his expression when he came back, the rib cage is gone. I guess that was enough to corroborate our story in his mind, so he's prepared to let us get a few digs in before he starts the interrogation proper.

It's petty considering I'm pretty sure the Prince is about to tear strips off Scarbo, possibly literally, but then so am I. I kick him clean in the ribs, hard enough to wind him, not hard enough to snap one off and impale his heart on it before I pull it out of his chest and use it in a raclette, pouring molten cheese fondue over it before I devour it, preferably still beating. Not that the thought of kicking him that hard ever crossed my mind. Obviously.

When Scarbo recovers the ability to draw air in without vomiting dribble everywhere, Leandre snaps his fingers, and suddenly the twat is sitting in the chair nearest to him. It makes me more than slightly nervy. No one should be able to do that without glowing like they just swallowed a ten tonne nuclear warhead when *looked* at. He should be awash with *talent*, and I don't understand how he isn't. It's unsettling. Scary. I guess this is the reason he still holds Paris, why people like La Guillaneu are ready to bend the knee to him. It makes even a hag's weird magic and chronomancy look piddling small in the power stakes.

No wonder he underplays himself. Otherwise, no one would even say boo to a goose in front of him (although, side note, you're a raving psychopath if you try to scare a goose, and I'll be the first to point and laugh when it pecks your eye out). This way, people might just forget how scarily powerful he is, relaxing in his presence enough to say something stupid that he'll never forget. Then one day you'll find yourself in a "PR review meeting" just like the one Scarbo's about to have.

'Now then.' Leandre bends down all casual-like, albeit business casual, and looks Scarbo in the eyes. He's just pulled off three sets of insane magic, and he's not even breaking a sweat. Terrifying. 'Where's my rib cage, Scarbo?'

Oh, damn. Oh, no. I squeeze my eyes closed, and although I don't believe in a god anymore, I can't help but pray. *Please don't say it, Aich. Resist the temptation. Don't take the piss out of the very pissed off, heart-stoppingly powerful lutin. Don't say it, Aich. Don't...*

'In your chest,' she says deadpanned.

My heart sinks in mine. I mean, he walked into that one to be fair, but he doesn't look in the mood for a bit of banter. I crack one eye open to see if he's, I don't know, about to turn up the gravity in our immediate locale and crush us with the air itself or something else equally impossible and comparable to what he's already done. Instead, he looks like he's choking, like maybe he's swallowed a bee, and it's now stuck in his throat. I'm just about to dive across to perform the Heimlich manoeuvre when he gasps in air, and I realise he's dying.

With laughter. Sorry, dying with laughter. I should have probably put that together considering the proceeding imagery.

'Oh, she's hilarious. Top drawer material, bish bosh.' He turns his attention back to the unfortunate prisoner. 'Don't you think so, Scarbo?'

All the attention swings back round to the little poet shitbag. Aicha's eyes narrow. 'I don't think he'll agree. What did you call me the last time we met? A mouthy bitch, wasn't it? Notice you're not mouthing off now.'

Unlike Leandre, Scarbo is definitely sweating. It's pouring off him by the gallons. I don't know how he's not rapidly emaciating considering what percentage of his own body weight he must be shedding each time he mops frantically at his brow with the back of his hand. I wonder idly if he'll end up as the equivalent of beef jerky if he carries on at this rate. Dehydrated Scarbo snacks. I can see the packaging now. 'Fill your mouth so you don't have to listen to him run his.' Marketing genius.

It's probably not going to massively reduce his life expectancy though. He stole from the Lutin Prince. He's not walking out of here. I know it. He knows it. Leandre knows it. Hell, I bet even Al-Ruhban knows it, and he managed to single-handedly miss us getting chased by the entire supernatural community of Paris while he indulged in some solo Netflix and chill. That brings some horrible images to mind that makes me want to reformat my own brain with an over-powered magnet. Wipe it all. Please. Anything to scrub that thought away.

Leandre leans closer. 'Where is it, Scarby, eh?'

Urgh. A nickname based on the actual name, no shorter than the original? Truly the stuff of nightmares. It reeks of boarding school bonhomie and privilege. I'm so horrified that I almost miss the answer.

'It's far away though I am not
Though hard to say quite what is what
How I was taken from the spot
My plans unmade and gone to rot.'

I groan. It's fucking painful. He obviously considers himself a genius rather than the hack he is. That's the worst part. Aicha apparently agrees. She answers him back.

'If you should rhyme another time

The next line, I'll write with your spine.'

I can't help myself from breaking out into applause. I mean, it's rubbish, but it's still a million times better than anything he's said. Leandre also gives it a somewhat distracted half-hearted clap too.

'Yes, very good, very good. Definitely hilarious.' His attention never wavers off Scarbo, pinning him in place, dissecting him with his eyes, looking for his answers. 'Now as for how you're called to order, well, you signed the contract. Full disclosure's always in the fine print. Devil in the details. The same optimisation applied to you that lets you into my boardroom also means if I call? Well, you come running. Willingly or not.'

Fascinating. There's almost something of a demonic contract to it. The irony being, of course, that demonic contracts don't exist, at least not in the way Christopher Marlowe presented them in his famous play *The Tragical History of the Life and Death of Doctor Faustus*. A title that made Mephistopheles cry with laughter for several weeks. I believe he's still ribbing Faust about it.

Leandre's magic doesn't seem to follow the same rules of any *talent* I've ever come across, and I'm trying really, really hard to ignore it. Otherwise, the electric ants are going to start working out their tap-dance routine on the outside of my cerebellum, and I won't be able to rest till I solve the mystery. And, frankly, we have bigger fish to fry.

As scared as Scarbo looks, he's not begging for his life or for forgiveness. I thought he might try to kiss up to the Prince, persuade him we're the ones in the wrong, charm him one more time. Not at all. The look on his face under the terror is anger, disgust even. Leandre sees it. So does Al-Ruhban. While the former looks mortified, the latter looks genuinely hurt.

'I gave you my friendship,' the half-djinn says. 'Not something I do lightly. Welcomed you to my table and broke my bread with you. Does that count for nothing?'

'And I,' Leandre adds, 'raised you up. Gave you the Thirteenth, promoted you to serve by my side. And the thanks I get are you breaking the non-disclosure clause and selling me out?'

Scarbo opens his mouth to answer and catches sight of Aicha. I watch her mouth, 'Speak plainly,' at him. He closes his mouth. Opens it again. Then a strange thing happens.

I don't know if you've ever seen the old John Carpenter film *Big Trouble in Little China*. At the end, when Lo Pan is killed, one of the Three Storms, Thunder, I reckon, kills himself by holding his breath till he swells into a huge blob and explodes. For a moment, I think Scarbo is going for the same effect. His face swells, and he turns red, Nain-Rouge-style red, like he's absolutely furious. Or he's battling high-grade constipation. Or he's absolutely furious at his high-grade constipation.

As he does so, Leandre cries, 'No!' and lunges forward, but at the same moment, Scarbo exhales. A tiny wisp of red smoke passes his lips as he does so, and he grins humourlessly at the Prince.

'Too late,' he crows and throws back his head, letting out a high-pitched cackle that's like nails down a chalkboard. Then he turns his attention our way. 'You want me to speak plainly? Fine. Why would I betray my prince? Have you heard him? Metrics this. Optics that. It's all business. I am Scarbo the Magnificent. I've spent hundreds of years feeding on the blood of artists in exchange for the fever dreams I give them back, driving them to the heady heights of creativity only such madness can produce. And when I come to spread my gift and take my drinks here, am I welcomed? Feted as I should be? Given my dues, set up in Montmartre, close to my flock, all who take pen or paints in the Artists Quarter? No.' The little creature's upper lip rolls back in a sneer, revealing the vicious points of his teeth. 'Instead, I have to scrape and bow for years to a man obsessed by numbers, by statistics. And when I'm finally granted territory, where do I get? The Thirteenth. Tell me, what artists have come from there?'

'L'Affaire. Lomepal. Georgio.' Aicha lists the names without blinking.

Scarbo spits. 'Rappers? I said artists.' Well, if we needed further evidence he's a fucking idiot, there we are. 'Regardless, I've never been treated how I should be, given my due. He promised me all of Paris, all the artists of France. Every poet, every painter, every tortured writer so I can sup their blood like an aged Bordeaux.'

'Who promised it to you?' I need the answer. 'De Montfort?'

Scarbo's eyes widen, perhaps shocked I know the name of his new patron. He opens his mouth to answer, but all that comes out is more red mist. Only now it's billowing out of his lungs, pouring out, settling on the tabletop in front of him like dry ice mixed with blood. It keeps coming, and a second later his head follows it, smashing onto the tablecloth with tremendous force as the smoke dissipates.

Aicha leaps forward, pulling him back upright, but it's too late. He's dead. Leandre hasn't moved, just looks at the little body with sad resignation.

'He knew the cost of breaking that curse. Damn fool.' He doesn't sound like an eighties stereotype this time. He just sounds very, very old and very, very tired from everything he's seen. For the first time since we've met the Crown Prince of Paris, I find myself relating to him intensely.

I look at the limp sack that was once a living, breathing creature that Aicha has propped up. It's amazing how jealousy, how that toxic mix of over-entitlement and under-achievement can fill a person's brain with poisons that rot away anything good from life, turning every mouthful that it feeds you into ashes just because the spoon it's on isn't silver. Or if it is, because it isn't gold. Or if it is gold, because someone else has a larger golden spoon than yours, which should be yours, and *it isn't fair*. So often, the ones with the most are the ones who feel most strongly the grievance that they only have most, not all. What a terrible way to live.

The only thing that can be said is that for someone as pretentious as Scarbo was, death by prose is a suitably melodramatic way to go.

Not that he would have ever been satisfied.

EPILOGUE - PARIS, 8 JUNE, PRESENT DAY

Wondering if I can get a T-shirt made up. "Survivor of the Great Chase across Paris". Or "I didn't get murderised by the Lutin Prince and all I got was this lousy T-shirt" maybe.

L eandre doesn't plan to stick around. I sort of hoped, considering his demonstrations of utterly off-the-scales levels of *talent*, we'd do some sort of crossover team-up now that De Montfort's stolen from him. Instead, he launches into some buzzword-laden corporate jargon about holistic synergy and incentivised retargeting.

It takes some work on my part, but I eventually distil it down to the gist. It's actually simple despite how overly complicated he makes it sound: we get safe passage out of here, and Al-Ruhban keeps Saint-Ouen, but he's not going after De Montfort. The Thirteenth is now leaderless, and there's going to be a power struggle to fill the vacuum. He'd really appreciate us dropping the rib cage back if we can, but that's about it. Oh, and if we spread word around that he got robbed, especially by Scarbo of all people, he'll kill us. Horribly and messily. And if I understand the subtext correctly, permanently in mine and Aicha's case.

He's already on his mobile phone, fielding some undoubtedly hyper-important call by the time we work it out, which is good news in some ways because he disappears without clocking onto Aicha's answer to being threatened. I can summarise it — death threats and asterisks. Which, incidentally, is going to be the name of my new bluegrass punk band. When I learn to play an instrument. And sing without sounding like someone is drowning a laryngitis-ridden cat.

We stay the night at Al-Ruhban's. Luckily, with his elemental abilities, he's able to seal up the gaping hole in the front of his house easily enough, and we share a few glasses of Kavalan, a particularly lovely Taiwanese whisky that goes down a treat. Then we crash out in the two respective guest rooms because, honestly? Today has been a lot. A whole lot. I'm more than ready to get some sleep.

The following morning, I have the delightful job of calling up Isaac and telling him we're heading back empty-handed while Aicha books train tickets. Catching the train isn't going to take us that much longer than flying would, and it saves me from having to be anywhere near Aicha inside an aircraft, which is something I'm happy to avoid for the rest of my existence if at all possible, thank you very much.

It's a bleak call to make, but at least it involves talking to one of my favourite people. I expect him to be more downhearted than he is, more matching in my "crowd from an eighties The Cure concert" mood. He tries to commiserate, but I know him too well. Despite our misadventures, he has something. Something positive. Whatever it is, after all we've been through, I want it. Gimme, gimme, gimme.

'Enough, 'Zac. What's going on? What's got your knickers in a twist?'

Of course he tells me. He was only being polite, letting me vent my misery beforehand. 'Well, that's a truly disturbing image, my lad,' he says. 'Still, you've caught me. There's something — Well, two things really, but one I want to keep as a surprise. I'll show you when you get back. But the main thing, lad, is the bones.'

I avoid hitting myself in the forehead with the phone till it breaks. The phone or the forehead, I don't care which. 'We know it's all about the bones, man. That's why we've been chasing after them since —' I check my watch. 'The day before yesterday.'

Has it only been two days? Good God, it feels like weeks, months even. When this is all done, I'm going to go and lie on a beach somewhere and have a decent break for like a century or two. It's well due. Then I remember I have to write all this down when it is finally done. Maybe I can stand it lasting a bit longer after all.

'Yes, but it's when the bones are, okay?'

'Hold on a sec.' I take the phone away from my ear and wiggle my finger in it, trying to clear it out. 'Right, say that again. Could have sworn you said *when* the bones are.'

'I did! Well, when the bones are from rather. Look, I started researching for a pattern. We know one skull was Almeric's, the other Torquemada's right?' I nod, then feel utterly foolish as I'm on a phone call. Luckily, Isaac's too excited to notice my awkward pause or care. 'Well, I did some digging. Looking for other bones that have gone missing. A thought came to me about Melusine's sceptre. How long was she gone before setting up in Lourdes?'

I wrack my brain. 'Nearly a thousand years?'

'Right. So what does that tell you about the sceptre?'

I shrug and then kick myself again mentally for the non-verbal communication. Aicha kicks me physically. She's stopped trying to get the booking done, drawn in by the conversation. 'She didn't have it initially.'

I can feel Isaac beaming at her from here, like she's a star pupil. Bloody swot. 'Right. I mean, it's not impossible she did, but considering how much she enjoyed being worshipped and adored? I doubt it. It might have taken some time for her to decide it was worth killing her sister but not a thousand years.'

It's a good point, and one that didn't even cross my mind in all the other madness I've had to deal with ever since Gil drove said sceptre into Melusine's heart. 'So you sound like this gave you a lead, 'Zac?'

'Absolutely. I started searching for any evidence of the sceptre anywhere. I found nothing — at first. It took a lot of digging before I found a tiny scrap of information in the diary of Franz Anton Mesmer. He talked about hearing of a working by those who paid heavily for their *talent* during the witch-hunting era. A group of those who lost loved ones apparently gathered together under a secret patron. Here, let me send you a photo of the excerpt.'

I avoid pointing out that it'll be a damn sight quicker if he just tells me and look at the screen, waiting for the beep of arrival. He's done good work. It's up to him how he wants to pull the big reveal.

My phone beeps a few seconds later, and I pull up an image of a book stained by the passage of time and covered in a scrawl that takes me a few moments to decipher. I get there, though, as does Aicha, leaning over my shoulder.

Word didst reach mine ear of a great magick, worked by those whom had paid prices most high, caught 'i the hunts of the temple and its empowered representatives. Great power was found, most terribly ironic, 'i the bones of Matthew Hopkins, witchfinder general of England, and Archbishop Johann von Schönenberg, leader of the Hounding of Protestants, Jews and womenfolk accused of witchcraft. These formed a wand of great power, 'i and of itself. Yet, when the bones contained within the hand of Cotton Mather, much hated minister of Salem, were found to bear also power, they were added to the working. Wherein mere twere a thing capable of great magicks. Yet all involved 'i it didst disappear, and the sceptre too, so as I never wot if it is a truth, or hold, but for a rumour.

I mull it over for a moment. 'You think the patron was Melusine herself?'

'Exactly. She took the sceptre once it was done. Probably the group too. Ate them and their *talent* all up to keep the sceptre secret. How Mesmer even caught word of it afterwards, I've no idea. But it tells us something incredibly useful. Whose bones it was made from. So what's the link between them?'

I think about it, scratching at my chin, baffled by how smooth it is despite the lack of grooming I've done in recent times before I remember I'm currently a woman, so facial stubble isn't such a pressing concern. 'Well, those three were all active in persecuting witches or anyone suspected of witchcraft.' I'm almost there. I can feel the neurones forming, making the neural pathways that'll get me to the answer.

Aicha gets there first, of course. 'They were all religious extremist wankshafts.'

Good God damn it, she's getting all the gold stars today. I'm pretty sure I hear Isaac clap his hands together through the speakerphone. 'Right! So I dug into bones of religious extremists, particularly those where the bodies or parts thereof have disappeared. I found it to be a recurring theme throughout the span of time since you destroyed the Grail. A pattern, even.'

One thing doesn't fit for me in this though. 'What about the bones from the dig in Leicester? The woman buried by the king?'

Isaac has the answer, of course. 'Think it through, lad. A woman. Buried in an abbey. By Dominican monks? Must have been someone the local Order considered almost saint-like. And the Dominicans always did like their saints liberally painted in the blood of sinners.'

So an informer of some sort or perhaps just a local harridan who terrified the population into religious submission. Okay. 'So you said there was a pattern to it?'

'Absolutely. A loose one but a pattern nonetheless. Seems to be every thirty to fifty years, a Christian extremist pops up —'

'I think you mean every thirty to fifty minutes.' It's a fair point by Aicha, however wryly delivered.

'Okay, yes, thank you. Valid. But the ones who come along in those time frames are proper fire-and-brimstone sods, and the thing that links them? Magical bones once they're dead.'

'So who was the last one then?' I wrack my brains for arsehole Christian leaders in the last few decades. There's a fair few that spring to mind.

'Before we get to that, who was the first one?'

And like that, it all slots into place. I can't believe I didn't click onto it. Now that Isaac's said that, it's so obvious. 'Almeric. They're all fucking Almeric. That son of a bitch keeps coming back.'

'And every time he does, he's just as much of an arsehole as the first time. Now. To answer your question. The last set of bones I can find is the rib cage that just got stolen from Leandre. Ludwig Muller, Nazi bishop. Died in 1945.'

'1945. So if Almeric comes back every thirty to fifty years...'

The realisation hits me like a tonne of bricks. That's where the last set of bones are. In his current body.

He's out there, somewhere in the world.

Arnaud Almeric is alive right now.

AUTHOR'S NOTES

There we are. The penultimate tale in the first story arc is complete and finally some answers are becoming clear. Almeric is alive but De Montfort is still loose, and so very close to getting his hands on all of the bones. What is his – undoubtedly malicious and utterly fucked-up - plan? You'll have to pick up 'imPerfect Gods' to find out...

Thank you for following me so far in this journey. I hope you enjoyed the sojourn across to my home town of Leicester, and then to Paris, where I also lived for some years. The story of the discovery of Richard III – including the mysterious woman's sarcophagus – are both true, although her bones didn't go missing – at least as far as I'm aware. Kenilworth Castle is much as described – and I didn't even give them chance to visit the Elizabethan Gardens! – and definitely well worth a visit should you ever head that way.

The Parisian locations are all real, with the exception of Scarbo's flat. That is the location of my own Parisian apartment, but it certainly wasn't as grandiose – or marble-coated – as Scarbo's is. The Musee Des Arts Forains – The Museum of Fairgrounds – is absolutely real, as is the Biblioteque Nationale De France. I did have Paul and Aicha initially plotting their next move – and discovering their wanted status via the radio – in my favourite watering hole in the Buttes Aux Cailles, Sputnik. It got cut by my editor for pacing, so perhaps I'll pop that in one of my newsletters instead at some point.

Craig, the Magus of Blackburnshire, is based on a real person, owner and presenter of Killa Tapes, the rapper Grimee Quick. I had the great chance to present a French version of Killa Tapes for a year for Booster FM, the radio station in Toulouse, and wrote a short story for Killa Tapes Magazine creating the Hob King, a link for which you can find after these notes. I loved the character so much, I wanted to include it in the series, and Craig kindly gave me permission to do so. My thanks to him and Emme for that and I hope I've done him justice with this particular fictionalised version of him.

In terms of the history, Otto Rahn was a real character, and one of the hardest ones to choose how to portray I've encountered. His motives and his true intentions are not really clear from any source, with each – as is often the case in history – providing personal bias. Some friends of his said he absolutely did not subscribe to the views of the National Socialists, that he was a liberal academic forced into something he could not escape from by Himmler's fanship. Other sources say he was delighted by the prestige and accolade, and perhaps happy to go along with the attitudes and actions of the Nazis, at least until he discovered the true horrors, on his tour of the camps. In creating his character I've done my best to include all those moral ambiguities and questions, but perhaps created a little redemption for this strangest of figures, this gay Jewish Nazi esoteric scholar, supposedly the inspiration for Indiana Jones. If you want more information about Rahn, I can highly recommend the excellent documentary 'The Hidden Glory' by Richard Stanley. His other documentary 'The Otherworld' about his own strange experiences around Montsegur, and some of the curious happenings and individuals around it, is also a fascinating watch.

As always my thanks go to my family, who keep me sane even if I tell them they drive me mad. My editor, Miranda, who might take me through the seven stages of grief each time she gives me back an edited book, but who undoubtedly makes them infinitely better with her red pen. Becca, Becky and Lauretta for their beta reading and brilliant suggestions. Athena for her proofreading of the audiobooks. All of my ARC readers, with particular mention to Leigh and Brenda for their fabulously detailed feedback notes. The imPs, my readers' group on Facebook, and Mel Mel and Jimmy for the work they put in corralling the madness. The FAKA author group who are always on hand to cheer me on, or cheer me up, and whose invaluable advice has been a major part in my successes. The Semper Eadem sisters and Craig Verbs for the love and support at all times. My mum and dad, my brothers and sister, who never cease to be there and never have. Every one of my friends and family. I love you all so much, even if there are too many to mention without writing a whole other book.

So, we have one book left, one more until this first tale of the imPerfect Cathar comes to completion. What is De Montfort's devious plan, and what will be the price to be paid? By him. By Paul. By the world.

Get a sneak peek on the other side of the opportunity to grab a special short story about Craig, the Magus of Blackburnshire, which was written for Killa Tapes Hiphop Magazine.

Then join Paul, Aicha and Isakob for imPerfect Gods, the last step in this first strange and wonderous journey for the imPerfect Cathar and his friends...

REMEMBER

Do please consider leaving a review, or clicking a star rating on Amazon. If you can click follow too, that'd be fantabulous. It keeps the terrible hungry demon Sozeb from clawing chunks from my very soul.

Just remember. Never say his name backwards. Especially when you're still in your Prime.

If you'd like to read a short story about Craig, the Magus of Blackburnshire you can do so here –

https://cnrowan.com/craig/

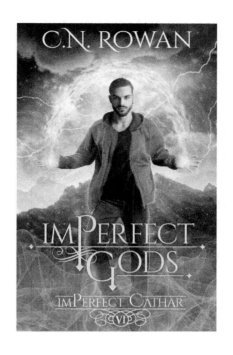

TURN THE PAGE FOR THE FIRST CHAPTER OF THE IMPER-
FECT CATHAR BOOK 6

'IMPERFECT GODS'

IMPERFECT GODS

There's always a price to pay for the choices we make, the paths we walk. In blood. In tears. In bones.

In those lost, sacrificed, willingly or otherwise. In the parts of ourselves consumed just as utterly as those who've fallen in our stead.

The higher the stakes, the higher the bill when it comes due. There's no avoiding it, no ducking out at the last minute. Once you start down the path, unsure where the twists and turns will take you, there's one certainty you can carry with you every step of the way.

There's always a price to pay.

CHAPTER 1 - TOULOUSE, 9TH JUNE, PRESENT DAY

Someone fetch me a pair of overly baggy trousers. I want to do the Hammered Dance.

By the Good God, I want to get drunk.

Let me be clear, I'm not about to crawl off into the gutter again. My days of drowning my miseries face-down in puddles of booze until they stop shrieking constantly in my face are done. For the time being at least. When your miseries swoop down on you like disease-ridden harpies to upset your banquet as often as mine do, the temptation is always going to linger.

No, I'm not about doing a booze cruise of the nearest alleyways and park benches. But I'd love the space to get a little buzz on, for the pressure to ease up enough that I could so easing of me own. Right into the nearest comfortable chair with a bottle of single malt, enough ice to sink a mid-sized ocean liner, and maybe even – wonder of wonders – a decent book. To have room to escape reality without it kicking my front door in and smacking me in the teeth.

But that's just a pipe dream. Because we're a long way from such hobbit-like dreams of quiet and calm.

The storm is arriving. And I feel like I'm stood in the middle of a field. On top of a metal ladder. Dressed in a suit of fucking armour. Holding a sign saying 'Zeus is a right twat'.

Of course, there's another good reason why I won't go off into another self-pitying pile of dejected spirits, both alcoholic and personal. Two good reasons actually. And they're both attached to the arms of the woman sitting next to me, who won't hesitate to wield her hands like the utterly deadly weapons they are, cracking me round the back of the skull if I decided to duck my responsibilities again. Those, I wouldn't be able to duck.

While we might be waiting metaphorically for the storm to arrive, physically it's already here. The night time sky is split regularly on all sides by electrical flashes, like the gods decided to have a disco and we weren't invited, just hanging around on the outside looking in while they get their rave on. Sheet lightning cracks off to the west; to the south forks dance between the bubbled-up cloud mountains that dominate the horizon, blotting out the Pyrenees, the sky mocking the earth, replacing its mightiest features with terrible, deadly imitations of its own.

And the rain sheets down, sluicing the streets, of my city washing them clean. I can't help thinking of a slaughterhouse getting sprayed down, ready for the next arriving cattle. Can't help wondering if these won't run red with blood before we get to the end of this story.

Except it's not really my city anymore. I'm still fed by the connection, still linked in. But just like I'm in a moving vehicle right now and I'm only a passenger, so it is with Toulouse now. Isaac – well, Isaac and Jakob and Nithael and Nanael because why settle for one person in a body when you can have two Kabbalah masters and two *freaking angels* took over the wards when my own magic got eaten. I have *talent* again now, but it's only the *talent* I get from wearing the body of a dead fae queen. Next time I die, I'll be back at shizzard levels all over again. They had no choice but to take the strain. Not only that, they've pushed the wards out a lot further – like a hundred kilometres farther in each direction, giving us all a better early warning system for whenever De Montfort comes calling. And he will because he needs Almeric's first original skull to complete his creepy sets. Someone really should get him into stamp-collecting or something instead.

So they hold the wards, meaning they hold the city. They're only doing what I asked them to do, what I told them needed to be done, but it still hurts in a way. Toulouse has always been mine, my one constant in a world changing at breakneck speed. Sure, I ended up co-habiting it with Franc, but somehow I always felt like the owner leasing out a granny flat to the local weirdo. I don't think Franc would have agreed, but it allowed me to sell it to myself. Plus, he was a scum-sucking shit heel. And now he's dead. Good. Fuck him.

'Any fresh ideas?' I don't have to spell out what I'm talking about. The same thing we've been talking about every time we've started up conversation the whole of the seven or so hours we've been travelling back from Paris. Sat in the uncomfortable train seats. As we walked to the car park next door. While stealing a pretentious penis extension from therein to get us to where Isaac is waiting. There's nothing else worth talking about, nothing else that's occupying a single braincell apart from the ones necessary to keep us safe on the road, moving in a straight-line home.

The only other thing occupying our thoughts is Simon De Montfort. Him and his macabre ossuary. And how that all ties into the apparently alive Arnaud Almeric.

'None.' A short, sharp answer. Not surprising. Short and sharp are two words you could use to describe Aicha Kandicha anyhow. If you were feeling suicidal enough to make cracks about her height. Even I'm not that stupid. Most of the time. She has plenty of short, sharp objects she'd introduce into your various cracks were you to do so.

I sigh, a sound which has been as much the soundtrack to our drive as the eclectic blend of songs from the radio. Our station selection has been as unsettled as our minds have been, fingers constantly jabbing out to try a different sound, searching for that elusive something that might allow us to relax, might bring us some peace.

That hyper-vigilant, utterly unsettled state of mind means that I feel it. The moment the thought strikes Aich. Her body language changes at the wheel, hands tightening, frame stiffening. 'Could Almeric be behind it all?'

I'm about to dismiss it, but I stop, consider it. We know that all the bones are from previous time Almeric's been alive, bodies he's reincarnated in throughout the ages, starting with his own skull from his first life as the Butcher of Beziers. The one that Jakob and Nanael spent centuries trapped in. The life that I'd ended, the first time I willingly killed anyone.

I rub my chin. 'I mean, he was certainly enough of an arsehole.' There's no question of that. Slaughtering twenty thousand people to kill a handful of Perfects, wiping out the town of Beziers with the now famous quote "kill them all, God will know his own"? Not exactly sainthood material. The only issue is, he might not have agreed with that. 'He was a religious extremist though. Simon doesn't strike me as thinking he's on a mission from God. Jake and Elwood would think him as much of a cockgoblin as we do.'

Aicha shrugs. 'People change over centuries. Especially when reincarnating. Look at Ben.'

It's a fair point, albeit a painful one. Reincarnating broke my once-friend. Ruined him. Tore all the goodness from his soul and left him twisted, bitter and ready to do anything to achieve his own ends. Of course, it's not true of everyone. 'Demon Fart hasn't changed.'

She nods acquiescence at the point. 'True. Neither have you. You're still a twat. Always have been, always will be.'

And, on those pearls of wisdom, we both fall silent once more, lost in the same thoughts that haven't stopped swirling around and around in our minds since we left Paris. Where is De Montfort? What does he want with the skeletons? What horrors will be unleashed if he completes both sets? And where does Almeric fit into all this?

By the time we turn onto the dirt path, my mood isn't so much soured as pickled, wrapped in slices of lemon and then painted with tamarind. Because every time I feel like we're getting closer to an answer, another hundred questions seem to pop up like the world's most unfair game of whack-a-mole. The reassuringly familiar crunch of the gravel chips under the tyres brings with a touch of upliftment, of returning positivity. Because if there are any individuals in the world capable of answering a hundred impossible questions simultaneously without breaking a sweat, it's the geniuses waiting for me inside the farmhouse folly that becomes visible through the parting forest boughs.

I walk into the comfortably familiar country-farm kitchen area. The warmth outside is mitigated instantly by the cool tiles underfoot, and it's a relief. After having visited Paris and the middle of England, the temperature on dismounting the train at Matabiau felt oppressively hot, and I'm still struggling to reacclimatise. Isaac stands and sweeps me up into a manly hug, and now I'm crushing the breasts currentl[1] y attached to me into my father figure, which is precisely as weird and uncomfortable for me as it sounds. I quite like this current body, apart from the gender dysmorphia it causes me. It'd be a shame if I ended up killing it trying to snort bleach powder to cleanse my brain of such terribly disturbing memories later.

Once we get past the entirely normal hug that I just succeeded in making unnecessarily weird, we all grab a seat. Different seats, obviously; otherwise, it'd just get weird again.

At Isaac's insistence, we fill him in on what happened during our time in Paris. Because I love him dearly, I do so instead of punching him repeatedly in the face and screaming in his ear until he tells me who Almeric is at this precise moment. It's a level of self-restraint that I think deserves a written commendation – possibly an actual medal. For resisting violence in the face of extreme provocation or something. I'm basically Gandhi and Isaac the rapacious British colonialists, here. And I'm definitely not exaggerating with that particular metaphor in the slightest.

Once we get Isaac caught up on our hi-jinks — and our low jinks and all the jinks in between — I'm ready to do my impression of Hiroshima if I don't get the answers I want. So, of course, Isaac changes subject.

'I said on the phone I have another surprise for you,' he says.

Now I'm in a quandary. I want answers regarding Almeric. Let's be honest, most of my mental capacity – which is fairly limited at the best of times– has been focused on the Grail-infused bone sets De Montfort has been collecting like Panini stickers. But there's a gleam in his eye that is tickling my brain. He mentioned he had a surprise for us before Paris, but frankly under the weight of exhaustion, and terror, and terrified exhaustion, I'd clean forgot. Plus, he's clearly having to work damn hard not to bounce up and down in excitement and to hold on to his scholarly poise. This is Isaac being a kid at Christmas.

'Go for it, man. Knock our socks off.'

Boy, does he. Does he ever.

From out of the doorway off to the right that leads to his workshop, comes what, I assume for a moment, is a robot sent from Skynet in order to stop me leading the human rebellion. Who am I kidding? The target would clearly be Aicha. That's beside the point though.

The point is, it's not every day a seven-foot gleaming chrome monstrosity, all burnished metal and walking death, strolls into your kitchen. If you're reading this and that isn't the case, then my sincerest apologies to the future. We fucked it up even worse than it looked like we had. Or if this is being read by a seven-foot gleaming chrome monstrosity, and I'm still alive, please let me say how glad I am to have handed over control to our clearly superior robotic overlords.

The automaton definitely resembles that skeletal badass underneath the fake flesh Arnie was in the original *Terminator*. I suppose "metallic murder skeleton" is a pretty go-to design strategy if you're creating a deadly robot. It's a fabulous feat of engineering, and I'd applaud rapturously if I wasn't currently tensing all the muscles in my body simultaneously in order to stop myself from wetting myself.

This isn't made any easier when it strides directly towards me, wraps its arms around me, and pulls me inexorably towards it. I manage a *meep* of dismay as it crushes me into what, I realise after a good few seconds of waiting for my head to pop like a grape, is a warm embrace.

'Hello, my dear boy!' The warm, almost plummy intonations are clearly identifiable, even warped by the harsh grate of the speaker apparently embedded in its throat. Or rather, his throat if it's who I think it is. Or even their throat, actually. I suspect both of them have gone along for the ride.

'Jakob?' I ask, blinking, trying to calm down my fight-or-flight instincts, which keep going into overdrive every time I catch the reflection of my own eyelids blinking in the metallic carapace. 'Is that you and Nanael? Really?'

'It is indeed! What do you think of my rather marvellous new body?'

I pull away to give myself the space to look more appreciatively now I'm not on the edge of gibbering in terror at its very presence. 'Very impressive,

Jak! Far better than the beaten-up old rust bucket you've had to ride around in until now.'

Isaac swats at my arm. 'Watch it, lad. None of your lip now. I'm ready to bask in all the praise for the miraculous creation I've made.'

I have to admit, this is beyond extra. This is master craftsmanship that'd make Hephaestus snuff out his forge and hang up his blacksmith apron for good. It's the kind of design work that would have haunted Steve Jobs' dreams and would make any government's military wing cream their pants in excitement. Still, one thing concerns me with the whole setup.

'Zac, it's amazing. Like, seriously incredible. But it's a bit...' I search for the right term. '"Exterminate all in my path. I have become Death, Destroyer of Worlds" for a pacifist researcher and a committedly non-violent angel, isn't it?' And there's another part of this that doesn't make sense for me as well. 'Also, how did you manage it? I thought you ruled out golems as an option for getting Jak his independence back?'

Isaac goes that delightful shade of glowing pink I always aim to make him turn when setting out to embarrass him. 'Well, yes. Admittedly, I may have gone a bit OTT with the design aesthetics. Still, we are effectively at war, are we not? And Jak and Nan need to be able to defend themselves. Especially considering they're now a major target – the major target, presumably - for De Montfort.'

I'm about to ask him what he means about them being a major target when a sneaking suspicion slides into my mind.

'You used Almeric's skull, haven't you? Put it inside the golem?' I almost whisper the words, as if saying them too loud will make them irrevocably real. It seems inconceivable that after centuries of emasculated imprisonment where Jakob and Nanael were helpless and out of control of their own power that they would willingly re-enter their prison cell. I can't help thinking about my own recent stint of captivity. Three weeks, give or take, and I'll never go willingly back into that dark hole. Hell, going near anywhere like it is going to be hard work for a damn long time. I can't imagine how much courage it must have taken for them to step back into the skull, to take up residence in it all over again, especially since the first time they had they'd also had someone they trusted. Love had led them to centuries of suffering. Ben's trickery cost them everything. That they can trust anyone again, that they can risk everything to go back into that skull? It shows two things. The unwavering faith they have in Isaac. And the incorruptible love they have for us all.

Jakob pats me reassuringly on the shoulder. This tells me just how recently they've made the transfer because he clearly hasn't even come close to learning his own strength yet. Were I not in the considerably tougher-than-human frame of a daoine sidhe, I suspect my shoulder blade would have just snapped in two. As is, I can feel some very pretty bruises blooming like flower petals where his heavy-duty fingers made contact.

'It was my choice, my dear boy,' he says as I step as tactfully as possible out of range of any more sympathetic gestures. 'We worked out the details together. Of course, obtaining this much titanium wasn't easy, but it was worth it.'

Bloody hell. Titanium might be cheaper and easier to get hold of than gold, but still. I can only imagine how many tonnes of the material they had to obtain. Fuck-tonnes would be my educated guess.

Of course, articulating and animating a structure based on modern robotics would be precisely zero problem for these two prodigies. Considering they are capable of making articulated clay, like the Golem of Prague, this must have been a doddle for them. It's also a lot easier when you can probably replace some of the trickier wiring components with Kabbalist runes and sigils. Still, to achieve this? To take the skull and all it must symbolise for Jak and Nan and transform it into a form of freedom for them, to give them back their independence and liberty? Not to mention giving us an even more formidable weapon than the mage and angel combination already were...

'Absolute fucking genius. The pair of you. Top marks. Seriously. Colour me impressed.'

Aicha's been quiet throughout most of this. I catch her eye, and note the furrow of the brow. She sees the moment when I work out what she's already worked out, though. Before, we had an easily transportable skull, a chess piece we could use and – if needs be – sacrifice in this fucked-up game we're apparently playing with Demon Fart. Now? Well now, it's infinitely more valuable. There's not one of us would sacrifice it for the world. And that makes it both more vulnerable, as well as more valuable.

She gives a shake of her head though, a subtle no. It's too late to start upsetting Isaac with those details now. All it'll do is make him worry more, second-guess himself harder, and we need him on his a-game. Instead she starts to applaud, and for once, it's not even sarcastic. 'Bravo, both of you. I think you should work out a song and dance routine to "Puttin' On The Ritz" for when you debut this to the Talented community at large.'

Jakob peers at her. At least, I think that's what the camera-lens-style optics he has in place of eyes mean when they whirr and narrow. 'Are you suggesting I'm Frankenstein's monster here, young lady?'

Well, well. Isaac's introduced Jak to the works of Mel Brooks. I'm surprised and impressed for the second time. Aicha, though, returns his look so impassively, it's a toss up which is the automaton. 'Tell me, in all honesty, there wasn't an operating table with restraints and plasma globes and probably even a thunderstorm. Also, 'Zac, if you didn't shout, 'It's alive!' after it worked, I'm revoking your mad scientist card.'

Isaac blushes that deeply satisfying colour again. 'I may have mumbled it,' he says, shuffling his feet.

Jak leans forward, a hand cupped to the side of his mouth. 'He screamed it to the heavens as I sat up. You'd have been very proud, my girl.'

Isaac coughs and harrumphs. 'Right, well, quite enough of that. We have other fish to fry. Let's get to the matter at hand, shall we? Quite enough of Paul's meanderings. We all know how incapable he is of focusing on the matter at hand and getting to the heart of the matter.'

Now, look. There may be some small truth in the suggestion that I can get side-tracked at times, especially when telling stories. That I might, occasionally, end up going off on a tangent or straying into some slightly elaborate flight of fancy that can keep me from reaching the point quite as quickly as some might like. Now and then.

But this time, it definitely isn't my fault. I've been raring to go since we got here, desperate to know the answer to the questions steadily burning a hole through my cerebellum. Sadly, by the time I consider this and reach that conclusion, the conversation has moved on, and my rebuttal is no longer timely. Good God damn it.

I'm still going to interrupt with it though. 'I know you are, but what am I?'

'A complete and utter dickhead.' No prizes for guessing who that one comes from.

'Anyhow,' Isaac says, 'we should get to the matter at hand.'

Finally, I think, finally we're going to find out who Almeric is in this life, and we can start making a plan to move forward. Then I see Isaac's eyes widen slightly. I have a brief moment to wonder why. Then I feel it too.

I'm still tied to the wards. I created them, after all. And I can tell precisely the moment they're breached.

We're under attack.

ABOUT THE AUTHOR

It's been a strange, unbelievable journey to arrive at the point where these books are going to be released into the wild, like rare, near-extinct animals being returned to their natural habitat, already wondering where they're going to nick cigarettes from on the plains of Africa, the way they used to from the zookeeper's overalls. C.N. Rowan ("Call me C.N., Mr. Rowan was my father") came originally from Leicester, England. Somehow escaping its terrible, terrible clutches (only joking, he's a proud Midlander really), he has wound up living in the South-West of France for his sins. Only, not for his sins. Otherwise, he'd have ended up living somewhere really dreadful. Like Leicester. (Again – joking, he really does love Leicester. He knows Leicester can take a joke. Unlike some of those other cities. Looking at you, Slough.) With multiple weird strings to his bow, all of which are made of tooth-floss and liable to snap if you tried to use them to do anything as adventurous as shooting an arrow, he's done all sorts of odd things, from running a hiphop record label (including featuring himself as rapper) to hustling disability living aids on the mean streets of Syston. He's particularly proud of the work he's done managing and recording several French hiphop acts, and is currently awaiting confirmation of wild rumours he might get a Gold Disc for a song he recorded and mixed.

He'd always love to hear from you so please drop him an email here - chris@cnrowan.com

f facebook.com/cnrowan

a amazon.com/author/cnrowan

g goodreads.com/author/show/23093361.C_N_Rowan

◎ instagram.com/cnrowanauthor

ALSO BY C.N. ROWAN

<u>The imPerfect Cathar Series</u>

imPerfect Magic

imPerfect Curse

imPerfect Fae

imPerfect Bones

imPerfect Hunt

imPerfect Gods

imPerfect Blood

imPerfect Blades

imPerfect Demons (Release date – 1st July 24)

Standalone Adventures

An imPerfect Trap (prequel novella to imPerfect Magic)

An imPerfect Samhain

An imPerfect Fable

Omnibuses

imPerfect Beginnings

imPerfect Villains